Summer Promises

Laura Simcox

This edition published by
Crimson Romance
an imprint of F+W Media, Inc.
10151 Carver Road, Suite 200
Blue Ash, Ohio 45242

www.crimsonromance.com

ISBN 10: 1-4405-5466-8
ISBN 13: 978-1-4405-5466-7
eISBN 10: 1-4405-5467-6
eISBN 13: 978-1-4405-5467-4

Dedication

FOR PAT

BRILLIANT MAN, WONDERFUL FATHER AND MY HUSBAND

Chapter One

Pacing the narrow shoulder of the road, Carly Foster tried to remember how far she was from the turn-off to the interstate. Could she really hike that far wearing new sandals? Didn't it get scorching hot in the middle of the day out in this part of the country? Weren't there rattlesnakes and stuff?

"Ick." She squirmed in her damp, coffee-stained shorts and kicked at gravel. New Mexico sucked. And so did her judgment.

The unwelcome feeling that she'd chosen her latest adventure very poorly crept into her mind, but she brushed it away and took a deep breath. She had to focus. She'd been driving for two days with no company except the ancient car's cassette tape deck. Until it chewed a tape to ribbons somewhere in eastern Colorado. After that, the radio died.

Since then, silence had prompted the conversation with her new boss to play over and over in her head like a crappy song and naturally, she'd gone just a touch nutso. Each time she thought about it, Carly got more nervous. The guy had sounded perfectly normal, right? But there *were* those tiny worries that she'd: A) never met him, B) never heard of him before she found his business on the Internet (How naïve could she be?) and C) driven halfway across the country to a job in a town that didn't seem to exist. A "bona fide Old West ghost town." That should have been a big fat clue right there. Ouch.

Picking out a summer job by closing her eyes and pointing at a map was probably not the best idea she'd ever had. Going online and finding the first theater in that location and calling the owner pretending to be a tourist was not super-smart either. And talking her way into a job out in the middle of the rattlesnake-infested mountains was proving to be, well, idiotic. She gave up trying to focus on how to get unstranded and sighed.

The hasty phone call from three weeks ago played like a crappy cassette tape on a loop in her brain.

"Ruby Spring Hotel, Daniel Day speaking. How may I help you?" The man's voice on the other end *had* been calm and friendly. And she really needed to get out of the city. Chicago sucked in the summer and so did her dead-end temp job.

Carly cleared her throat. "Yes, sir. I am calling to inquire about space in your hotel for this summer."

"Oh, well, I am afraid you're wasting your time, ma'am," he said, "Our hotel is reserved this summer for our theater employees."

She fumbled on the desk for a pen and a scrap of paper. "Oh, really? What type of theater are you producing?"

"Normal type, I guess?" he said after a moment of hesitation.

Normal? This guy was not in the business. Warning flag for most people, but not for her. Curiosity killed cats, not women. She had to know. "Tell me about it," she said.

That's all it took, and the guy began babbling about the project. The theater really was in a ghost town called Ruby Spring, and it was in the mountains, about a half-hour north of Albuquerque. All of the buildings were intact and the theater itself was an old opera house with balconies and boxes. The hotel was already a tourist destination and apparently had been for some time.

Despite having no theatrical experience, he intended to revive an old play from the turn of the century, one that hadn't been produced in seventy-five years. Carly was dubious about his plan, but if he would pay her to work there it was perfect, and *so* far removed from the cheesy musicals she'd been surviving on the past few summers. She listened to him talk about the play and the renovation of the theater, her excitement growing, while she took notes.

"So, you say that you are hiring a full crew this summer, Mr. Day?" she finally asked as she toyed with her coffee mug.

"It's Daniel. Yeah. But I haven't found half the people I need yet," he said with a sigh.

"Aw, that's a shame," she sympathized. "Just what are you looking for?"

"I still need two actors, and a director, and a set designer. The only catch is the designer has to know how to do restorations, too. Now where I am going to find that?"

She grinned. *Jackpot.* She took a quick swig of lukewarm coffee, her mind racing for just the right words. All she could see in her head was the ghost town and her in it, lounging at the hotel with booted feet propped up on a porch railing. She'd have a big tin mug of coffee and fresh air. No subways. No dumpsters outside her apartment window. No crowds. And this summer, no men. She could make it happen.

"Ma'am? Are you still there?"

Taking a deep breath, she spoke. "Sir, I have something to confess. I'm not looking for a hotel. I'm looking for a job. And you probably won't believe this, but I am a scenic designer." She paused, waiting for a response, but there was silence. "And I am sitting in an office right now doing research for an architect who specializes in historic restoration. In Chicago." Silence. "And I have a friend who is a brilliant director who is also looking for work this summer." Carly waited a bit longer. "But I don't know any available actors. I'm sorry," she finished lamely. There was still no response, and she sighed in frustration.

"Me and my big mouth," she muttered as she reached over to disconnect the call. As she moved the receiver back to the cradle, she heard his voice again.

"When can you start?" he said.

Carly laughed and brought the phone back to her ear. "Seriously? Don't you want to see my resume?"

Daniel chuckled. "I have caller ID. I can see the name of your company right here. We may be in the middle of nowhere, but we are not totally out of touch. If you feel better about it, e-mail it to me. But I can read people, and I know you're not lying to me," he declared.

"No, I'm not," she said, "and I really appreciate the opportunity."

After a few more minutes of chatting, she hung up and called her director friend, Ross. He was thrilled with new adventures and was even more impetuous than Carly. When he told her, "Sure, why the hell not?" she had already known he would come along for the ride. Except . . . Ross hated to drive, so he suggested that Carly drive his car out west. The car that by all rights should have died about ten years ago. He decided to fly out and meet her. Good for him, bad for her.

Now here she was, sitting in said car on the side of a mountain, starting her summer escapade in the grandest of ways. Stranded, lost, and freezing, with wet, coffee-stained shorts. Plus, it was probably six a.m. or something. Nice. Like she ever got up before nine. Just thinking about it made her yawn.

Making a new resolution to stay focused, she grabbed an old sweatshirt and wiped at the rivers of coffee in the driver's seat. Frowning, she unfolded a paper map with a snap (GPS was for sissies, plus she couldn't afford it) and began to trace her route south from Colorado with her index finger. Somewhere along this two-lane highway, somewhere very close by, was Ruby Spring, her very own custom-made, perfect-in-all-ways summer adventure. Probably.

Every summer for the past four years, though, she had come back to Chicago gushing about some guy she had met. Except . . . it never worked out. Sam turned out to be gay but straight-curious, Joey dumped her for one of the size four chorus girls, George accused her of being too absorbed . . . whatever that meant, and Ivan had never actually acknowledged the fact that she breathed the same air as him. Getting over Ivan was the worst. Theater sucked.

This summer had to be different. She was here to work, not develop adolescent crushes on men. In fact, on men who were emotionally little more than adolescents themselves. Most women her age were in serious relationships and in stable careers with amazing things like health insurance and retirement accounts. But she had chosen theater, not the other way around. And right now, she needed to make a decision about how to get herself out of this latest mess.

She looked up one side of the road. Scrubby bushes and dry brown dirt arched steeply into the mountainsides. The road quickly curved into nowhere. Wrinkling her brow, she squinted and looked the other way. The same desolate scenery greeted her. "No trees, no water," she muttered to herself. Suddenly, she was very thirsty. Carly licked her lips and began to pace across the narrow two-lane highway. Someone had to come along soon.

With nothing better to do, she popped the trunk and began to rummage through her luggage for snacks and water. After a few minutes, she produced a small crumbled package of cheese crackers, but no water to go with it. Her stomach rumbled, but her dry mouth held her back. She walked back to the open window, reached in and turned the ignition. Maybe now that the fossil had rested, it would cooperate. Click, click. Sputter. Wheeze. Silence. Panic began to creep in and she tamped it down with ruthless determination.

"I am not going to cry. I am not going to freak," she declared, even as tears formed in the corners of her eyes. As far as she could tell, no other vehicle had come by since she stopped . . . what was it . . . hours ago? But she *had* fallen asleep holding a cup of horrid gas station coffee. How could *that* have happened?

Hands shaking, she reached into her pocket for the cell phone. Turning it on, she squinted at the vibrant blue sky again and wished for a hat. As the phone came to life with a little beep, she breathed a sigh of relief and waited for the signal to appear. Calmer now, she smiled as the precious word "roaming" appeared on the screen. The smile soon turned into a frown when she saw the battery level. Low.

She had to swallow her apprehension and call Daniel Day. Maybe Ruby Spring was real. Maybe he wasn't a psycho. The phone issued a tiny warning beep.

"No, no, no," Carly screeched as she scrolled the contact screen for the number to the theater. When the phone beeped again, she grimaced and cursed her memory. Where had she stored that damn number? There was one final, mocking beep and the screen was blank. In stony silence, she threw the phone on top of her makeup case and slammed the trunk.

Less than thirty seconds later, the distant sound of an engine echoed through the mountain pass. Her head whipped around and she rubbed her at her blurry eyes. "Too good to be true," she whispered as she peered down the road. The rumbling grew closer and she leaned back against the trunk in relief. Along with the engine, she began to hear the faint sounds of heavy metal music, and as the vehicle came around the bend, she straightened and waved her arms like a crazed fan at a concert.

"Hey!" she gasped in a hoarse whisper. The big white sedan with lights on top slowed and pulled in beside Carly. A sheriff's car. She grinned. Then her mouth dropped open as the occupant stepped out of the idling vehicle. *Holy shit.* He had to be the hottest cop she'd ever seen. Her gaze raked him as he reached in and switched off the engine and her grin froze in place. A giggle threatened to erupt from her parched throat. Too good to be true for sure.

He adjusted his wide-brimmed hat and cocked his head to the side, smiling at her. He was movie star-beautiful, with long, lean legs and an impossible tan. "Having a little picnic, are we?" he grinned. His voice was like smooth honey.

"Uh . . ." Carly croaked, "Uh . . . picnic?"

Hot Cop swaggered toward her, stopping inches from her body. He reached out and grasped her crackers with a strong, warm hand. "Doesn't look much like a very good lunch to me, miss." He smiled again and all Carly could think about was how hot the trunk of the car might be. Would it completely fry her butt if he lifted her onto it, leaned between her thighs and . . . *bad. Bad, bad girl.*

"No, I suppose not," she attempted, "Lunch? I thought it was morning. I'm lost. I think. The car is old and I think it's pretty cranky. Or not. No pun intended. Ha. And my cell isn't working. Probably because I might have forgotten the charger. And I put it right by the door on top of the bills. Although it might be in a suitcase. The bills, too. Crap. Anyway. I, um . . . am babbling," she finished. God, she sounded lame.

He reached over and pressed the crackers back into her palm. She wrenched her gaze from his hand and looked up into his crystal blue eyes. Big mistake. Carly tried to control it, but the nervous giggle came bursting out. *Brear chicka brear brear.* Porn guitar began playing in her head and another burst of giggles slipped out. She clapped a hand over her mouth and looked back down at the crackers. He gave a polite cough and she groaned to herself. Yep, he thought she was nuts. Great.

She had to focus. He was just a sheriff. He was here to help her. But he was also the hottest guy she'd ever met. She banished the cheesy porn music from her head and bit the inside of her cheek to suppress more maniacal giggles. Taking a deep breath, she inched her way along the trunk (which actually was hot enough to fry a T-bone) to put some distance between herself and the object of her sudden lust.

"I would appreciate some help," she said and stuck out her hand in what she hoped was a professional manner. "My name is Carly Foster. And you are, Officer . . . ?"

The patrolman smiled and tucked his thumbs into his belt. He stared up at the sky for a second and then closed the distance between them again. Taking her hand, he bent forward. "Deputy Sheriff Barstow. Wheeler Barstow. And it would be my pleasure to help you, Mrs. Foster."

"Oh, I'm not married," she declared, and snapped her mouth closed. *Dammit.*

Wheeler grinned and released her hand. "I didn't think you were, but I had to make sure," he said with a laugh and stepped around her. Carly opened her mouth in annoyance and stared after him. Realizing she looked like a deranged fish, she clamped it shut again and pressed her lips together before sneaking a peek at Hot Cop. He was leaning into the driver's side window of her car and the view was almost as spectacular as the mountain scenery.

Swallowing her giggle, Carly asked, "And just why do you have to make sure, um, Deputy Barstow?"

"It's Wheeler," he said from inside the car, "and I had to make sure because I normally don't take married ladies out on dates." He pulled his head out and turned to see her reaction. Stunned, all she could do was stare at him and blink.

A gorgeous smile spread across his face. "Don't have a lot to say, do you, girl? Well, that's OK. Let me, ah . . . jump you and we'll discuss it over some drinks tomorrow night." He ambled past her and walked to the trunk of his cruiser.

Jump her? Carly was tempted to play along, but it had been a crap-tastically long night. She looked down at her coffee-stained shorts and ran her hands through her hair. It probably looked like a nest for gophers. *Gophers, really?* She needed more sleep.

"Um, Officer. I mean, Wheeler. That would be very nice, I'm sure, but how do you know I'm even from around here?"

"Not many people come up this road with Illinois tags that aren't headed to Ruby Spring," he said as he opened his trunk, grabbed jumper cables and walked to the front of his cruiser. He raised his eyebrows at her as he felt under the hood of his car for the catch to raise it. She narrowed her eyes. Was it psycho to be jealous of a car hood?

"Oh. Well, how do you know that I'm not just passing through and staying at the hotel there?" she tried again, folding her arms.

"Because the hotel isn't accepting guests. There's a big sign at the entrance that says so. You have to be one of the drama people." As he walked by her, he winked and patted her head. Carly stomped after him.

"Now how would I know that? I didn't see any entrance," she demanded.

"Then you should have been looking closer about an eighth of a mile ago." Wheeler straightened up and held out jumper cables. "Here. Hold this, Miss Explorer."

Carly snatched them from his hand and looked down the road. "You mean to tell me the ghost town is around that bend back there?"

He winked again and began humming as he connected one

end to his battery.

She rolled her eyes and ran her hand through her hair again. "Great. Just great." Embarrassed, she looked down at her new red wedge sandals. They were covered in coffee stains, too. Feeling Wheeler's eyes on her, she looked up and caught his intent, almost ferocious stare.

What was with this guy? She normally didn't fall for smooth lines and men who were way too delicious for their own good. And she certainly didn't fall for pushy guys. But this guy *did* rescue her. Her resolution not to lust after, develop a crush on, and/or date people from summer theater jobs didn't include tasty cops she met on the side of a road, did it? No, it certainly did not.

She cleared her dry throat and Wheeler's lips curved in amusement. "So how about that drink tomorrow night?"

She grinned. "OK. Yes. And thanks for your help." Hell, it was summertime and she could allow herself some adventure. Still smiling, she ambled back to her car and watched with pleasure as Wheeler attached the jumper cables and then turned the ignition in his cruiser.

"Start it up, just to make sure," he yelled over the heavy metal. *Good God, he was hot.*

"Sure thing." Carly gritted her teeth as she slid into the sticky seat and fumbled with the key. The engine came to life and she gave him a thumbs-up.

"Don't forget to buckle up, sweetheart," he shouted. She hadn't been called that in ages. Her face turned red and she glanced over at Wheeler. He was seat-dancing to the music, trying to make her laugh. And she did. How could she not be sucked in?

He removed the cables, threw them in his back seat and then slid into the driver's seat. "I'll call you," he mouthed with a wink and with a spin of tires he was off. He was around the next bend by the time the dust cleared.

Chapter Two

Still smiling, Carly made a U-turn and headed back down the highway. She braked around one sharp curve and immediately saw a huge sign for Ruby Spring. How could she have missed it? Pulling across the road to the entrance, she slowed down and peered at the writing on the bottom.

"Guest services unavailable this summer but please join us for live professional Theater. 7:30 nightly, opening July twentieth," she read aloud. "Nice," she said wryly as she drove up the gravel road. It twisted and turned, much like the highway, for about a mile and then opened out into a spectacular little valley.

Neat, weathered wooden buildings lined the single-wide dirt throughway that passed for a street. The largest and nearest building on the right side of the street was painted in vibrant Victorian colors reflecting the mountainous desert setting. An elaborate, antiquated sign read "Ruby Spring Hotel." Next to the sign was a paved parking lot with several cars.

"Civilization!" Carly exclaimed and steered around the hairpin turns down to the valley. As she approached the hotel, she saw a tall blonde woman waddle onto the front porch. The woman shaded her eyes from the sun with one hand and pressed the other over her swollen abdomen. Carly turned off the car and hopped out.

"Carly?" the woman inquired.

"That's me," Carly called and bounded up the steps. She held out her hand and smiled.

Taking it, the woman beamed and said, "I'm Sophie. Daniel's wife. Did you have any trouble getting here?"

Carly laughed and shook her head. "I'll tell you about it later. Daniel told me all about his theater, but he didn't tell me you were expecting."

Sophie rolled her eyes and held open the screen door. "Men. It's OK, though. I would rather have him fussing over that than fussing over me."

Carly followed her into the lobby, bracing herself for the possibility of decay in the old building. Her eyes were drawn instantly to the front desk. It was a large semi-circle, of intricately carved dark oak and built into the banister of the wide, curving staircase.

"Wow." Carly ran her hand over it. "This is amazing. I have to tell you, I didn't know what to expect when Daniel said 'restoration needed.' I guess he wasn't talking about the hotel."

Sophie chuckled. "No, the hotel is in great shape. It's been in operation since it was opened in 1885. This summer is the first summer we won't have guests, but it's worth it if we can get the theater restored."

Carly wandered over to the built-in bookshelves to the left of the staircase. "These are great, too." Lost in her favorite pastime, old architecture, she didn't realize someone was behind her until cold hands clapped over her eyes. She yelped and struggled to turn around.

"Nope, gotta guess first," whispered a familiar voice. Carly smiled hugely and grabbed the well-known hands that covered her eyes. "Ross, you're here!"

Turning around, she gave him a giant hug and then looked him over. Dark, almost black, hair peeked out from under a rag of a baseball cap and his jeans fit him like a second skin. His tight T-shirt showed off smoothly muscled, deeply tanned skin. He had a dancer's body, and he showed it off to his best advantage. His wide smile was infectious as he winked at her flirtatiously. Ross was completely the same, except, of course, for the fact that he had pierced his left eyebrow.

She gave him a light punch in the stomach. "When did you get here?"

"Mark dropped me off at O'Hare and I flew into Albuquerque last night. He cried buckets, but honestly, I don't miss him all that much. I'm terrible. But, really, we had only gone on a couple of dates. To tell you the truth, he was getting kind of creepy. So, it's over. I'm such a slut. Ha. Did you make it here OK?"

Carly sighed and patted his shoulder. "I'll tell you about it over a huge glass of water and some lunch."

Sophie walked to the other side of the lobby and pushed open a swinging door. She was all business. "Carly, hope you don't mind living on the third floor. Most of the guest room furniture is in storage and a bunch of rooms are bare, awaiting renovation. We have another empty room on the second, but it's kind of small. Since you'll be here for a while, I gave you the bigger one. Daniel will be home in a little while and he'll help you with your things. In the meantime, come on into the kitchen and you'll get that water and a sandwich right now."

Ross clasped her hand and pulled. "Carly's here, Carly's here," he chanted as he dragged her toward the kitchen.

"You're such a little kid," she retorted, elbowing him in the ribs.

"And you're not immature?" he shot back.

"At least I don't leave bawling boyfriends at the airport," she teased, pulling them both through the swinging kitchen door.

"No, you leave cops swooning over you in the mountains."

He opened his mouth, mimicking her shocked expression. Carly's face turned bright red for the second time that day.

"What? How do you know about that?"

"I went for a little hike up the south ridge about fifteen minutes ago and stopped at a cliff. I saw the whole thing, you shameless whore."

She gasped and sank down at the kitchen table. Still laughing, Ross handed her a large glass of ice water. Her face heated, she took a long drink and then peeked at Sophie over the rim.

"Which cop?" asked Sophie in a casual tone as she began to pull sandwich makings out of the refrigerator.

Carly's eyes went liquid and she sighed. "His name is Wheeler. And we have a date tomorrow night."

Sophie dropped the bread on the counter and turned around.

"Um . . . not a good idea. You are begging for trouble if you get mixed up with him."

Carly glanced at Ross. He shrugged. "Seemed cute enough to me," he said, "plus he saved this aging damsel in distress."

Sophie shut the refrigerator with her hip and unscrewed a jar of mustard. She didn't respond, and Ross and Carly looked at each other in confusion. After a minute or two, she turned and placed a sandwich on the table in front of Carly. "Look, I don't mean to be negative," she said as she lowered herself to a chair, "but Wheeler is a . . . well, he's quite a handful. To be diplomatic about it."

"I get it," Ross said. "You mean he's an asshole."

Carly slapped her hand over his mouth. "I appreciate your concern, Sophie. But I can handle Wheeler. It's really just one date, just to thank him for helping me out." She paused. "If you think about it, he was a gentleman. He didn't even touch me except to shake my hand," she added.

Ross smirked and reached over to squeeze the back of Carly's neck. "Plus, our girl here is old enough to take care of herself. Almost thirty, hmm? When's your birthday? Isn't it sometime in June?"

Carly narrowed her eyes and pushed his hand away. "I don't see how that is particularly relevant, Ross."

Sophie drummed her fingers on the table and looked back and forth from Ross to Carly. After a moment, she shook her head. "OK. Why don't you finish that food and then you can take a tour of Ruby Spring?"

Ross jumped up. "I'll meet you out front," he said and bounded out the door.

Sophie chuckled. "Does he always have that much energy?"

Carly nodded her head yes, her mouth full of food. Ross never got tired and put his work above everything else. Two of the many reasons he made such a great director. Carly swallowed the last of her sandwich, and then drained the last of her water. She gave Sophie a sheepish grin. "Guess I was hungry."

Sophie looked at her with amusement. "Ross makes me jealous," she said. "Not that I am lazy, but being eight months pregnant sucks the ambition right out of a person sometimes."

Carly patted her hand. "From what Daniel says, you *are* the ambition behind this entire project."

Sophie grinned. "Well, now that you mention it, the only way that man stays on track for even twenty seconds at a time is if I manage his every move." They both laughed as the kitchen door swung open with a bang.

"Manage this!"

Carly turned at the deep, familiar voice and saw a tall, thin man with dark hair entering the kitchen. He was loaded down with Carly's luggage and was attempting to balance an open bottle of grape soda on top of it.

Sophie jumped up from the table, faster than it would have appeared possible. "*Daniel Henry Day.*" She reached out and plucked the soda from its precarious position on top of Carly's makeup case. "What do you think you're doing?"

Daniel winked at Carly. She couldn't help but laugh as she stood and grabbed some of her luggage from his arms. He dumped the rest on the table and turned to Sophie, enveloping her in a warm embrace. He placed a loud kiss on her neck and she squealed, smacking his arm.

"What does it look like I'm doing? I'm making out with Miss America," he said into her shoulder.

Wiggling free, Sophie held him at arm's length and her expression softened as she looked into his eyes. He brushed a lock of hair from the side of her face and lowered his head to kiss her reverently.

Carly stared at them, embarrassed. They looked so perfect together. It was ridiculous to feel like a third wheel with people she didn't even really know, but all the same, she felt minuscule. She used to long for a man to look at her like that. But not anymore. Not this summer. The next three months were supposed to be completely devoid of theater romance.

Irritated with herself, she shook it off and snapped her fingers.

"Earth to Daniel and Sophie," she said. "Is it about time for that grand tour?"

With reluctance, Daniel let his hands slide from Sophie's shoulders. She leaned up and kissed his cheek. "Go on. Ross is waiting on the porch. And he isn't getting any more patient."

"I can attest to that," Carly said as she pushed open the kitchen door.

Ross was waiting as promised, a play script and pen in hand. "Come on, cop lover . . . what's taking you so long? Did you forget to grab your night stick?" he laughed as Carly rolled her eyes and bounded down the front steps of the hotel.

"Always working, aren't you?" she teased back as she flicked his script with her index finger. He responded by tugging on an imaginary police hat, whistling and licking his lips. "Shut up," she declared as she sailed past him. Ross reached forward to grab her hand.

Daniel loped ahead of them, staring up at the façade of the building next to the hotel. Following his gaze, Carly wrestled her hand loose and looked. A few weathered clapboard shingles hung above a big, faded sign that read "General Hardware Store." Her gaze trailed down the grayish-brown building, noting the simple doorframe and leaded plate glass windows. Amazing. It was like being on the set of *Tombstone* or some other Western movie. Except it was real.

She shaded her eyes and peered up the street. Next to the general store was what had to be a stable because of the hitching post out front and the hayloft on the second story. She squinted at the building beyond the stable and started toward it. It was smaller than the general store, but still had the remains of faded and peeling red paint.

"What's this one?" she asked.

"That, my dear, is the saloon," declared Daniel in a proud voice.

Stopping in front of the entrance, Carly ran her hands over the smooth wood and eased open the ancient screen door. She turned an old brass knob and the thick door creaked as she entered. "What, no swinging shutters?" she joked as she stepped through into the dim interior.

Directly in front of her against the wall was a huge bar, carved much the same as the front desk in the hotel. Scattered around the room were square plank tables, with chairs upended on top of them. Dust sifted through light made by cracks in the window shutters.

A staircase curved from the right side of the bar into a wide gallery-style balcony that encircled the room. Several stools and an old piano perched up there, as if waiting for customers to come and observe the action below. Carly was in her element. She stood motionless, her tired eyes straying around, darting here, resting there.

"We could leave her here for ten years and she'd still be in heaven," whispered Ross.

Daniel smiled. "Just wait 'til she sees the theater."

The theater was far beyond Carly's expectations. Standing at the back of the house, she swiveled her head in amazement. "This is like winning the lottery," she whispered, looking up. A generous, sloping balcony arced in a semicircle overhead. On either side of it, quaint boxes with red tattered curtains nestled into the old plaster walls. Wide, curving rows of faded velvet-covered wooden seats sloped down before her, ending in an elaborate, soaring proscenium arch. The arch framing the stage was painted a dull white, but Carly knew that a treasure was hidden beneath.

She meandered down one of the two side aisles, looking at the chandeliered ceiling as she walked. "This used to have a mural, didn't it?" she asked.

Daniel stomped past her and flopped into a seat in the front row. A cloud of dust rose into the stuffy air. "Yeah. Although the only pictures we have of the original aren't all that great. My brother, wonderful man that he is, offered to help you out with the ceiling restoration."

"Oh yeah?" Carly answered and climbed the narrow steps in

front of the stage. Making sure to be gentle, she scratched a corner of the proscenium with a fingernail. "OK by me. This was gilded, I would imagine," she muttered.

"What's 'gilded'?" Ross asked. He was behind her now, looking up into the cavernous area above the stage. The backstage door of the theater flew open with a thud, jolting Carly from her inspection.

"Gilded means golden, and unfortunately for you, Daniel, that's not the term I would apply to that dangerous witch you hired to be your lead actress."

Carly swiveled and saw a tiny woman slam the door shut, a tape measure looped around her neck, her hands jammed on ample hips. A puffy red scratch mark marred one round cheek. Throwing back her frizzy lion's mane of hair, the woman clomped on platform sandals to the front of the stage. She leaned down and stuck a finger in Daniel's face.

"She has to go. I can't work for twelve weeks with a diva like that! You're the producer. It's either her or me. I won't stand for co-workers who assault people!"

Daniel's eyes widened and he looked at Ross for help. Ross rolled his eyes and walked over to the woman and took her by the shoulders.

"Sweetie, are you Nancy? My brilliant costume designer?" he cooed. "I am SO excited to be working with you. I've heard so much about the show you just opened in L.A." Taking her arm, he steered her down the narrow steps and up the central aisle of the theater.

The door banged open again. A beautiful cover-model redhead in stiletto heels covered the stage in wide strides. Standing near the footlights, she swept her dainty arm through the air.

"That's right, leave. You obviously don't have the ability to handle *real* talent anyway." Sniffing, she looked down at Daniel and pouted, batting her lovely eyelashes.

"Give me a break," Carly muttered as she leaned against the arch. The young woman's spine stiffened, but she didn't turn around.

"What did you say?" she demanded.

Carly bounded across the distance between them and stuck out her hand. "You must be one of the actresses. Hi, I'm Carly."

The beauty didn't spare her a glance. "Hi, I'm leaving," she retorted as she picked her way down the steps and past Daniel.

"Let this be a lesson to you in the future, Mr. Producer," she snarled over her shoulder, "No decent actress has to put up with some low-budget designer telling them they're too fat for costumes." She shoved open the double doors of the theater and disappeared into the sunlight.

Carly pressed her lips together to keep from laughing and looked at Daniel. Shock froze his handsome, angular face. He sat in silence until a car started up in the distance, screeching its tires and spinning gravel.

Slowly Daniel put a hand over his eyes and grunted. "Sophie's gonna kill me. She told me to wait for Ross before introducing everybody. Why don't I listen to her?" He moved his fingers apart and peered up at Carly. "Are all theater people this volatile?"

Laughing, Carly sat next to him in a dusty seat. "Not the ones who keep getting work . . . unless they are talented beyond belief. Was she that good?"

Daniel sighed. "She *looked* that good. And I know that would have sold tickets. Man, I'm a pig."

He gazed at Carly with puppy dog eyes. A few years ago, she would have fallen all over herself to convince him otherwise, but now that she was older and hopefully wiser, she held back her sympathy.

"Even pigs deserve second chances," she declared, patting his shoulder. "You'll find another actress. Don't worry about it." Rising and dusting off the seat of her shorts, she was suddenly exhausted. "Look, I don't want to leave you here in your hour of need, but I really have to change my hideous clothes, take a shower, and unpack."

Daniel stood and put an arm around her. "Carly? Did I tell you yet that I am so happy I hired you?" He grinned and gestured around the theater. Carly laughed, despite her tiredness.

"Daniel, again. You don't have to worry. From what I have seen of Ruby Spring today, wild horses couldn't drag me away."

*

Later that evening, clean, rested, and refreshed, Carly dragged a pink sundress out of her suitcase and slipped it on. Standing in front of the large oval mirror in her guest room under the eaves, high on the third floor of the Ruby Spring Hotel, she tried on a hesitant smile. Her shoulder-length light brown hair lay in soft, damp waves against her sun-pink cheeks. Large gray eyes, although tired, sparkled in her heart-shaped face. Her cheekbones actually looked elegant in the dusky light peeking through the recessed windows.

Satisfied that she didn't look like she'd been gnawed half to death by raccoons, Carly pushed her suitcase over on the four-poster bed and smoothed the old quilt. Grabbing a plain white pair of sneakers, she slipped them on her feet and made her way down the curving staircase of the hotel to the lobby. The air had cooled considerably outside, and she shivered, wishing for a sweater as she passed the front desk to head for the kitchen. Rummaging in the refrigerator, she heard the door swing open.

"Ross, I'm not raiding your food for much longer. Tomorrow I'll go into town and get some groceries," she said, pulling out an orange and a tub of chicken salad. A large, tanned hand came around her shoulder and reached for a beer.

"You could raid mine anytime you want to, good lookin'."

Carly's heart dropped to her stomach. *Wheeler!* But what was he doing here? Their date wasn't until tomorrow night. She took a deep breath, inhaling the scent of leather and woodsy cologne. She closed her eyes for a second, reveling in the pure maleness of him.

"I thought you were going to call me, Wheeler," she said in a quiet voice.

Placing a gentle hand on his hard chest, she pushed him back and sat down at the table, smoothing her sundress. He pulled out the chair next to her and turned it around, straddling it. Sipping his beer, he flashed her one of his sure-to-charm grins.

"Couldn't wait on that, Carly. I had to see you," he stated.

She gripped the orange in her hands and looked across the table to the coffeemaker on the counter. The clock on it read 9:30. It wasn't really all that late. Tipping her head, she looked into his blue eyes. They left her weak, just as they had that afternoon.

He reached over and covered her hands and the orange with one of his large, smooth palms. "This doesn't look much like a very good dinner to me, miss," he joked. Carly threw her head back and laughed. A strap of her dress slipped from her shoulder.

"I wasn't aware that you were keeping such close tabs on my eating habits, but whatever floats your boat, I guess," she replied with a grin.

Wheeler's magnetic eyes slid from her face and he caught his teeth in his lower lip. He moved his hand from hers and reached for her shoulder. Grasping the strap of her sundress, he raised it back up to her shoulder, skimming her soft skin and instantly raising goose bumps.

"C'mon, Carly girl. Come with me," he whispered.

She was lost.

Chapter Three

This had to be the worst night of her life. After a dinner of a dry hamburger, soggy fries and uncomfortable conversation, Wheeler had insisted they go dancing. Not taking no for an answer, he had driven across Albuquerque to one of the seediest dumps she had ever seen. In a loud voice, he'd ordered her a watery drink and proceeded to introduce her as "his hottie for the night."

After ignoring her, shooting a couple of rounds of pool and losing a wad of money, he had started drinking in earnest. It was well past time to go. The country music at the cramped, hazy bar was pounding into Carly's brain and the thick cigarette smoke stung her eyes.

Gazing down at her half-finished cocktail, she played with the straw and glanced at her watch. Two a.m. She should be asleep right now. There was a production meeting at the theater tomorrow morning . . . wait . . . this morning. Shit. It wasn't like her to show up unprepared and exhausted. She was beyond irritated that the bonehead hadn't taken any of her subtle hints. But one way or another, she had to get out of there. Pasting a bright smile on her face, she looked up at Wheeler.

"Hey there, handsome," she began. "Have you looked at a clock lately?"

She was alarmed to see that his gorgeous eyes were now red-rimmed, and he had a nose to match. His leather jacket was stained with mustard and a toothpick dangled from the corner of his mouth.

"Whats'a matter, good lookin'? Doncha like to party?" he retorted, grabbing her shoulder with a rough hand.

He shoved her toward the dance floor, crashing into a table as they went. *What in the hell was she thinking?* This guy was completely different from the dashing officer who had rescued her that afternoon. She looked up into his foggy eyes and decided to take matters into her own hands.

Carly wrenched her shoulder from his grasp and turned, heading for the exit. Images of a handsome and charming Wheeler flooded her tired mind, but she pushed the bitter thoughts away. She slammed open the door and walked into the dark parking lot past the blare of the music, pulling her completely charged cell phone from her purse. Tapping an impatient foot on the gravel, she fretted for a minute before scrolling to the number for the hotel. Just as she was about to hit "send," Wheeler grabbed her arm and spun her around.

"Where do you think you're goin'?" he demanded.

His breath was a fog of whiskey and his eyes glittered in the dim light provided by the neon sign above the bar. This time, Carly was way too angry to be intimidated by him.

"I'm going wherever I want, and believe me, you aren't invited!" she shouted, shoving him in the chest.

In the flash of an eye, Wheeler snatched the phone from her hand and hurled it into the bushes across the parking lot. Stumbling, he hooted as it connected with a rock.

"Always did have good aim," he crowed, making shooting motions with his fingers.

Disgusted with Wheeler, and though she hated to admit it, furious with herself, Carly stalked back across the gravel to the roadhouse door. Before she even got halfway, Wheeler's hands were on her again.

"Dammit!" she yelled and struggled to free herself.

This time, though, his grip was like iron. He whirled her around and pinched her face in one of his large hands.

"Carly girl, you are just askin' for it."

He lowered his head and enveloped her lips in a sloppy wet kiss. Carly gagged on the taste of cheap alcohol and cigarettes. Panic kicked in and she brought her knee up into his crotch. Hard. He released her and doubled over.

Howling, he stumbled backward and slammed his head on a truck's side mirror. Cursing at the top of his lungs, he grabbed the mirror and wrenched it off the truck. He stomped on it until it cracked and then gave it a violent kick. Fear replaced Carly's anger.

Not taking her eyes from him, she inched her way through the dark toward the bar as Wheeler stumbled to his car and still cursing, managed to start it and back up.

She squeezed herself behind some bushes next to the door as he careened around the parking lot, looking for her.

"Carly. Get out here. NOW!" he screamed, "You better listen to me, girl. You'll regret this."

Every part of her wanted to go back inside, but she *had* to make sure he left. After a few endless minutes, Wheeler gave up and pulled out of the lot with a screech of tires. Her knees shaking in relief, Carly eased out of her hiding place and took a deep breath.

She looked up at the stars and set her mouth in a grim line. "I am not going to cry. I am not going to freak," she said. Her voice shook.

"No reason to."

Relief flooded through her and she searched the dark for the source of the familiar voice.

"Daniel? Daniel? Where are you?" she asked.

A tall, thin, dark-haired man emerged from the shadows near the bushes and walked toward her. He was holding her cell phone, but he wasn't Daniel. He stopped in front of her and held it out, a compassionate smile warming his deep brown eyes.

"It's not broken," he stated. His voice was warm and soothing.

"But . . . Daniel . . . " she began.

The man's smile widened and dimples formed in his gaunt cheeks. "I may sound like Daniel and I may look like Daniel, but I am definitely *not* him. I'm Asher."

"But . . . " she started again.

He held the cell phone closer. "You can call Daniel if you really want to, but you would most likely wake up Sophie . . . and she isn't in a great mood these days."

Carly understood then. "Why didn't you just tell me you're Daniel's brother?" she asked, taking the phone.

"Just wanted to see how quick you are," He gave her another smile and thrust his hands into the pockets of his old jeans.

Carly stared at him. "Well, I appreciate you finding my phone, but I am absolutely not in the mood to be judged by any more men this evening." She narrowed her eyes. "And by the way, what were you doing hiding in the bushes? If you saw that loser attack me, why didn't you do something?"

The smile wiped from his face, Asher pulled his hands out of his pockets and laced them behind his head.

"Look, I didn't want to interfere as long as you were kicking his ass on your own. Believe me, I was watching. If that asshole so much as raised a hand to you, I would have been on him like a shot." With that, he turned on his heel and stomped back toward the edge of the parking lot.

Carly shoved the phone in her purse and followed him. "Where are you going?" she asked.

"Home," he answered.

"Ruby Spring, I hope?" she asked, catching up to him as he opened the door of an old VW van.

Asher turned and gazed down at her. His expression softened and in the glow of the van's interior light, his face was all compassion. Carly glanced into the side mirror on the door and noted her smeared lipstick and the dark shadows under her eyes. No wonder he felt sorry for her. She looked like a train wreck. And she couldn't quit staring at him. With a hint of a smile, he reached out for her shoulder.

"Get in."

They rode in silence for a while, the winking lights of Albuquerque dimming as they climbed into the mountains. The moon was bright overhead in the clear sky and Carly rolled down the window to let the cool breeze ruffle her hair. Pretending to close her eyes, she peered at Asher from beneath her lashes. The glow from the dashboard illuminated his features.

He *did* look like Daniel. But Asher was much thinner, if that was even possible. The gauntness made him look severe, but his dark eyes were thoughtful and expressive. Magnetic, actually. Thin streaks of gray peppered his wavy brown hair and faint lines etched the corners of his well-formed mouth. Large tapered fingers gripped the steering wheel. His legs were wide apart, his left knee drawn up to rest against the door. Carly glanced back up at his face again. A small smile curved his lips and she realized with dismay that she had been busted staring at him.

She gave a huge fake yawn and looked around the interior of the van. Suitcases, boxes and several stacked canvas frames were wedged tightly into the back seats.

"What's with the paintings?" she asked in a casual tone.

Asher glanced at her, then back at the road. A pained expression clouded his eyes.

"Oh, just some dabbling," he answered, just as casually.

"That's a lot of work for just a dabbler," she stated, "and a lot of luggage for a person who lives around here." She peered over at him again.

His face remained blank as he concentrated on the road. "I used to live here. Now I do again. End of story."

Silence again. She toyed with the door lock and smoothed the skirt of her sundress. "So what were you doing at that dump?" she tried again.

"Just having a drink before going home. You have a problem with that?" he responded.

Carly mentally kicked herself. "Hey, I'm not usually that nosy. Today I've been finding myself making a lot of extra chit-chat. Meeting new people and all that." She laughed. "I'm not a ditzy woman or anything. Quite a few people even tell me that sometimes I'm too close-mouthed, but I'll bet you wouldn't believe them, would you?" She looked over again, a hopeful smile in her eyes.

Unfortunately, Asher didn't look amused. Slowing down, he turned the van up the bumpy road leading to Ruby Spring.

"You worry way too much about what other people think of you, don't you?" he replied, still staring at the road.

She turned back to the window, blinking as the truth of his words buzzed through her. The van bounced along in silence and she gripped her purse, suddenly wanting more than anything to be in bed, completely under the covers, and fast asleep. She sensed Asher looking at her, but refused to move her head. Finally, the van rolled to a stop and she yanked off her seatbelt, wrenched open the door and jumped to the ground.

"Thanks for the ride," she shot over her shoulder and ran for the steps of the hotel. Tears stung her eyes as she turned the doorknob.

Asher's deep voice reached her as she shut the door. "Wait! What's your name?"

She ignored him.

Chapter Four

Carly woke with a start and stared in confusion around the unfamiliar room. Soft morning light beaming through the lace curtains made patterns on the old hardwood floor. An antique rocker stood near the door; her pink sundress lay in a crumpled heap on its seat. Realization dawned on her and she pulled the comfy quilt over her head.

What had she been thinking last night? She knew better than to go out the night before starting a new summer job. On four hours of sleep the night before, spent in a car. And with a stranger, nonetheless! *A stranger who turned out to be a grade-A asshole*, she thought with resentment. Carly turned over on her side and stared at the lavender floral wallpaper.

And then last night, three hours of sleep. Impressive. She had to slow down. Just because she had finally taken a job that she really and truly cared about, one that was going to be exciting and professionally fulfilling didn't mean that she had to lose her senses and act on instinct every moment of the day. But why not? She was twenty-nine years old . . . not fifty-nine. *I'm too anal. It's just two night's sleep messed up. What's the big deal?*

But it was a big deal to Carly. This summer . . . well, this summer was somehow supposed to be different. She'd promised it to herself. She shut her eyes and willed her body to relax. She needed to take care of herself, for God's sake. And the best way to start was by not beating herself up. She needed another hour of sleep.

Willing herself back to snooze-land, though, proved fruitless. Through one of the cracked-open windows, she heard familiar voices. Carly crept out of bed and opened the window the rest of the way. Ross stood in the dusty street in front of the hotel, a giant travel mug of coffee in hand, the requisite baseball cap jammed onto his head. Sophie, one arm full of scripts and pencils, stood next to him rubbing the small of her back.

"She got back here *when?*" Ross exclaimed.

"About three in the morning, I guess, give or take," Sophie replied, "I woke up when I heard the van, and I knew it was Asher. Danny got up and came around front to meet him." She gestured to the back of the hotel, where she and Daniel shared an apartment in the basement.

Ross's brow furrowed. "We should have taken your advice, Sophie. If I ever see that cop again, I'm gonna kick his ass into next week." He looked up at Carly's window.

Busted again. She drew back into the room and chewed on a fingernail. Tears sprang to her eyes for what seemed like the umpteenth time since she had arrived in New Mexico. What kind of shitty luck was she having, anyway? Embarrassed over and over in a little more than twenty-four hours, and insulted by two first-rate losers last night, too.

"Hey, sweetie. Good morning." Ross's voice drifted up to the window. "Are you coming down for the meeting?"

The meeting. Carly's eyes widened and she looked around for her travel alarm. It was nowhere to be found, which meant it was probably still in a suitcase. She clapped a hand over her eyes and breathed in. Her luck absolutely had to change. Vowing to make the best of the day, she hurried back to the window. She pasted a merry smile on her face and poked her head out.

"Hey there, Mr. Director. Hope you slept well . . . I sure did. Be down to the theater in about fifteen minutes. I just have to unpack something to wear."

Not waiting for a response, Carly slammed the window shut and ran for a suitcase. Upending it on the rumpled bed, she grabbed her bathrobe, underwear, a fresh T-shirt and a pair of shorts. She stripped off her nightshirt and threw on the bathrobe, holding the silky fabric closed around her nude body, the ties flapping behind her. Barely stopping to grab her shampoo, she scurried into the hallway and pulled open the bathroom door.

Asher stood in front of the mirror wearing nothing but a towel wrapped around his hips. His face covered with shaving cream, he stopped short with a razor in mid-air. Although he was whipcord thin, the muscles of his arm bunched as he raised the razor to his chiseled face. He observed her without interest for a split second and went right back to shaving.

Carly's mouth dropped open and she took a step backward. A small sound escaped her lips and she hastily pulled the robe closer around her waist. He turned to her and moved forward, bracing himself against the doorway with a lazy smile.

"Hey, Carly."

His voice was deeper and more melodic than she remembered. Glancing up at his amused expression, Carly frowned.

"I thought you didn't know my name. And what are you doing in my bathroom?"

"This bathroom isn't private property, I'm afraid," he stated and gestured to a closed door across the hall.

Still frowning, Carly stepped around him and opened it. It was another bedroom, a mirror image of hers. Except in this one, a pair of old jeans was thrown over a rocker instead of a sundress. She closed it and turned back to him.

"You mean you are going to be living next door to me? I thought the hotel was reserved for the theater employees."

Asher chuckled. "I guess being family rates somewhere." He reached out and stuck a dab of shaving cream on her nose. "Don't worry, Carly. I won't be long." He flashed another devilish smile and shut the bathroom door in her face. Carly knocked on it immediately.

"Could you get out of there for just five minutes, please? I have a meeting." She tapped her foot and waited. Asher began to sing on the other side.

"Come on, buddy," she said with a sigh, "It's my first day of work. Give me a break."

He turned the water on full blast and raised his voice. She thought she detected a chuckle breaking into the chorus of his song.

Oh, he thought he was really cute, didn't he? Well, two could play that immature game. Banging on the door now, she kept it up until her knuckles were stinging. She gritted her teeth and leaned against it, pounding even harder.

Suddenly the door swung open and she lost her balance. Tripping forward, she screeched as she stumbled straight toward the enormous claw-footed tub. A strong pair of arms caught her just before her head came into contact with porcelain.

"Whoa!" Asher pulled her upright and grinned. He was clean-shaven, but still wore nothing but a towel. "You should pay me, you know. It's a full-time job keeping you out of trouble."

They were locked in an intimate embrace, squeezed between the tub and the wall in the tiny room. Carly tried to ease out of his gentle grasp, but only succeeded in nestling her head against his shoulder. She was uncomfortably aware of her heartbeat pounding into his body. And the firm warmth of his chest against her skin.

Flustered, she pulled as far away from him as possible and looked down. Her bathrobe was completely open. And her breasts were smashed into his abdomen. Oh, Lord, had he noticed? *Of course he noticed. What kind of idiot are you?*

Panicking, she glanced back up, a flush spreading across her already sunburned cheeks. Smiling, he hauled her out of the corner, still keeping her close in his arms.

"Yeah, I know," he whispered, "And don't worry. As much as I would like to, I'm not about to touch you after what happened last night with Wheeler."

Carly winced at the sound of the name, and the mood was broken. Jerking her bathrobe around herself and stepping to the door, she gestured toward the hallway.

"Thanks for your help. Again. Could you please leave? I'm really very late."

Scowling now, Asher stopped in the doorway, his eyes locked with hers. He brushed his hand across her cheek and then gently wiped the shaving cream from her nose. He took a deep breath and opened his mouth. She flinched and braced herself for his retort, but he said nothing.

Dipping his head, he came closer. Carly shivered and closed her eyes as she felt the warmth of his lips near her mouth. Did her really mean to kiss her? While they were both half-dressed and standing in a hallway? Her eyes snapped open and met with his.

At the last second, her turned and placed a sweet kiss on her cheek. His face lingered near hers for a few seconds, his eyes on her lips. Then he straightened and strolled into his bedroom, closing the door behind him.

Carly shut her eyes and stood completely still, but all she could see was the image of Asher's lips. Reaching up to her face, she pressed a palm on her burning cheek. This craziness had to stop. She was here to do a job, and for once, a job she really and truly cared about. Nothing was going to get in the way. Not this summer. She had sworn it to herself.

*

A few days later, after a round of get-to-know-you meetings, Carly sat on the front porch of the hotel with Ross, blueprints spread on the weathered boards beneath them. The afternoon sunlight winked over the mountaintops, warming her face. She smiled and settled back against a wall, relieved that her life was going so much more . . . well . . . smoothly this week. Rehearsals had started, and her paperwork on the restoration was well underway.

"So you think the ceiling of the theater can be repainted in enough time?" Ross asked, sipping yet another cup of coffee. "I mean, I'm kind of worried about that. The show has to come first, and I *have* to have an authentic oleo curtain. Daniel told me there's big money tied up in local sponsors who have paid to advertise on it. Don't you have to go visit them and get the logos and—"

Carly held up her hand as she doodled on a sketchpad. Placating Ross was second nature.

"It'll be tight, hon, but Daniel really wants this, and I agree with him. We need the audience to be drawn into the magic, and not just the show. No offense." She looked up, wincing, to gauge his response.

Ross waggled his eyebrows. "You know you can't offend me, partner. If I wanted someone to lie to me, I'd hire a hooker." He grinned when she gasped.

"For a woman who's almost out to pasture, you sure haven't been around the block much."

Carly shoved his shoulder. "Most men would consider that an *attractive* quality in a girl!" she retorted, smiling in spite of herself.

Gazing up at the brilliantly blue sky, she sighed. Things had settled down somewhat after her crazy first day at Ruby Spring. Nancy, the costume designer, was not a psycho, as Daniel and Ross had feared. Just a little bit high-strung, which could be interpreted as normal, as far as theater designers under tight deadlines were concerned. Carly doubted that she would have reacted any differently if a wound-up actress had raked fingernails across her face, either.

The rest of the remaining actors seemed to be decent people, if not predictably flaky. Daniel had been nervous when he gave his opening speech, but his excitement for the play and the restoration soon overcame his shaky voice, and he had managed to suck all of them into his enthusiasm for this unique project.

Carly's greatest challenge now was to not only design and supervise the build of the set for the show, but also to somehow manage to restore the inside of the grand, but decrepit old theater. Fortunately, the work was almost all cosmetic. The largest project was the repainting of the mural on the ceiling, and Carly knew that she had to talk to Asher about that. Daniel wanted him to help her. Butterflies swirled in her stomach as she thought again of the memory of his lips so close to her own. She'd talk to him sometime soon. Like maybe tomorrow.

Frowning, she glanced down at the rough sketch for the oleo curtain. Where had Asher been, anyway? She hadn't seen him since that morning when . . . well, that morning when they had bumped into each other in the bathroom. Not that she had been looking for him.

Late in the evenings, when she had been snuggled in bed, she had heard the door to his bedroom open and then click shut. In the mornings, the infamous bathroom had been unoccupied. After a few days, though, she hadn't even heard the sound of his bedroom door. Where had he gone? Although she shouldn't have cared, it made her peevish.

Just that morning, as she went down to the kitchen, she had heard voices inside and stopped, her hand on the swinging door. Although she hated it when people spied on her, just this once Carly couldn't resist doing the same. She had stayed there, motionless, and listened to the conversation.

"So why did he disappear this time?" Sophie murmured.

"Same old, same old," Daniel sighed, "He said he had some thinking to do, and he'd be back in ten days."

"Well, he'd better be back in time to help Carly with that ceiling. He promised you, Daniel."

A chair scraped on the floor and Carly jumped back. She heard the sound of the refrigerator door open and then the sound of someone sitting down. She relaxed again and cocked her ear to the door, straining to hear Sophie's voice.

" . . . I know that horrible woman hurt him. And I can't blame him for running away from New York after she skipped town with most of the paintings for his gallery opening. But all the same, Asher's thirty-five years old. If he's going to come back here and stay in Ruby Spring, he really needs to help us out, Daniel. He owns half, just the same as you."

Daniel sighed. "I know, Soph, but Asher is . . . well . . . he's different. He doesn't take love that lightly. And he *is* an artist. Just give him a few days. I am. Part of the reason I asked him to help with the ceiling is to get his mind off of it."

"Well, I guess. But Daniel Day, you have to get used to dealing with *artists*. If you handle them with kid gloves constantly, they'll walk all over you," she stated in a gentle tone.

Daniel cleared his throat. "I think I'm handling the *artists* here just fine, thank you very much. This is the first time I've ever produced a show, for God's sake. Give me a break Sophie!"

"I didn't say you were doing a bad job, dearest. Quite the opposite. Don't forget that I am always . . . and forever, absolutely proud of you."

Carly heard Daniel's chuckle and the unmistakable sound of a loud kiss. Sophie giggled and Carly back away from the door and tiptoed quietly across the lobby.

So, that was Asher's problem. His girlfriend screwed him over. Her brow puckered and she ran her hand over the carving on the front desk. But why did *she* feel sorry for him? All he had ever done was insult her. And save her from danger. In a completely dashing manner. Twice. She sighed and tried to force her over-organized mind *not* to count the calendar days until he would be back.

She still felt guilty for having listened in on what had to have been a completely private conversation between Daniel and Sophie. Debating about whether to confide in Ross, Carly drew circles on her sketchpad. But confide what? That she might possibly have the hots for the producer's brother?

Someone shouted in the distance, pulling her back to reality. Carly brushed her hair out of her eyes and looked up.

Nancy was tottering down the dusty street on her platform sandals at a fast clip, her cell phone grasped in a pudgy hand. Her eyes were wide and she was panting. "Hey, Ross. You gotta come quick. Something bad," she wheezed as she hauled herself onto the porch.

Carly and Ross jumped up at the same time. "Nancy, what's wrong, sweetie?" Ross grabbed her by the shoulders. She gulped and pressed her cell phone into his hand. "Use . . . yours," she gasped, "I . . . can't get a . . . signal." Flopping down on a rocking chair, she took a couple of deep breaths.

"Use mine for what?" Ross asked.

"To call an ambulance, of course!" Nancy cried. "Daniel just fell off a ladder. I think he broke his leg."

Barely stopping to grab his phone from the porch railing, Ross jumped over it and onto the street. He was halfway to the theater before Carly could open the hotel door. "Nancy, go inside and get Sophie," Carly demanded, "I have to get down there and help them."

She didn't wait for Nancy to mobilize. Yanking the woman up from the chair, Carly turned and ran to the theater with her heart in her throat. She slipped through the front doors. The stage was empty. "Ross . . . Daniel," she called, sprinting down a side aisle and onto the stage. "Daniel! Where are you guys?"

A faint moan came from beneath the stage. Hastily, Carly darted stage right and clattered down the narrow metal spiral staircase to the dressing rooms. Daniel, his face pinched and white, was lying on the floor, his left leg at a sickening angle. Ross was crouched next to him, gripping his hand, speaking into his cell phone.

Carly's eyes flew to the tall ladder at the end of the room. The top three rungs were cracked clean in two, hanging at haphazard angles. Her mouth dropped open and she squatted next to the two men. "Isn't that the ladder you bought for me yesterday?"

"Yeah," Daniel managed through gritted teeth, "Guess I'm getting my money back, huh?"

Carly murmured in sympathy and stroked his forehead. "Just try to lay still. I'm sure an ambulance will be here soon."

Ross snapped his phone shut and stood up. "They said fifteen minutes. Can you hang on for fifteen minutes, buddy?" Daniel nodded and released Ross's hand. "What were you doing up there anyway?" Ross asked.

Daniel laughed weakly and closed his eyes. "Sophie's gonna kill me. I was just making a little joke. Just going to post something funny, just for grins." He gestured to a makeup table with lights. "See that head shot?"

Ross picked it up and frowned. It was an eight by ten picture of the beautiful red-head who had walked out before rehearsals even started. "What the hell, Danny?" Ross demanded, "I thought you would have torn this up and used it as kindling by now."

"I was going to put it up on that old bulletin board we don't use anymore . . . with 'employee of the week' underneath," Daniel muttered.

Ross shook his head and snorted. "That's a good one. *Almost* worth a broken leg, but somehow . . . I don't think so." Glancing over at the ladder, he shook his head again. "Why is the bulletin board so high on the wall, anyway?"

Daniel waved his hand noncommittally. "I don't know. To make more room for makeup mirrors, I guess. God, Ross, what is this, the third degree? I'm kind of occupied right now."

Carly glared at Ross and moved her lips. *"Shut up!"* Ross gestured toward the ladder, his eyes wide. *"This was no accident,"* he mouthed. Carly narrowed her eyes in confusion. *"What?"*

Before he could explain, voices overhead interrupted. A radio squawked and Carly sighed in relief. "Hey, down here!" she shouted.

A pair of boots and tan uniformed legs descended the spiral stairs. They were followed by an impressively buff body, and then, to Carly's horror, Wheeler's face. "Well, well, well." He smirked and folded his arms.

Carly scrambled up and ran to stand beside Ross. Daniel raised his head from the floor and frowned at Wheeler. "Did you bring an ambulance with you, Barstow?" he whispered gruffly.

Wheeler jerked a thumb upward. "They're comin'." Immediately, he turned to Carly. He smiled, running his tongue across his perfect teeth. "What's up, good lookin'?"

Uh-oh. Ross was her best friend and she knew him almost as well as she knew herself. He was about to pick a fight. With a cop. She grabbed his hand in an iron grip, but it was no use. He snarled at Wheeler and tugged himself free.

"Why don't you just do your job, you ass . . . "

Carly clapped her hand over his mouth. "Wheeler, could you wait upstairs, please? This room is pretty small, and they have to get a stretcher down here, don't they?" Wheeler gave her a fierce stare and remained where he was.

"I think I need to stay down here and survey the situation, but thanks for the suggestion, cutie," he scoffed, plunking down on a bench. He folded his arms, slumping, and glared at Ross.

Ross glared back and stomped over to the broken ladder. "As long as you insist on staying down here, again, I'll ask you to do your job." Placing a hand on the ladder, he crooked his index finger. "Come here. If you have any investigative skills, now is the time to put them to use, *Officer.* This ladder has been sabotaged."

Chapter Five

Sophie stood at the hospital bedside, a soggy tissue clenched in her fist. She reached down, careful not to bump Daniel's left leg. It was in a cast from ankle to hip, and was raised into the air, thanks to traction. Brushing a lock of damp hair from his forehead, she gazed anxiously at his pale face. Dark lashes shadowed his cheeks, and his breathing was quiet. Leaning closer, she whispered, "Dear heart? Danny? Can you hear me?"

Daniel moaned and opened his eyes a crack. He reached up and weakly grasped her hand, bringing it to his lips for a kiss. "These drugs are awesome," he murmured.

Smiling, Sophie kissed his forehead and perched on the side of the bed. "Well, don't get used to them, Mister. That's all I need, a brand new baby *and* an addict on my hands."

His eyes opened wider and he clenched her hand. "Baby? My God, Soph, did you have the baby?" He lifted his hand to her face.

She laughed and moved it to her belly. "No, silly. Feel. He—or she—is still in there. For three more weeks or so. You'll be home by then, and I'll be where you are."

Daniel exhaled and looked around the room. His eyes found the television and went wide. "This is awesome."

Sophie raised an eyebrow. "What is, dearest?"

"I can watch cable," he exclaimed, grinning.

Sophie shook her head and squeezed his hand. "I thought you said you didn't miss cable when we moved up to Ruby Spring," she said.

He snorted matter-of-factly. "I lied."

They both turned their heads at the soft knock on the door. Carly opened it and poked her head in. "Hey, Boss," she whispered.

Daniel grinned and motioned her in. "What's up, Carly? Hey,

I can't feel a thing." He reached down and rapped on his cast. Sophie snatched his hand away and stood up.

"Daniel Henry Day. What do you think you're doing?"

"Drugs," he promptly replied.

Sophie rolled her eyes and walked to the door. "Carly, keep him out of trouble for a few minutes. I need to stretch my legs." Shaking a finger in his direction, she admonished, "Danny, I want you to be asleep in one hour."

He made little effort to remove the smile from his face. "Yes, ma'am."

Carly flopped down in the chair next to his hospital bed. "So how long are you in for?" she asked, careful to keep her tone light.

"I dunno. Probably a few days at least. Hey, could you hand me the remote?" he replied.

Carly rose and crossed her arms. "Sophie said you have to rest, Daniel."

He sighed and folded his hands across his middle. "Fine." He turned his face toward her and pressed his lips together. "If I can't watch TV, maybe you could tell me something, then."

Carly sat back down and took his hand. "What is it?"

"I want to know how that ladder came to be broken."

Carly frowned and crossed her legs. "I don't know if now is the best time, really," she began.

"Now is a great time. If anyone has the right to know, it's me," he pushed. She pressed her lips together.

"OK, but you're not going to like it. Not one little bit."

"Try me."

Carly nervously laced her fingers together. "Well, here's the thing. After they put you on the stretcher and managed to get you upstairs, Ross made Wheeler stay and take a statement. Wheeler didn't want to. Go figure," she said with a snort. "Anyway, after Wheeler left, Ross and I looked more closely at that ladder. There was dried glue on the center of the rungs that broke, Daniel." She glanced at him, but he was looking at the ceiling, his face expressionless.

"Go on," he replied.

She got up and began to pace. "We went back up to the stage and started looking around. Ross noticed that the stage door had been jimmied open. There was also a bottle of wood glue in the dumpster," she continued. "And boot prints all over the dirt behind the theater. Whoever this jerk was, he was pretty damned stupid about leaving evidence behind."

Daniel rubbed his eyes and groaned. "Great," he muttered.

Carly looked at him with sympathy and walked to the door. "Well, now you know. If it makes you feel any better, I have this feeling . . . and it may be paranoid . . . but I think that ladder was meant for me."

Daniel frowned. "Why would that make me feel better?"

Carly sucked in a breath. "No, no, that's not how I meant it. It's just that the ladder was probably not meant to hurt *you*. I'm pretty much the only person at the theater who's been climbing on a ladder in the last couple of days." She pushed her hair out of her face and continued. "I almost hate to say it out loud, but . . . I'm pretty sure . . . Wheeler did it."

Daniel's face was grave and he stared at her for a few seconds. A lump formed in her throat. Carly looked away, blinking up at the ceiling, willing the tears to stay put. "Carly," he said in a soft voice, "I want you to be very, very careful."

Squeezing her arms about her middle, she could only nod.

"Get better soon," she whispered, not trusting her voice. Thank God the room was dark. That's all she needed; her boss seeing her as an emotionally unstable crybaby. Reaching for the door, Carly slipped outside into the empty hallway and then on to the elevator.

Once in the parking lot, she took a deep breath of the cool evening air. Better now. Reaching for her car keys, she glanced over her shoulder. Although the lot was well-lit, it was also pretty well deserted. There was no reason to be freaked out. None at all.

It's not like she was back in Chicago.

Carly squared her shoulders and shook off the prickly feeling at the back of her neck. Jogging to her car, though, she couldn't help but scan the edges of the parking lot for a tall, well-built blond man with blue eyes in a cop uniform. And she couldn't help but wonder if a tall, thin dark-haired man with brown eyes would show up, too. Dammit! This was ridiculous. Wheeler was not going to materialize out of nowhere and try to hurt her. And Asher was not going to appear like magic to save the day, either.

Wrenching open her car door, she scrambled in and slammed it behind her, locked it and turned to check the back seat to make sure it was empty. Of course it was. Carly leaned her forehead against the steering wheel and exhaled, trying to calm her galloping heart. What was wrong with her? Almost wishing for Wheeler to show up so that Asher could come and save her? What kind of sick fantasy was that?

She sat up and slumped in the seat for a few minutes. OK. OK, she had to be honest with herself. On some well . . . elemental level, she found Asher extremely . . . compelling. And mysterious. And . . . magnetic. But why? He was just the brother of the guy who had hired her to do a *job*. And the job was what was important here.

There were tons of men in Chicago who were equally as handsome as Asher, she reasoned. And some of them were artists, too. Moody artists, who were completely self-involved. And that was the catch. Asher didn't seem to be selfish. He seemed decent. That was it; that was the attraction. Carly sighed in frustration and pulled on her seatbelt.

She couldn't obsess. Not this summer. There had to be something about Asher that would make him unappealing. Carly wracked her brain as she pulled out of the parking lot. A few drops of rain hit her windshield, and she turned on the wipers. Merging onto the interstate, and then onto the two-lane state highway, she still thought. And as she turned into the bumpy road leading to

Ruby Spring, she came up with it.

What kind of person moved back home and then took off again almost right away? Especially if he had a responsibility to a family business? Now, that *was* selfish. And it was even more selfish to make himself completely unreachable, too. Carly doubted if Asher even knew that Daniel was lying flat on his back in a hospital bed, his leg in traction.

Bouncing up the rutted, muddy road, she peered out the windshield through the drizzle. Maybe Asher was a decent guy in some respects, but he was also irresponsible and unpredictable. She should be disgusted with him. She should be completely unimpressed by him. She shouldn't give him a second thought. But God help her, she just couldn't help herself.

*

Asher sat disconsolately next to the window, watching rivulets of rain run down the pane. He shivered at the chill in the cabin and got up wearily to stoke the fire. Wrapping a quilt around his bare shoulders, he carefully placed the cell phone back in its charger. Sophie's call had unnerved him, it was true.

He'd felt . . . well, infuriated since coming back to Ruby Spring. An oppressive, panicky feeling that had nothing to do with being here. And had everything to do with New York. Escaping to the cabin up the trail from Ruby Spring had helped some, but didn't take the sting completely away. And now this. His brother was hurt, and he, Asher, was sitting on his ass licking his wounds. Like a little boy.

Most annoying of all was that his thoughts kept straying back to Carly Foster and her laughing eyes and pretty caramel-colored hair. What the hell was wrong with him? He wasn't a masochist. Not a month ago, a similarly pretty girl had taken his heart and his trust, and stomped all over them while she laughed all the way to Europe. His paintings and his girl were gone in the blink of an eye. So how in the world could he be finding another female attractive so soon after being crushed so completely?

It must be pure physical attraction, he reassured himself. Nothing more. Just his body reminding him after all, that he was a healthy heterosexual man.

He ran a hand through his wavy hair and glared over at the pristinely white, empty canvas sitting on the easel. The box of paints next to it had actually gathered dust in the week he had been up at the cabin. Abruptly, he made a decision. No more big baby crap. Daniel needed him, and so did Sophie. And flirting with little Miss Carly would certainly take his mind off of things.

He wandered to the window again and was surprised to see the sun peeking over the horizon. The rain had stopped and steam was rising up from the damp earth. Soon, the sun would burn it off and turn it back to crumbly dirt. The single street in Ruby Spring would quickly be blowing with dust. All of a sudden, Daniel wanted to get back home. He threw off the quilt and started to pack.

*

The afternoon sunlight streamed through the open stage door in the back of the theater. Carly, sitting in the front row, shaded her eyes and peered up at the stage, apprehension growing in her stomach. Next to her, Sophie sighed and shifted uncomfortably.

"Why is Ross so tense?" Carly whispered.

Sophie covered her mouth and leaned toward Carly's ear. "We have to get a replacement for our leading lady," she whispered back, "Soon. Having Nancy stand in is just making everything so . . . well . . . awful." She leaned back and massaged her giant middle.

Carly glanced at her. Sophie was exhausted, and rightly so. Two weeks away from her due date, and she was managing the theater *and* shuttling back and forth to the hospital for the past couple of nights to visit Daniel. And where was that jerk brother of his, Asher? Nowhere to be found.

Carly pressed her lips together and focused on the stage. Ross was pacing in one corner, a script and pencil in hand, his eyes daggers. They were focused on Nancy, who perched on a stool, her face frozen in a comical expression of shock. She waved a pudgy arm in the air.

"Oh, no! Save me! Save me!" Nancy shrieked in a fake, high-pitched voice. Looking at Ross, she giggled and batted her eyes. He slammed his script shut and stared helplessly at Buddy, the leading man, who was sitting on an upstage platform.

With flowing shoulder length hair and an impressive physique, Buddy *looked* like a hero from a melodrama, but certainly didn't act like one. He had his legs folded into a pretzel, his hands in a praying position. His script was clasped between them, and he hummed in a monotone.

"Buddy," Ross hissed. Buddy cracked one eye open.

"Yeah?" he answered.

Ross raked a hand through his dark hair. "Buddy, you idiot, that's your cue," yelled Ross, unable to control his frustration.

Carly grimaced. She knew today was one of those days that Ross regretted giving up smoking. Good thing the nearest pack of cigarettes was at a convenience store at the end of the highway, because if there'd been any in Ruby Spring, Ross would have lit one up by now.

Buddy unfolded his legs and stood up, stretching. He scratched his chest and ambled over to Ross. "Relax man. It's all good. I know my lines already." He tapped the side of his head. That's the power of concentration. You should try yoga sometime, dude. It would really make you a lot less uptight."

Ross stared at him for a few seconds, and then broke his pencil in two. "Ten minutes!" That's a ten-minute break, everybody," he shouted, "Parker. What's the time?"

The gangly acne-prone stage manager jumped up from a desk placed in the center aisle. A college theater student from

Albuquerque, he hung on Ross's every word. A pile of papers slipped to the floor as his fingers scrambled on the desk for the stopwatch. Patting his chest, he exhaled as he found it hanging around his neck. "Hold on a sec . . . uh . . . I got it."

Ross raised an eyebrow and crossed his arms.

"3:32, everyone," Parker exclaimed, "We're back at . . . hold on . . ." He carefully pushed a button on the watch. 'We're back at 3:42."

Rolling his eyes, Ross jumped from the stage and stretched out on his back at Carly's feet. He threw an arm over his eyes and exhaled.

"Sophie?" he said in a weary voice.

"I know. I *know*," she replied, "I'm looking, Ross, really I am. It's hard to get a decent actress at the beginning of the summer, you know."

"It's just that Buddy is great when he has someone to keep him focused up there," Ross said, sitting up. "We are getting nowhere fast, and Nancy, as much as she loves being actress-for-a-day . . . or more like . . . a week . . . really needs to get back to the costume shop."

"I KNOW!" Sophie repeated, her fists balling in her enormous lap.

Carly reached out her foot and nudged Ross in the ribs. Placing a soothing hand on Sophie's arm, she said, "Look, we both have a friend we worked with about five years ago. He's an actor, but has moved to L.A. and is working in an agent's office. Maybe he knows a good actress who is available. You want me give him a call?"

Sophie reached her hands out to Ross, who jumped up and heaved her out of the seat. Groaning, she leaned against the edge of the stage.

"Yes. Do that. I absolutely have to take a nap. Right NOW." She smiled feebly at them and waddled up the aisle.

Ross and Carly shrugged at each other. He grabbed her by the arms and dropped his head to her shoulder. "Oh no. Save me, save me," he mimicked Nancy.

Carly chuckled and pushed him away. "You'll be OK."

The theater doors at the back of the house creaked open and

they heard Sophie's voice faintly from outside. "Hey, Asher, where have you been? Well, I know, but I haven't seen you since yesterday . . . Yeah, she's in there. Daniel said what? Well it's about time . . . OK . . . See you later tonight."

Carly's heart plummeted to the pit of her stomach. Asher was back! And had been, apparently. She hadn't seen him in well over a week, although it seemed like much longer. But why should she want to see him? He didn't care about anyone but himself. He kept creeping into her mind, all the same. Maddening. She heard his muffled deep laugh outside and her stomach dropped to her knees. Suddenly, she knew she couldn't handle it. Trying to maintain a calm expression, she turned to Ross.

"Hey, I forgot . . . something. I'm just going to go back up to the hotel and grab it, okay?"

She wheeled around and scrambled up on the stage, running to the backstage door. Poking her head out, she glanced around and stepped out into the sunlight, deciding to sneak back to the hotel behind the buildings. She turned the corner of the theater and stopped short. Too late.

Asher was strolling toward her, a hint of a smile playing around his fantastic lips. He was so much more handsome than she remembered. His wavy hair was pulled back into a small ponytail at the base of his neck; loose strands floated around his lean face. His hands were shoved into the pockets of stained painter's overalls, and his white T-shirt was ripped at the neck. He could have been in a thousand dollar tux as far as Carly was concerned. Stopping in front of her, he gestured toward the theater with a shoulder, looking at the side of the building.

"So, when do you want to get started?"

Carly's gaze followed his. It was easier than getting lost in his hypnotic eyes. She wanted to be mad at him. Wanted to ask him where the hell he had been while his brother was suffering in extreme pain. But that's not what came out of her mouth.

"Oh, any time. Mornings are good. They don't start rehearsals until eleven. You know actors, late night people," she gushed, kicking herself all the while for sounding like a dimwit.

Asher laughed. "Well it doesn't really matter when we paint, Carly," he said, drawing out her name, caressing it.

She shivered and clenched her fists, willing her stomach to calm down. Looking at him, she flashed what she hoped was a warm, friendly, and completely *professional* smile.

"Why is that? Do you have all of your time free just for me?" she bantered.

Asher gently clasped her shoulder. "As a matter of fact, I do. And will. Hasn't Daniel talked to you?"

Carly's eyes widened. "No, I haven't spoken with him since I visited at the hospital. What are you talking about?"

He cleared his throat and grinned at her. "Carly Foster, meet your new bodyguard."

Her mouth opened and she stumbled backward. What *was* he talking about? She didn't need a bodyguard, dammit. Jamming her fists on her hips, she recovered her composure. "That's nice and all, but I can take care of myself, thanks."

He laughed and leaned a shoulder against the wall of the theater. "Daniel told me you would react like this. Man, he sure can peg people. I have to hand him that."

"You mean you've actually bothered to talk to him this week?" Carly burst out.

His eyes narrowed and he stepped forward. She pressed her lips together and stepped back. Where did that come from? Why couldn't she just keep her big mouth shut sometimes?

"What do you mean by that, Carly?" he asked.

She took a deep breath and shrugged. It was better not to try to explain. It usually got her into trouble. "Nothing. You've been gone, is all."

Unsatisfied, Asher scowled and began pacing around her. Like a hunter. He circled behind her, so close that she could feel his breath on the back of her neck. He was trying to intimidate her. Well, she wasn't having any of it; no man was going to make her feel uncomfortable this summer. Not even one she kind of, maybe, in a way, had the hots for. Deciding to play it off, Carly cocked her head to the side and sighed, feigning boredom.

Despite her many resolutions to herself, she couldn't resist the opportunity to touch him. She leaned over as he passed again and patted his shoulder in a patronizing manner. A split second later, Asher reached up and clasped her hand in his warm, powerful grasp. Her stomach plummeted again and she stepped back.

"Look, Carly. You're going to have to let Danny have his way on this one. I'm afraid you don't have a lot of choice in the matter. You spend a lot of time down here by yourself at night, don't you?"

Carly wrenched away from his grasp. "So what?" she retorted.

'So, that makes you vulnerable. And I have volunteered to keep you safe. It's the least I could do for my brother."

Carly bit back her retort. *Yeah, the very least you could do!* She swallowed when he placed his hand on her shoulder. He smiled at her and she lifted her eyebrows.

"Daniel and Sophie were adamant. And you don't want to upset those dear people. A gimp and a pregnant lady?" He smirked.

Carly stared at him for a few seconds, and then sighed in frustration, hating that she would cave in. "No, I suppose not. So, what, are you going to follow me down to the theater and sit there while I work at night?"

"Yes, and follow you to meetings, and follow you on trips to town, and follow you to the breakfast table, and—

She gasped and stomped her foot. "No way. What are you going to say next? You'll *follow* me into the bathroom?"

A slow grin spread over Asher's face. His dimples seem to mock her as he laughed. "Honey, you've already taken care of that job. I think I can manage to stay *outside* the bathroom while you are . . . ah . . . bathing."

Her face bright red, Carly glared at him. "That was a low blow, Asher," she whispered.

He chucked her under the chin and pulled her in for a friendly hug. "Oh, come on. I couldn't resist. You know you would have said the same thing if the tables were turned."

His arms were like bands of steel, but gentle. Her face buried in his chest, Carly breathed in the scent of pure, clean male, tempered with a hint of oil paint. Her head swam.

Asher pulled back and looked at her. He wasn't smiling anymore. Her mouth opened slightly and her tongue snaked out to wet her dry lips. His gaze wandered over them and she drew in a breath. Still, he held her close. Carly's heart hammered and she shifted slightly in his arms.

"Carly," he whispered, and ran a hand from her back up to her hair. "Damn."

She felt the gentle tug as her face was lifted upwards, and then his lips were on hers. He kissed her slowly, exploring. Her hands found his solid shoulders and he pulled her in closer as she began to slide to the ground. Her breasts were flattened against his chest. His mouth was firm and insistent and Carly's hands rose to tangle in his hair. She lifted her chin, parting her lips in welcome.

Asher groaned, but hesitated. He pulled away and cupped her face in his hands. Deep brown eyes met yielding gray eyes, and neither of them moved. His mouth against hers, he whispered, "Not here. Not now. But soon."

Their eyes locked for a few seconds more. She could barely breathe, much less blink. Slowly releasing her, he crammed his hands into his pockets and stepped back. Her eyes fluttered shut and she lifted a hand to her hammering chest. Dimly, she heard the theater door slam shut. Raising a trembling hand to her lips, Carly Foster smiled like a fool.

Chapter Six

"So you think you have the perfect match for us, huh?" Carly asked her friend Mike.

Pushing her cup of coffee away, she shifted the phone to her other ear, reached over the pile of drawings on the kitchen table and grabbed a legal pad. She grinned as she thought about how relieved Sophie was going to be.

"Sure thing. I wouldn't steer you wrong, Carly," replied the voice on the other end of the phone, "Plus I stand to make a good commission from this; that never hurts."

Carly laughed and settled more comfortably in her chair, smoothing the soft cotton of her jeans skirt. "Okay, Mike, give me the details."

"Well, she retired . . . I mean, *left* a soap opera about three years ago. She was on it for about . . . well, quite a while. *Passion Sunset.* Have you heard of it?" he asked.

"I can't say that I spend much time watching soaps, but yeah, I've heard of it," she smiled, "go on."

'Well, as you can imagine, she can learn lines in the blink of an eye, with all of that soap experience. Plus, she's quite beautiful, and a decent person to boot."

"What's the catch, Mike? Why would she want to come out to the middle of nowhere in New Mexico to do a play no one's heard of in a hundred years?" Carly asked.

"No catch. And hey, why did *you* go out to the middle of nowhere to a theater no one's ever heard of?" he countered.

She laughed again. "Point taken. So, tell me more."

"Well, here's what I'm thinking," he began, "because she is a minor celebrity, we could work it into her contract so that she could make a few appearances in Albuquerque before your show opens. You know, radio spots, that sort of thing. Drum up some publicity."

"Oh, that's a great idea. And maybe she could go on TV, too. So, give me her name."

Mike chuckled uncomfortably. "I'll have to ask her about television, but we'll see," he replied.

"What's her name?" Carly pressed.

"Oh. Well, her name is Marilyn Masters," Mike said, "and you won't regret it, Carly. Your producer will be getting a gem of a lady here."

After making a few more notes on her pad, Carly stretched and stood up. "It's nice talking with you, but I had better go down to Daniel's apartment and let him know about this, Mike. I wouldn't worry about it though; I think he'll be sold. Poor guy, the more pressure we can take off of him right now, the better. And Ross will be your best friend for life."

Mike laughed. "Ross, Ross, Ross. What a man. He could be a lot more than a best friend, as far as I'm concerned, Carly."

"You are so bad," she said, "But really, I've gotta go. Daniel will call you back right away, I'm sure."

Satisfied that the burden of finding a replacement actress was lifted, Carly stretched again and yawned. Walking to the sink, she began to dump her cold coffee. Lost in thought, she looked out the open window to the right of the sink. And jumped.

"Dammit," she swore, as dark coffee splattered down the front of her white top.

Asher's grinning face was two inches from hers. "Good going, Carly," he smiled. "Hey, aren't you glad I'm your guardian angel? Like you said, anything we can do to help Daniel."

Carly rolled her eyes, put the cup in the sink and grabbed a dishtowel. She sponged at her damp top and threw the towel back on the counter. Leaning on the windowsill, she regarded him through the screen that separated them.

His eyes sparkled as his gaze shifted to her lips. She felt her face flush as his gaze slid next to her tank top, which had slipped low enough to expose the top of her bra. Yanking it up, she narrowed her eyes at his amused expression.

Carly poked a finger at his face through the screen. "I thought you were supposed to be a bodyguard, not a stalker," She reached up to slam the window for effect. It was stuck. She grunted and shoved on it, but it didn't move.

Asher chuckled and disappeared. Seconds later, she heard the kitchen door swing open, and he was behind her. Close behind her. "Need some help with that?" he murmured, his breath on her neck.

Carly whirled around and ducked under his arm. "No thank you. What I need is help laying out a painting grid on the ceiling in the theater."

Asher glanced at his watch. "The actors started early today . . . so rehearsal ends at one p.m. It's only nine a.m. What do you suppose we should do for four hours?" He hopped onto the kitchen table, his long legs swinging his feet onto the seat of a chair.

Opening her mouth to yell at him, Carly stomped over and punched a finger close to his face. He caught it and brought it to his lips, his eyes sparkling in amusement. "Yes?" he went on.

"It's not necessary to make plans with you every second of every day," she countered, and snatched her finger away. Why did he keep doing this? Antagonizing her constantly?

Ever since the day he told her that he was her "bodyguard," Asher had turned up like a bad penny everywhere she went. And each time she spotted him, her stomach jumped like crazy. It made her so mad at herself . . . that she couldn't control her reaction to him. And it made her cranky and sleepless, knowing that he was just a few feet away across the hall at night, behind a closed door, lying in a warm bed, his long eyelashes brushing his strong cheeks. His solid chest rising and falling in dreamless sleep. His long, warm limbs wrapped around a pillow. A pillow that she wished was . . . bad. *Bad girl.*

Carly shook herself and frowned. Eye to eye with Asher, she clasped trembling hands behind her back. "Well, I'm waiting? Why do you think I have to make plans with you all of the time?" She tapped her foot.

He raised his hands to her shoulders and began to massage. "Carly, Carly," he sighed, "You've gotta loosen up. You ought to take some pointers from Buddy. Maybe yoga would alleviate some of that sexual tension you seem to carry around."

Her mouth dropped open.

Grinning, he slid off the table and opened a cabinet door. "Here's how I'm going to help you out." He shoved a picnic basket in her direction. "We're going to make a nice little lunch and take a hike. The exercise will do wonders for your black mood this morning."

Carly grabbed the basket and sputtered, but was too embarrassed to take the bait. Sexual tension? Where had that come from? Well, she wasn't going to run away from him. That was just what he wanted. Then he could run after her and make fun of her until she got even angrier. Wrenching open the refrigerator door, she turned to him and raised an eyebrow.

"Asher, you're on. I suppose it wouldn't kill me to get away from work for a couple of hours." She slammed a jar of pickles on the counter. "But don't think that agreeing to go hiking with you constitutes permission for you to touch me." Her chin shot up into the air. "Since it was your idea, you make the lunch. I have to change my clothes." Sniffing, she pushed open the swinging door, the sound of Asher's deep chuckle mocking her as she crossed the lobby.

After telling Daniel the good news about Marilyn Masters, Carly went to change clothes. Up in her room, she pulled open a dresser drawer and began rummaging through her shorts and tops. She'd show Asher. All she had to do was get a grip on her nerves. Pulling on a fresh pair of shorts and a T-shirt, she laced up her hiking boots, grabbed her brush and ran it through her hair. She jammed a baseball cap on top, pulled her hair through the back opening and took a quick look in the mirror. Good. A no-nonsense hiking look. Satisfied, she nodded to herself and tied a sweatshirt around her waist.

Asher was waiting in the lobby, stretched out on top of the front desk. "You done primping for me?" he asked in a smooth voice.

"You really shouldn't lounge on top of antiques, Asher," she admonished as she sailed past him, picking up the picnic basket on window seat next to the door. "C'mon, let's get this over with."

*

Asher chuckled and hopped down. She sure was something. Catching the screen door and following her outside, he took the opportunity given to him with pleasure. His gaze examined her from behind, noting the sway of her silky ponytail and the gentle curve of her hips. And the way they moved as she jogged down the front steps. He took a deep breath. She smelled like spring flowers.

He shook his head. It really wasn't wise to be playing this game with his feelings . . . and hers, but she was proving to be irresistible. Well, for as long as it lasted, it was something to keep his mind occupied, and off of New York City. And his lost paintings. The paintings that had taken two years of his passion and energy to complete. Frowning, he shook off the unwelcome remembrance of what could have been. The past was just that, and damned if he was going to torture himself thinking about a part of his life that caused pain. It just wasn't worth it.

Quickening his step to catch up with her, he reached out and grabbed the basket. "Do you even know where we're headed?"

Carly's head whipped around and she gave him a smile that made his stomach flip. "Does it really matter? A mountain is a mountain. And there are plenty of those around here."

Asher jogged in front of her and pointed toward the end of the street. "See that path up there? That's the one that leads to Ruby Spring."

"We're *in* Ruby Spring, Einstein," Carly retorted.

Asher laughed and grabbed her hand. "Just wait, Ms. Foster, just wait."

*

"Hold. HOLD!" Ross shifted in his seat in the front row of the theater, raised his hand and made a note in his script. "Buddy, do you have that new blocking? I didn't see you write it down."

Buddy strolled downstage and peered down at Ross. "Dude . . . yes." He grinned and tapped the side of his head.

Ross crossed his legs and pursed his lips. "Really. So then I guess you wouldn't mind repeating that back to me?"

Buddy yawned and plopped down on the edge of the stage. "OK. Here goes: Cross from the down left chair up to the up right corner and jump up on the sofa. Sword fight, sword fight. Knock the sword out of the villain's hands, turn down right and check on the girl tied to the bar. Turn back upstage when he comes after me. Punch his lights out, untie the girl, pick her up and cross back up right to the sofa. Dump her on it, and then kiss her. Correct?"

Ross pursed his lips again and considered Buddy for a few seconds. "Yes," he said carefully, "But it's hard to tell if you know what's going on half the time."

"Dude, I know I'm frustrating. But I know what I'm doing. Trust me."

Ross sighed, giving up. "As long as you stay in character when we get to tech week, just do what you have to for now, I guess." He craned his neck to look back at Sophie, who was pacing the center aisle near Parker's stage management desk. "Soph, how are you feeling?" he asked.

"OK, but pretty tired. I'm trying not to think about it." She gave him a weak smile.

Ross gauged her mood and ventured, "Any more on when Marilyn Masters is getting here?" It was a poor choice.

"ROSS. Daniel told you an hour and a half ago that her plane lands tomorrow. I told you an *hour* ago that her plane lands tomorrow. Quit asking me. If something changes, you'll be the first to know." Sophie's outburst was so loud it echoed. She glared at him and massaged her back.

He blinked for a few seconds in astonishment. "Yes ma'am," he responded, turning around and shaking his head.

The theater was dead quiet and the actors on stage were motionless. Buddy looked over at Nancy, who was examining her nails, and then back at Jack, an older gentleman from Denver, who was playing the villain. Jack raised a white eyebrow at Buddy, and then opened his script, pretending to frown in concentration.

Parker, rising from his desk, cleared his throat. "You wanna take a break now, Ross?"

Sophie moaned and sat down. She glared at Ross and clasped her hands over her swollen belly.

Ross glanced over at her and shook his head silently at Parker. "*Not now,*" he mouthed. Sitting up straight in his seat, Ross clapped his hands. "Okay! Let's get back to it. Go back to the top of page forty-six and Jack, this time you need to be quieter. You're supposed to be *hiding* behind the sofa."

Sophie moaned again.

Sighing, Ross jumped up and walked to where she sat with her head bowed. "What? If you don't like the blocking, I can change it. You're the producer of course; I'm just a director," he said, trying to keep the testiness out of his voice. He failed.

Sophie lifted her head and looked up at Ross. Tears ran down her sweet, puffy face. "No, it's not that!"

"Whoa," Ross exhaled. His frustration fizzled and he took her hand. "What is it then? Come on, let me help you up. We can go outside and get some fresh air, huh?"

Sophie wrestled her hand loose and grabbed the front of his shirt in her fist, yanking him in close. "I can't get up," she cried out.

He rolled his eyes. Sophie had been difficult all week, but today took the cake. "Why not, sweetie?"

She rested her head against his chest. "Because my water just broke and it's embarrassing and scary and well . . . not FUN. Not fun at ALL." A sob ripped out of her throat and she began to cry in earnest.

A jolt of adrenaline running through his gut, Ross stroked her hair and reached in his pocket for the cell phone. "Don't worry," he soothed, all business again. "We knew this was coming, and we have a plan. Asher's going to drive you, and I'll follow with Daniel. Don't cry, sweetie. We'll be at the hospital quicker than a rattlesnake." He looked back over his shoulder. "Guys, rehearsal is obviously canceled for the day. You can go on back to Albuquerque. And Nancy . . . go sew something."

*

After an hour on the trail, Carly's chest was burning and she had a stitch in her side, but she kept going. She would be damned before Asher knew that she was having difficulty on the steep path. Trying to keep her breathing quiet, she leaned against a tree for a minute, wiping the sweat from her neck. Her legs felt like rubber bands.

Asher looked back in amusement. "Having trouble?" he asked, holding out his hand.

"Not a bit," she replied, barely able to keep the huffing and puffing out of her voice.

"It's only another couple hundred yards. You'll make it." Asher turned and continued up the rocky trail, more slowly this time.

Despite her discomfort, Carly couldn't help but admire him from behind. The soft dark hair, blowing in the wind . . . the strong shoulders and broad back. Deliberately, she skipped his jeans-clad backside . . . it was too much to think about . . . and continued her examination . . . those strong thighs and lean calves . . .

Suddenly, a pine branch whipped across her face. *Ouch!* She wanted to squeal, but also didn't want to give him the satisfaction of knowing she wasn't paying attention. Because she could pretty well tell that he would know just *why* she was distracted. Which made her even more determined to stick with the plan of driving him crazy . . . by being as cool and calm as possible.

Sucking in a breath, she forged ahead and met Asher at the top of the crest. Spilling out before them was another valley, this one even more beautiful than the one that contained Ruby Spring. It was lusher, for one thing. Tall pine trees thickly covered the mountainsides and a sparkling, clear lake, which was obviously the authentic Ruby Spring, rested at the base of the valley. A tiny cabin sat on a ridge above the lake, a winding dirt road snaking away from it. Asher's familiar old van was parked next to the cabin.

"Wow." Carly's feigned nonchalance dissolved and when he draped an arm around her shoulders, she didn't lean away. In fact, did her body just sway closer to his? Yep. It was probably because her legs were so shaky from the hike. That's all.

Asher grinned with pride. "*This* is the real Ruby Spring, my dear," His eyes twinkled and his face somehow seemed younger. His smile was relaxed and genuine. It was . . . revealing. She looked away.

Tipping her head up to the sun, Carly beamed. "I see that it is. And I'm really glad that you made me come here," she admitted.

Catching her hand, Asher pulled her farther down the trail. "C'mon, let's go to the cabin. You shouldn't be in the sun too much longer. I don't want Daniel accusing me of French-frying his set designer."

Laughing, she trotted along beside him. Now, this was more like it. Fighting with him was fun, but also tiring after a while. And it was fairly obvious how comfortable he was in this setting. Was the cabin where he had been for that week? If so, his grumpy ass should spend more time here. Carly giggled to herself as they reached the cabin door.

"Why is your van here, Asher?" she teased, "Did you plan this trip, knowing that I would say yes?"

"Yep. And I figured that you might be too tired to hike back down. Or that we might run out of time. I didn't want a hysterical employee on my hands."

Carly punched his solid shoulder and grabbed the picnic basket out of his hands. "I'm *never* hysterical. Just very dedicated to my work."

"What, no sassy comeback? You're in a good mood, finally." He pushed open the door.

"I could say the same to you, Mr. Grouch," she retorted.

What a cute little cabin. A wide bed covered in an old quilt was built snugly in to one of the walls, and a plank table and benches rested next to another wall. The large fireplace was blackened with use, and a small set of shelves sat near it, holding simple ceramic dishes and cookware. A folded up easel and a box of paints were propped in a corner next to the single large window.

"Home away from home?" she inquired, her eyes resting on the art supplies.

Asher cleared his throat. "You might say that, but let's not talk about it right now. Let's eat." Placing the picnic basket on the table, he began to pull out sandwiches and bottles of water.

Watching him to make sure she hadn't broken the pleasant mood, Carly crossed over to the bed and sat down. He wasn't frowning, which was a good sign. Pulling off her baseball cap, she shook her hair free and slipped off her hiking boots. They were new and still pinched just a bit. She glanced over at Asher, her eyes drinking him in. God, how she wished she could give in and just flirt with him. Just a little bit. She sighed.

Asher met her gaze; the hungry look in his brown eyes making her stomach flutter. "Getting ready for bed?" A smile played over his sculpted lips and he moved toward her. "You want some company?"

A delicious shiver ran down Carly's spine and it was all she could do not to scream out *"Yesss."* Primly, she sat up straight and smoothed the hair out of her eyes. "Oh, I'm not sleepy!" she said, "Just hungry." Her eyes widened. *Crap.* Why couldn't she keep her big mouth shut?

Asher stepped closer, leaned down, and placed his palms on her bare thighs. "I'm hungry, too," he whispered.

Carly's lips parted and she tried desperately not to look into his eyes. She failed.

"Really?"

"Really," Asher replied. Slowly, his palms moved up her thighs and caressed her hips. He rested them on her waist and she closed her eyes. *Oh, God.* Struggling for a good reason to stop him was pointless, though. She couldn't think.

Asher nudged her thighs apart gently with his knee. The soft cotton of the jeans and the warm firmness of his leg sent electric thrills to the very center of her. His knee sank into the bed between her legs and his hands moved up to her ribcage. Carly's face was close to his chest, and she let her head sink onto it as his hands moved further still, now resting under her full breasts.

"Carly?" he whispered.

She couldn't speak, but nodded. *"Yes."*

Asher groaned and pushed her backward until her head was resting on the pillow. Instinctively, her legs opened wider as Asher's other knee swung onto the bed. Pulling himself over her, he nestled between her thighs.

Slowly, Carly reached up with trembling fingers and touched his lips. "If you want to . . . I want you to kiss me," she murmured.

His eyes darkened and he slipped his warm hands under her T-shirt to rest lightly on her belly. "Are you sure?" He began to slowly rub her stomach, his hands brushing against her lacy bra.

Carly nodded and opened her mouth slightly, pulling his head in for a kiss. He resisted and continued his delicious assault, this time his hands slipping under the bra, lifting it up. Her shirt followed. His eyes burned fire as he observed her building passion, his hands light as feathers as they cupped her breasts. Carly's head dropped back and she moaned.

"I hope you're sure, because I doubt it will stop with a kiss,"

Asher whispered.

Still he denied her his mouth, but his thumbs were driving her into insanity.

Carly reached up blindly and grabbed his taut shoulders. "I hope it doesn't stop with a kiss . . . God, I hope it doesn't," she breathed, and pulled him down. His lips were so close, but still he hesitated.

And waited just a few seconds too long. The sudden high-pitched trill of a cell phone jolted them both out of the trance. Hovering above her, his expression changed and she blinked, rolling her head to the side in embarrassment. Asher groaned and clapped a hand over his eyes. He sat back on his heels, still between Carly's thighs.

Wrestling the phone from his pocket, he looked at the caller ID on the screen and rolled his eyes. "What, Danny?" he said in a tight voice.

Gingerly moving her legs, Carly wriggled out from under him and slid off the bed, her heart hammering in her throat. What the hell had just happened? Her summer promise was to stay *away* from prickly men, not have sex with one of them in a deserted cabin. Dammit. She had to stay away from Asher as much as possible from now on. She had to.

"Carly?"

She turned at Asher's voice, and met his gaze. The passion had been replaced by anxiety. Great.

"We have to go. Now. Right now," he commanded, striding to the table and throwing sandwiches back into the basket.

Mortified, she shoved her boots on and began lacing them up. "I know," she replied, "I didn't mean for . . . *that* . . . to happen either."

Asher let out a rueful laugh. "No, no, no. *That* was amazing . . . or was going to be," he said. "We have to go because Sophie is in labor."

Carly's mouth dropped open and she laced faster. "Good thing you have your van up here, Asher, or you'd be in deep . . . without a paddle."

Chapter Seven

Daniel Day shifted his weight in the uncomfortable chair as he flipped through the channels on the hospital waiting room television. Sighing, he threw the remote on a side table and glanced up at the clock for what seemed to be the hundredth time that night. There was absolutely nothing on television in the middle of the night.

"Tell me again why they won't let me back there?" he groused.

"Because you just got out of the hospital yourself, and they don't want to risk infection, Bro," replied Asher, swirling the grounds in his questionable cup of coffee.

Daniel shifted again and stared down at the cast encasing his leg from ankle to hip. "All I did was break my leg."

"Yeah, but badly," replied Asher, "Remember . . . you had a fever for two days afterward."

Daniel knew it was true, but he wasn't finished complaining. "I'm sick of wearing sweatpants and . . . and . . . showering with trash bags taped to my thigh."

"And I'm pretty sure that your wife is sick of being in labor," said Carly, as she walked in to the room, "but life is life, boss man."

Handing him a sandwich, she sat down in a corner, picked up a magazine, and started flipping through it. She didn't want to be unkind, but she also didn't want to get sucked into a conversation that included Asher. Daniel wasn't a fool and he'd figure out quick enough that Carly wanted to jump his brother's bones. She wasn't a very good liar.

It didn't help that Asher had been pushing her buttons since they'd arrived at the hospital. Every time she turned around, he was staring at her with intense eyes, and over the past few hours in the waiting room, he had taken each and every opportunity to touch her. Granted, it was casual . . . a squeeze of the hand, a brush of a shoulder, but it was driving her hormones wild. She wanted him. Really bad. And he wanted her back. That thought alone caused the butterflies in the pit of her stomach to flit again.

"Carly? Car . . . lee?" Daniel's whimper broke through and she raised her head. "Could you please go and check at the nurse's station again?"

She had been six times in the past hour, but how could she say no? Rising, she stretched and zipped up her comfy, baggy sweater. And saw Asher staring at her out of the corner of his eye. *Dammit.* Flashing a nervous smile, she darted for the door. "I'll be happy to, Danny. But I'm afraid that the news will be the same."

Daniel sighed and turned the TV back on, flipping to a home shopping network. "There's some cool stuff on here, huh, Bro?"

Asher shook his head. "Give me that remote, you dumbass. That stuff's a bunch of crap. Are you crazy?"

"No, but you are," retorted Daniel, "*Lust*-crazed."

"What?" *Crap.* He should have known better than to try to play games with Carly in front of his older brother . . . the only person who knew him like he knew himself.

Daniel stared at him, a smug look animating his worn-out features. "Don't play stupid." He waggled a finger. "I can totally see that something is going on there."

Asher rolled his eyes and wandered over to the door, peering out the small, long window. "Nothing's going on, Danny. You're seeing things because you're tired."

"See there. You're looking for her." Daniel goaded.

Shaking his head again, Asher leaned against the door. "I most certainly am not. I'm just bored is all." Trying his best to fake a world-weary attitude, he exhaled and gazed up at the ceiling.

"Pining for your lover?" Daniel chuckled.

Asher gave him a wary glance. If anyone knew how to push his buttons it was Danny. Or maybe Carly Foster. But time would tell on that one.

"No. I don't *have* a lover, thank you very much. Women are not at the top of my list these days." Asher pushed away from the door and advanced into the room, glowering at Daniel, his hands on his hips.

Daniel glanced at the door and cleared his throat. "Sure, sure. I understand. So why is it, then, that every time you look at Carly, your eyes are unsnapping her bra?"

"Not true." Asher said through gritted teeth.

"And why is it every time she looks at you, she's unbuttoning your . . . ah . . . shirt?"

"Again, decidedly, untrue."

Daniel reached up and thumped Asher's chest. "Oh, come off it. You're *so* full of shit, man! Mark my words, if we're here another two hours, you two will have abandoned me for an empty broom closet."

The door clattered open and the two brothers turned sharply at the gasp behind them. Carly stood behind a wheelchair, her mouth hanging open. Her face was beet red. She looked back and forth between them.

"If this was any other time, I would have a bone to pick with each of you. You guys get off lucky this time, though." Pushing the wheelchair into the room, she glared at Asher as she passed. He, in turn, gazed at her butt, winking at Daniel over her head.

Daniel let out a hoot of laugher. "That's my boy."

Carly ignored his outburst and stopped in front of him. "C'mon, Danny Boy, it's really happening this time. The doctor agreed to let you in the delivery room, but you have to get suited up first."

"You're going to be a daddy, bro." Asher sprang into action and heaved his brother into the wheelchair and rolled him to the door. For once, Danny was speechless.

*

Four hours later, as the sun was peeking over the mountains in the distance, Carly found herself again entering a hospital room. Sophie lay on the bed, her blonde hair smoothed back in a headband. Her eyes gleamed as she looked down at the tiny bundle nestled in her arms.

"Hi there, mommy," whispered Carly. She glanced over to the corner of the room. Asher and Daniel were sound asleep in a heap on a small sofa, Daniel's broken leg propped up on Asher's chest. Each of them snored, and each of them did so through a wide-open mouth.

Sophie pointed down at her son. The baby's mouth was wide open, too, and he let out a little groan. "Like father, like son," she whispered, "And like uncle, too."

Carly reached out and held his tiny hand. The baby grasped it. She smiled in wonder and looked down at Sophie. "Wow . . . he's strong."

Sophie gazed serenely down at him. "Yeah. He's that for sure." She gestured with her head toward the two snoring men on the sofa. "You wouldn't think it to look at him now, but my husband is the inspiration for this little one's name."

Carly raised an eyebrow and grinned. "Which is?"

"Daniel Henry Day," declared Sophie.

Daniel snorted awake in the corner and lifted his sleepy head. "Huh? Coming," he mumbled. His head fell back again. Asher shifted and moved Daniel's leg to the floor, waking him in the process. Yawning, Asher smiled and turned a bleary gaze on Sophie.

"Your husband barely recognizes his own name, sis," he chuckled. Stretching, he turned his head and saw Carly. His eyes focused on her and she stepped back from the bed, smiling hesitantly at him.

"Good morning, Asher," she began.

"Hi, Carly. Did you stay all night?"

"Um . . . yeah," she fumbled. "Hey . . . uh . . . I'm sure all of you want some family time, now that everyone's awake," she said, looking around the room.

Asher shrugged and ambled to the bed. "You can stay if you want, I guess . . . right, Sophie?"

Sophie looked up at Asher and raised an eyebrow in interest. She turned her gaze to Carly, who blushed and looked down at the blanket on the bed. Clearing her throat, Carly pressed her lips together and reached out to grasp the baby's hand again.

A small, satisfied smile played around the edges of Sophie's mouth. "Oh, I think she'd *better* stay, don't you, Asher?"

*

"I'm sick of waiting rooms," complained Carly, as she stood up and stretched. Ambling over to the monitor on the wall, she checked again to make sure Marilyn's flight was on time.

Ross sighed and continued to type away on his laptop. "Then why don't you go down to the end of baggage claim and get us some coffee?"

"What's the point? Her flight lands in ten minutes. Did you remember to bring her head shot?"

Ross pulled it out from his backpack and waved it, his eyes still on the computer screen. "Yeah, I printed it off my e-mail this morning. Just give me a sec, Carly; I have to get the rest of the stage directions down for Marilyn. Nancy sure made a mess of it," he muttered.

Carly walked back over and took the photo from his outstretched hand. She gazed at the face and shook her head. Marilyn certainly was beautiful; Mike hadn't lied about that. Large, almond-shaped eyes sparkled with mischief in a heavily made-up, but flawless face. There were hints of wrinkles around the forehead, but they were so small they would never be seen from the audience. The lovely mouth revealed perfect, even teeth, and the hair was a gleaming blond waterfall. *"At least Asher will have something new to occupy himself,"* Carly thought with a hint of jealousy.

Sighing, she reached down to the floor and picked up the large hand-lettered sign with Marilyn's name on it. She held it up to her chest with one hand, face out. Adjusting the photo, she placed it next to the sign in the other hand. "I look like a limo driver for a movie star, Ross."

"Marilyn's not a movie star, but close enough, I guess," he muttered.

"Helloooo, there!"

Carly turned at the voice and saw a dumpy middle-aged woman trotting across the hallway. The woman waved and heaved a strap of her sequined faux-leopard bag further onto her shoulder.

Carly nudged Ross. "Hey. Do you know this person?"

Ross looked up and frowned. "Nope." He went back to his typing.

Carly peered closer. The woman had long, blonde hair . . . kind of strange for a soon-to-be senior citizen. Her baggy violet terry jogging suit looked as if it came straight out of a retirement village in Florida, and the gold lamé sandals screamed "Gambling Granny." The woman waved again, and smiled. She certainly looked familiar. Carly knew that smile. Nervously, she smiled back, and tried to place her.

"Helloooo!" the woman called again, and raised her large, black movie-star sunglasses to the top of her head. Carly's mouth dropped open and she kicked Ross.

"She's here."

Ross looked up again. "Where?"

Carly pasted a fake smile on her face and said between her teeth, "Just smile and wave, just smile and wave."

Ross scanned the crowd. "Holy . . . shit."

Jumping up, he placed the laptop on the seat next to him and began to grin and wave like a robot. He glanced quickly at the photo in Carly's hand and then back up at the flamboyant woman barreling toward them. "Are you sure? Please tell me this is your idea of a sick joke."

The woman lumbered closer and struck a pose in front of

them, scanning the crowd. She dropped her sunglasses back down and leaned in close. "I'm early. No one recognized me, did they?"

"I doubt it, seeing as how we didn't even have a clue, Grandma," Carly thought. Grinning still, she threw the sign and photo onto a chair and stuck out a hand. "Marilyn? How nice it is to finally meet you."

Marilyn reached up and placed a finger over Carly's lips. "Shhh! I *never* manage to get out of an airport without having to sign autographs, and believe me, today is going to be a first. I'm much too tired to deal with my fans." She raised her sunglasses again, and looked around expectantly.

"Something tells me you don't mind all that much," Ross said with a chuckle.

"*Ross.*" Carly kicked him. "Marilyn, this is our director, and he seems to have a case of foot-in-mouth disease this morning."

Marilyn stepped back and surveyed Ross. She swept her glittering scarf over her arm and looked around. No one seemed to notice. She looked him up and down, and then thrust her gaudy bag in his arms. "You'll do, young man." Sniffing, she turned and started for the exit, the scarf floating behind her.

"Way to go, you just pissed off the star of the show," Carly gathered up the sign and photo. She nudged Ross and hurried after Marilyn.

He grabbed his laptop with his free hand and rolled his eyes. "I know what I'm doing, Carly," he replied, "You know me . . . I could charm the crown jewels out of the Tower of London. I'm just establishing my territory is all."

Catching up with Marilyn, Carly looked at the picture in her hand and shook her head again. How in God's name were they going to pull this one off? Mike *promised* her that Marilyn could play an ingénue. But what ingénue had a body shaped like a potato and an outfit that belonged in an arthritis medication ad? She reached over and shoved the headshot back into Ross's backpack.

"Uh . . . Marilyn? Shouldn't we be getting your luggage before we go?" Carly asked.

Marilyn threw her head back and laughed. "*Darling.* That's what boyfriends are for." She leaned back and peeked around Carly. Waving her sparkly fingernails, she called out in a loud voice, "Nicky, darling, make sure you have everything."

Carly and Ross turned together and saw Nicky, whom they both instantly recognized as a tall, bronzed surfer-type model from a sports drink commercial. He ambled toward them, his arms full of luggage, turning heads like "the wave" at a baseball game. Clad in skintight red leather pants, a snug T-shirt and dark sunglasses, he oozed sex appeal.

Ross whistled between his teeth. "Sweetie, I'm jealous." He flashed his never-fail grin at Marilyn and wiggled his eyebrows.

She regarded him for a moment, and then thawed. "Yeah." Reaching up and pinching his cheek, she declared, "Honey, you should be." With another flounce of her scarf, she walked through the automatic doors into the brilliant sunlight.

"Marilyn Masters!" screeched a voice behind them. "OHMYGOD. It's Marilyn Masters." A little old lady shoved past Carly and Ross and knocked them backward into Nicky, who lost control of the massive bags. They ended up in a heap of arms, legs, and bright red leather suitcases. Ross groaned, clutching his precious laptop and Marilyn's animal print bag to his chest.

"Dammit," Carly muttered. Hastily she extricated herself and yanked on a five-hundred pound garment bag. She uncovered Nicky, the Greek god, who gave her a sheepish smile.

"Here we go again." he said. "Gotta love her, Marilyn gets mobbed everywhere we go."

Ross gripped Carly's arm. "Jesus. He's hot, I'll grant her that, but she dressed him to match her luggage."

"Shhhh," Carly admonished him, giggling.

By the time they had righted themselves and sorted out the bags, Marilyn was holding court outside the terminal. She stood on the sidewalk like a queen, surrounded by a gaggle of old women. "Just one more, darlings, and then I simply *must* fly," she exclaimed, as she signed a wrinkled airline ticket with a flourish.

"What on earth brings you to Albuquerque, Marilyn?" cooed one of the women, thrusting a piece of ripped notebook paper in her direction.

"Why, I'm starring in a play, naturally, darling," said Marilyn, "and all of you must come see it, yes?"

"Yes," the women chorused.

One of them piped up. "Where is it? When can we get tickets?"

Marilyn raised her eyebrow and glanced at Ross. "Yes, muffin, where can these fine ladies get tickets?"

Flashing a nervous smile, Ross shifted the luggage in his arms and cleared his throat. "Uh . . . Ruby Spring Theater. They go on sale . . . day after tomorrow . . . aren't you lucky?"

"Oh, yes," the women said in unison.

"Remind me to remind Asher to call and get that box office phone installed *today*," he whispered to Carly.

Carly frowned. "Asher? Why is he doing it?"

"Because daddy Daniel is a little preoccupied right now. I thought I told you . . . Asher is taking over producer responsibilities for the next couple of weeks." Ross groaned and shifted the bags again. "I hope he knows which end is up."

Carly gave him a reassuring smile. "You worry too much, Ross. I think he knows exactly what he's doing."

Ross looked her up and down and grinned. "I'll just bet you do, hon."

She flushed and looked back at Marilyn. Still surrounded. "Well, that remains to be seen." Time to change the subject. "Let's see if we can't pull her away without losing some precious ticket sales, huh?"

Nicky, who stood next to them watching Marilyn with a fond smile, spoke up. "Allow me." He winked at Carly and strutted over to the throng of white-haired women. His tanned biceps flexed as he bent to kiss the papery hand of one of the fans. "Ladies, ladies. Don't you all look pretty today?" They looked him up and down in shock. More than one pair of eyes came to rest on the crotch of his red leather pants.

As soon as their attention shifted, Marilyn made a hasty exit and stomped into the street toward the parking garage, giving the finger to a car that came screeching to a halt in front of her. Once across, she waved at them. "What are you waiting for? Let's get the F outta here." She reached up to her shoulder and yanked on a bra strap.

Ross and Carly glanced at each other, grinning. "Well, what do ya think, partner?" he asked.

Carly shrugged. "I'm not sure yet, but at least she's a character."

Ross grunted under the heavy load and stepped off the sidewalk. As he began to stagger across the street, he threw back over his shoulder, "That she is. And . . . just think of the box office. Ka-ching!"

Chapter Eight

Marilyn, it turned out, was more than just a character. She was a comedienne extraordinaire. Carly wiped her eyes as they parked in the lot next to the Ruby Spring Hotel. "No more, please. I can't take it." she gasped and looked sideways at Marilyn.

Marilyn pursed her lips and waggled her fingernails. "Cougar? I'm not a wild animal. That's absurd. Think of me as a sinfully sexy Robin Hood. I rob from the cradle and give to myself."

Bursting into another gale of laughter, Carly pushed open the car door and jumped onto the pavement.

"What's so funny? What could possibly be so funny?" called a sobbing voice from the front porch.

Carly turned and shaded her eyes. Nancy was crying again. What was wrong now? Sighing, she stomped up the steps and sat in a rocker next to the sniffling woman. Still smiling, she reached out and massaged her shoulder. "Hey, Nancy . . . what's got you so worked up?"

Nancy burst into another round of blubbering. After wiping tracks of mascara off her plump cheeks with the tape measure around her neck, she held up a folded costume in trembling hands. "This," she wailed, "this is what's wrong."

Carly frowned and took the dress, shaking it open. Immediately, she gasped and threw it to the porch. "What the hell?"

The bodice of the dress was still beautiful, a deep pink satin, edged delicately with black lace. But the front of the skirt was another matter. It was ripped angrily in several places, and covered in smears of mud. Carly spread it out gently and sighed.

"Oh, Nancy, what happened?"

"That's not all . . . that's not *even* close," cried Nancy, "Turn it over."

Ross bounded up the steps, skidding to a halt when he saw the ruined costume. "Oh, hell. Nancy, what happened?" he echoed Carly.

"Just turn it over, Ross," Nancy whimpered.

Ross raised an eyebrow, bent down and flipped the dress over. The zipper was ripped out and lay ragged near the waist. All over the back, streaks of black spray paint covered the skirt. Near the hem he spied the words, scrawled in paint.

"Bitch, go home," he read. Sinking onto the steps, he covered his head with his hands.

Carly sucked in a breath and glanced over the railing. Marilyn was only a few feet away. She kicked the dress into a pile. "Hey, funny lady. Do you want to see the theater, or go to your room first?"

Marilyn hopped up the steps and peered down at the shiny pink lump. "I hope that's not mine," she stated, noting Nancy's tear-stained face. "I look terrible in pastels." Opening the screen door, she slipped inside, calling over her shoulder, "Nicky . . . come along now. I need my things."

Ross raised his head and looked at Carly. "Wheeler," he said.

"Wheeler," she agreed, narrowing her eyes.

Ross rose and gathered up the pitiful dress. "Nancy, did you see anyone down at the theater this morning?"

"No. I was at the costume shop. Well, for about ten minutes, anyway. Until I saw . . . this *thing* spread out on one of the counters." She gestured at the dress.

Because there wasn't a true costume shop, Nancy had been using the old hardware store next door to the hotel. It served well, because the large windows allowed for good light, and the many counters were useful space for cutting out garments. The only problem was security. The keys to the front and back had been lost years ago, and the old doors were too rotten to hold a padlock in place. So, Daniel had said to just let it be . . . who would want to bother a rickety old store, anyway?

Carly brushed the hair out of her eyes and peered down the street. "I'll have to replace those doors soon, and fit them with deadbolts. Authenticity be damned."

"Could you do me a favor and at least wait until Asher can go down there with you?" Ross asked.

Carly opened her mouth to refuse, but saw the concern in his eyes. She turned to Nancy and saw the utter terror in hers, and relented. "Yes. Of course. It's not like we can call the cops for protection is it?"

*

Asher paced in the hotel lobby and cursed himself. He should have left the hospital earlier and stayed with Carly. Not that Ross couldn't protect her, but Asher had promised Daniel that he wouldn't let sweet Carly Foster out of his sight. What if she had been the one to find the ruined dress? He brushed the thought away. There was no reason for Carly to be down at the costume shop, anyway.

Which was why it was odd that Wheeler had vandalized a costume. What did a frilly pink dress have to do with anything? Either Wheeler was as stupid as he looked, or he was completely erratic. It was probably the latter, and that's what scared Asher. This meant that he had to stick to Carly like glue, no matter how much she squawked about it. And she would. Now all he had to do was try to keep his hands off her. With danger lurking around them, it would be completely irresponsible to try to get her into bed. He needed to focus on keeping her safe . . . and catching that bastard red-handed.

Fantasizing about smashing a fist in Wheeler's pretty-boy face, Asher gave a grim smile. He had always despised Wheeler, anyway. In high school, the idiot had broken into his locker, smearing motor oil all over the drawings he kept in a sketchbook. So what if Wheeler's cute date to the senior fall dance had dumped him for Asher? Wheeler should have done what any other normal boy would have done, challenged him to a fight behind the locker room. Not ransacked personal property. The guy was unhinged, and Asher should have seen it coming. This was all his fault.

He slammed a fist down on the front desk and cursed again. Looking up the stairwell, he cleared his throat. "Carly? Hurry up. What are you doing up there? We're just going down to the theater to work, for God's sake."

Her door creaked open and she poked her head out, staring down at him. "What's the big rush? It's not like we're headed to a fire," Her head shot back inside and she slammed the door.

"I *hope* we're not headed to a fire," muttered Asher.

He walked to the window and peered into the dim, dusky light. Wheeler could be out there. Asher folded his arms and frowned. Well, so what? Ruby Spring belonged to the Day family, and had for nearly twenty years, since an old family friend "Aunt Ethel" had died and left them the property. It was his to take care of, and his to protect. Asher gripped the windowsill and cursed yet again. Behind him, Carly bounded down the stairs, rolls of drawings under her arms.

"Ready?" she asked in a bright tone.

Asher ignored her cheeriness. He grabbed her by the shoulders and leaned in, his stormy eyes an inch from hers. "Do not . . . and I mean . . . do *not* get ten feet away from me, do you hear?"

She sucked in a breath at his closeness. It never failed to make her weak in the knees. God, even when he was angry, he made her want to kiss him. Maybe even more so. She looked up at his intense expression and caught her lower lip in her teeth. This was ridiculous. Here they were, in an anxious situation, and all she could think about was sex. Ridiculous. But her willpower was pretty much nonexistent. It was probably the stress. And she knew a good way to relieve stress.

Smiling, she leaned up and kissed his lips. "I promise."

The kiss worked, because the cloud of anger lifted from his face. He grinned and placed a finger over her lips. "And none of that, which is unfortunate." He sighed and caught her hand. "C'mon, it's time to work."

Walking hand in hand with Asher down the dusty, darkening street, Carly's heart soared, despite the awfulness of the costume situation earlier that day. She knew he wanted her. She was sure of it. What was wrong with flirting with a handsome man? As long as it didn't go too far . . . and she kept her heart out of it, it was nice to feel attractive. Shifting the rolls of drawing under her arm, she smiled. Asher Day had to loosen up. Wasn't that what he had told her not two days ago? Well, it was good advice.

Once at the theater, Asher adjusted the grasp on her hand and switched on the lights. They walked down the center aisle, gazing at the ceiling. "We certainly have a lot of labor ahead of us. Talk about a blank slate," he said.

"Yeah," Carly said with a sigh. "But I don't want you to get worn out. Ross told me today that you're taking over producer duties for Daniel for a while."

"It's no big thing. Besides, I *have* to keep tabs on you. The fact that I am a world-famous painter is just a bonus." He winked at Carly and began to set up a tall ladder.

She cocked her head in curiosity. "Really?"

"Really, what?" he answered.

"Are you really a world-famous painter?"

He laughed uneasily and took a roll of drawings from her. "Be serious. I'm just trying out . . . being dramatic. We are in a theater, right?"

Carly stepped back and folded her arms. "Somehow I think you're not exaggerating about your fame, but I'll leave you alone about it." She put another roll on the stage manager's desk and spread it out.

"Thanks," Asher replied in a wry tone as he climbed the ladder with a charcoal pencil. He seriously doubted if she could leave him alone about it for any length of time. It was better to throw her a bone. The last thing he wanted to talk about was his damned career.

"Carly?"

"Yes?"

"I will tell you about my paintings sometime. It's just that they're . . . not that particularly important right now. This theater is. My brother is. His wife and child are . . . and . . . and you are."

*

What? Carly couldn't believe her ears. She stared down in shock at the drawings in front of her. What did he mean by that? He *didn't* mean it, couldn't . . . at least not the part about her. He was trying to throw her off track. Well, so be it. It was shameful to pry anyway . . . she *knew* the reason why he didn't want to talk about his work. It was none of her business, and she shouldn't care. All she wanted was to flirt with him anyway, right?

She forced a coy smile on her face and looked up. "Sure. Sounds good to me, handsome. Now just tell me where that other ladder is, and I'll get started on the border."

Lost in their own thoughts, Carly and Asher worked in peaceful silence, managing to get a rough outline of the ceiling mural laid out by midnight. Although the pattern was full of leafy twists and turns around the edges, the central image of cherubs in a heavenly sky was easy to accomplish. Gazing up at their work from the aisle, Asher put his arm around Carly and squeezed.

"Not bad for two professionals, huh?" he said.

"Not bad at all," she replied, "And you can't imagine how relieved I am. As soon as we have this painted, I can actually work on the set for the show."

Gazing around the theater, Asher raised his eyebrows. "I'd say you don't have a lot to worry about."

The wooden floor gleamed; the walls were completely re-plastered, and well over half the seats reupholstered. The proscenium arch stood bare, all of the old white paint painstakingly removed from the intricate carving. All that remained was to paint it with a thin layer of gold, finish the seats, and hang new curtains in the private boxes.

Carly rolled her eyes. "I'd say I do. I *have* to say that, even if I'm in good shape. It's what keeps me under deadlines. Besides, aside from building the entire set, I still have to paint the graphics on the oleo curtain. I haven't even ordered the fabric for that yet."

Asher chuckled and pulled her up the aisle. "Well, when that time comes, I *think* I'm capable of helping you out. In the meantime, let's get you into bed."

Get her into bed? A delicious shudder ran up Carly's spine. *Careful.* She needed to slow it down. It's not like she actually planned to share a bed with the man, did she? Well . . . no. She couldn't possibly. That would complicate things far beyond what she could handle right now. But she couldn't let him know how his words affected her.

Pushing back her hair, she looked up at him and raised an eyebrow. "And just how do you plan to get me into bed, Asher Day?"

"Very cautiously, Ms. Foster," he replied, laughing. "And very sweetly."

"Sweet like sugar?" she teased.

"No, sweet like honey. Like warm honey," he whispered in her ear.

Dammit, he was good at this.

Embarrassed, Carly switched on her flashlight in the inky blackness and walked ahead of him back to the hotel. Lights were on in the lobby. Who was still up at this hour? Pulling back the screen door, she peered inside.

Marilyn, in a black satin dressing gown with marabou feather trim, lay on a brocade sofa near the fireplace, cucumber slices over her eyes. The waist of the gown was cinched tight, accentuating a surprisingly small waist and rounded ample hips. Nicky knelt in front of her, massaging her feet tenderly. A pedicure set rested on a side table, a bottle of bright red nail polish next to it.

"What . . . are they playing beauty parlor?" Asher whispered behind her head. He bit back a chuckle as Carly elbowed him in the ribs.

Stepping in, she crossed over to the sofa. "I'm so glad to see that you've made yourselves comfortable, you two," she said with a sincere smile.

Marilyn raised a slice from one eye. She grinned at Carly. "This place is wonderful, darling. So quaint. And I *must* thank you . . . you're so generous."

Carly's brow furrowed, but she continued to smile. "You're welcome, Marilyn, but what for?"

"For giving up your room, darling. Oh, you don't mind, do you? I didn't even bother to *look* at mine until after we took a glorious walk and cooked dinner. When I saw how teensy-tiny it was, I gave it to Nicky and took yours. But don't worry. We moved your things to the bedroom next door to your old one."

Carly gasped.

"Oh, I *do* hope you don't mind." Marilyn sat up. "I mean, yours was so cute with the wallpaper, and the other room was practically empty. Just a few art supplies and I assumed those were yours anyway . . . you were storing your things in that room, weren't you?"

Carly's eyes opened wider and she stared. What was she supposed to do now? She couldn't share a room with Asher. No way. Out of the question. Suddenly she felt strong arms encircling her from behind. Her stomach plummeted as she felt Asher's lips near her ear.

"We don't mind, do we honey?"

Marilyn let out a belly laugh. "I *thought* there was something going on between you two. Well, then . . . it's all settled isn't it?"

No. This couldn't be happening. Carly had to try to work something else out. She opened her mouth. "But I thought that you and Nicky would be sharing a room, Marilyn," she said.

"Oh, honey, we *do*. But not all night. He's a scrumptious man, but he snores like a bear," Marilyn said, reaching out to tousle Nicky's blond surfer locks. Nicky grinned and licked his lips.

Deep laughter burst from Marilyn's throat. "Gotta love him. Oh, Nicky, you're too much. Well . . . almost too much if you know what I mean."

Carly chuckled weakly and closed her eyes as a not-so-unpleasant thrill ran through her. There was no way out of it now. Well, she would just have to convince Asher to leave her at the hotel and go to his cabin. Or at least try. Though she knew it wasn't going to work.

Asher tightened his grip and rested his head on her shoulder. "It's late, sugar plum. Don't you think it's time you went on up to . . . hit the sack?"

Carly stiffened in his embrace. Of all the nerve. Who did he think he was, anyway? Well the games weren't over, but he had lost this match for sure. Forcing a smile, she extricated herself from his arms and turned to face him, making sure to brush every possible part of her body against him in the process. She gave him a light shove, and he stumbled backward, his eyes betraying his astonishment at her boldness.

Cornering him at the kitchen door, Carly ran a hand down his chest and then curled her fingers into the waistband of his jeans. He sucked in a breath.

She leaned closer and purred, "Oh, honey pie. How sweet of you to suggest it. I'd be so relieved to get that big ol' bed all to myself tonight. But don't worry; I'll toss your favorite pillow and blankie down the stairs for you."

Enjoying his shocked expression, Carly leaned up and nibbled on his chin, then kissed him soundly. "Good night . . . lover." She shoved him again.

*

It was all he could do to catch himself before falling backward through the swinging door.

Okay. So the lady knew how to play games. Well, he'd give points for this one tonight, but it wasn't anywhere near over. Asher turned to watch her from behind as she pranced up the winding staircase. Damn, she was something else. So smart. And funny. And so talented . . . she had proved that earlier down at the theater. He had doubted her artistic abilities . . . didn't a set designer just draft and measure?

Well, she had proved him wrong. And did again, tonight. Asher sighed, leaned on the banister and looked up. A fluffy pillow tumbled down and smacked him in the face, followed by a scratchy wool blanket. He spit a piece of lint out of his mouth.

"You've got it bad, don't you boy?" Marilyn asked. She heaved herself up from the sofa and slipped her feet into black satin stiletto mules.

Asher turned and opened his mouth. Then closed it. Marilyn stood, tapping her foot, determined, mischievous eyes boring holes straight through him. There was no arguing with this battle axe. He raised a finger and jabbed it in her direction.

"If you tell her, I'll make sure that you end up on stage from head to toe in bright, shiny pink," he whispered. "With a clown wig. I'm a producer, and I can make it happen."

Marilyn threw her head back and hooted. "Child, I'm not scared of you." She sauntered over and pinched his cheek. "And neither is Ms. Carly Foster. Although I can see why she's attracted. You're a stud." Laughing at his glowering face, Marilyn eased past him and glided up the stairs, her hips swishing. "Don't worry, though . . . your secret's safe with me."

Nicky followed after her, slapping Asher on the back on his way up. "Tough break, man. See ya tomorrow."

Grumbling, Asher took the bedding and stomped to the sofa, flipping off the lights as he passed the front desk. Settling down in the chilly darkened lobby, he folded his long legs onto the short sofa and pulled the rough blanket to his chin. He lay still for a few minutes, listening to the sound of the wind blowing through the pine trees. That should be enough to lull anyone to sleep, he reasoned. But not him. He shifted and then sat up, his body still smoldering from the memory of Carly's hands.

This was stupid. He had a right to sleep in a bed in his own hotel, didn't he? He should just go up there, open her door, and . . . and . . . what? Do what? Exactly. He knew what he *wanted* to do. What, deep down, *she* wanted to do. But actually seducing her would not be in anyone's best interest right now. Sighing, Asher laid back down, turned over and jammed the pillow over his head.

*

Out in the shadows, Wheeler Barstow crouched by the hotel's porch and slammed his large fist into the dusty ground. Damn them. It was pretty obvious that Carly had quickly forgotten about the man who had rescued her on her first day in Ruby Spring. And it was pretty obvious just who had helped her forget.

Pulling a pint of whiskey from his shirt pocket, Wheeler took a greedy swallow and wiped the burning liquid from his wet lips. He narrowed his eyes as he thought again about his girl running her hands all over Asher Day. Wheeler had suspected something was going on there, but now he had proof. Solid proof.

Asher Day. That artsy-fartsy bastard. He had stolen a different girl from Wheeler years ago, and Wheeler had made him pay then. Well, it seemed that Asher hadn't learned his lesson, had he? Felt that he had to have Wheeler's woman panting after him even now. It was enough to make any man furious, but Wheeler wasn't just any man. Fuck, no! He was Deputy Sheriff Barstow, and he made the rules.

Unscrewing the top of his bottle again, Wheeler stood up and drained it. It was a long walk back up to his cruiser, but he didn't care. He had to see for himself what his girl had been up to, and now he knew. And it was gonna stop. With a vicious throw, he sent the bottle sailing into the nearby bushes and began to weave up the road.

Chapter Nine

Ross burst through the back door of the costume shop. "Carly, are you in here?"

He ran through the back hallway and into the large, sunny work area. Carly, wearing overalls and a baseball cap stood by the brand new front door, adjusting a deadbolt lock with a screwdriver.

"There you are." Ross plopped down near the door on one of the large window seats that had served as a display area when the costume shop had been a hardware store. "I've got it. I've got it all figured out."

Carly turned the screwdriver one last time and shoved it into her pocket. "Yeah? What's that?"

"It seemed impossible, but I know what to do with Marilyn . . . who is a fabulous actress, by the way."

Carly made a cutting motion across her throat. "Shhh," she whispered, looking over her shoulder.

"What?" Ross demanded, looking around. "No, no, no. I'm not complaining. She's like a modern-day Mae West. All I need to do is shift some dialogue and blocking around, and the ingénue role becomes the full-figured, older, sexy, heroine role."

Carly widened her eyes, made the cutting motion again, and jerked her head toward the racks of costumes standing in the middle of the shop. "Ross! Keep your voice down. She's back there," she whispered in an anxious voice.

Ross raised an eyebrow. "What's with you today? It's okay. Nancy needs to hear this anyway. I hate to do this to her, but she has to get rid of all the frilly stuff she designed for the ingénue. We need sexy . . . like whorehouse madam sexy." He jumped up and began pacing. "I'm thinking . . . something in a deep blue . . . with some kind of swishy trim or something . . . "

Muffled giggles came from between the two racks. The costumes rustled and swayed. Smiling, Ross tiptoed over.

"Nancy . . . are you hiding from me? Don't worry, Sweetie, I'm only asking for three or four new costumes."

Nancy poked her frizzy head out from between the men's suits, grinning. "How about one costume? At least for now . . . and I mean *right* now." With a flourish, she pushed aside the trousers and gestured grandly. "Ladies and gentlemen, presenting Madame Marilyn Masters."

Marilyn stepped boldly forward and posed one hand in the air and one on a hip. Ross's mouth dropped open and Carly clapped her hands in delight. Marilyn was absolutely stunning.

Clad in a deep wine-colored taffeta 1880s bustle gown, she was corseted tightly. The resulting effect whittled her waist to nothing and pushed her wide hips out in a provocative way. Her generous cleavage spilled out of the top of the square neckline, and short satin sleeves covered her arms, ending in froths of black lace just below the elbow. Yards and yards of foot-long black fringe swished on the skirt as she turned slowly in front of Ross. Her long blonde hair was caught up in a graceful sweep behind an ear, secured with a jeweled clip containing two large ostrich plumes.

Teasingly, Marilyn pulled aside a slit in the skirt to reveal black fishnet stockings. Never wasting an opportunity to be funny, she had stuck a dollar bill in the red garter around her thigh. She pulled it out, dropped the skirt, and sashayed over to Ross.

"Hey, big boy. Take this and buy me a shot of whiskey," she said in a throaty voice.

Ross snapped it up, playing along. "You'll get all the shots you want if you look like *that* every night until this show closes," he responded.

Carly clapped again and walked over to shake Nancy's hand. "I am duly impressed, colleague."

Blushing, Nancy began plucking imaginary lint off the skirt of Marilyn's costume. "It's not that big a deal. Marilyn came and talked to me a couple of days ago. I'm not always the calmest person, but I *do* know how to communicate with my actors."

"That's undeniable," Ross commented, after he walked around Marilyn slowly and whistled. Impulsively, he grabbed Nancy in a giant bear hug.

"You're so awesome," he declared, "Filling in onstage for the lead, dealing with your costume being trashed, and now building this beautiful dress in less than two days." He kissed her cheek and held her at arm's length.

Nancy blushed again. Tears glimmered in her eyes, and she brushed them away impatiently. "Now see? I've turned from super woman back into psycho woman."

"What costume was trashed?" Marilyn asked as she adjusted her cleavage and pursed her lips.

Carly raised an eyebrow at Ross. "I don't mean to change the subject, but I have an idea. If we use Marilyn dressed like this in our publicity photos, we'll sell out the house every night."

"Imagine that, little ol' me on a poster," cried Marilyn, fluttering her fake eyelashes.

"Oh, please. How many theater posters have you been on in your life?" demanded Ross.

"Sixty-two," said Marilyn matter-of-factly.

"I believe it," Carly said, shaking her head in admiration. She glanced at Ross. He looked completely relieved. And though he hadn't talked about it much, she knew that he was worried about the show being a disaster. Now it was almost guaranteed to be a hit. As long as nothing else happened to upset things, they were in good shape. So far, though, the track record for smooth sailing wasn't good at the Ruby Spring Theater. Carly thought of Wheeler and shuddered.

Damn him. She was sick of worrying about that pathetic excuse for a man. Shaking it off, she walked back to the front door and turned the bolt. "Well, guys, this seems to be working just fine. I have to get back over to the hotel to get ready to go to Albuquerque. Asher told me that if I was gone more than fifteen minutes, he was going to come and find me."

Marilyn smiled struck another pose. "You should *let* him come and find you, honey. Keep a man guessing, that's what I always say."

Ross chuckled and laid a hand on her outstretched arm. "It's not that simple, I'm afraid. Asher is kind of looking after her. Carly has been having . . . issues with some idiot she dated who's been, well . . . bothering her."

Marilyn dropped her arm. "What? I thought that she and lover-boy were just hot and heavy." She paused. "Do Carly's issues have something to do with the mysterious trashed costume?"

Carly laughed nervously and opened the door. "Ross, you never fail to suck the life right out of me."

"Well, she has a right to know," he retorted.

"That's fine," said Carly in a level voice, "but could you please not remind me about it? I'm trying to get a job done here." Sticking her nose in the air, Carly walked through the door, closing it behind her.

She had done fine for the past three days, changing the subject every time Ross had mentioned Wheeler. She knew he didn't mean anything by it, but the constant worry was wearing on her nerves. That and having to deal with Asher in her room every night. Poor guy, he was getting sick of sleeping on the floor. Carly sighed and kicked at a rock in her path.

The situation was making her as tired and uncomfortable, too. Pretty much every evening after rehearsal and a casual dinner, the cast and crew sat in the lobby and talked for a while. It was a nice diversion, and it was surprising just how much she didn't miss television. But when she sat next to Asher, it made her nervous and self-conscious. Especially since she knew that later, they would be climbing the stairs to her room together.

Just last night, Ross had been telling a story about the previous summer, when Carly had managed to dump a whole bucket of paint over his head in a ladder mishap. Everyone listening had laughed uproariously, she along with them. Asher had caught her eye, and she had blushed at the expression on his face. It was loving fondness, pure and simple. Then to make matters worse, he had reached for her hand and then kissed it. In front of everyone. Mortifying.

Ross had made some crack about, *'Wasn't it time for them to go to bed?'* or something like that, and she, being the big mouth that she was, had protested, pretending to be repulsed. No one believed her. It was written all over their faces.

She sighed, shaking off the embarrassment. Sooner or later, she was going to have to let him have the bed and offer to sleep on the floor herself. The mere thought of it made her even crankier. *"Nicky should be sleeping on sofa in the lobby,"* she thought. He wasn't even a part of the theater company! That way, Asher could have a room of his own, and Carly could have some peace at night.

Hopping up the hotel's front steps, Carly resolved to talk to Nicky about it as soon as she saw him. She pulled open the screen door and walked through the lobby toward the kitchen. She pushed open the swinging door and stopped short. Asher and Nicky sat at the table, two bottles of beer in front of them. Nicky was on the phone, a serious expression on his face.

"Yep. Yep. That's what I'm saying. I'll come down to the college and give a couple of on-camera lessons to your summer school students tomorrow. Yep. Right. And then you send them up here to help build the set. One hour of lessons for four hours of work." He smiled and held his finger up to Carly, whose mouth had dropped open in surprise.

"I think that's fair, too, professor, considering that I have been in six national commercials. And if they want more lessons, we'll work out something for . . . say, twice a week until the set is built. Right. Great. Well then, I'll see you tomorrow."

Nicky snapped the cell phone shut and turned to Asher. "I'm going to need a car tomorrow."

Asher scribbled on a pad of paper and looked up, grinning. "Done. And good work, man. Way to strike a deal." He reached up and grabbed Carly's hand. "Aren't you going to thank the nice man?"

Carly frowned and wiggled her hand free. *Dammit.* Now how could she possibly ask Nicky to sleep in the lobby? He had just scored her an indefinite supply of semi-skilled labor. She forced a smile and half-heartedly punched Nicky's shoulder. "Thanks. That'll really help."

"Hey, no problem. But it wasn't really my idea. It was Asher's." He shrugged.

Asher took a swig of beer. "Just trying to stay on top of my duties as a producer until we pick up Daniel and Sophie this afternoon." Yawning, he stood up and stretched. "Let's go make a list of your lumber supply, Carly. We can't make another trip back into town tomorrow if Nicky's got the van."

Hastily, Carly pulled a folded sheet of paper from the bib of her overalls and waved it at him. "Quit worrying. Let's just go right now. I want to get it over with and back here in time to paint tonight." She adjusted her baseball cap and pushed open the swinging door.

Nicky waited until he heard the sound of the screen door bang shut in the lobby before he turned to Ross. "Whoa, she's tense. What's up with that, man?"

Asher rolled his eyes and rubbed his tired face. "I don't know. She's always worked up. Part of it is Wheeler, part of it is worrying about her deadlines, and part of it is . . . " He trailed off, shrugging.

Nicky chuckled and slapped Ross on the back. "Part of it is *you*, buddy. That's as clear as the sky is out here in New Mexico."

Asher ignored him and walked to the window, peering out. Carly stood by his van, writing in a little spiral notebook. "She's remaking her list, I just know it. You're right, Nick. She really needs to calm down."

"Oh, I can think of a really good thing to calm her down, man." Nicky pushed open the swinging door and gestured for Asher to follow. "And *you* are the only person who's capable of providing that for her, if you know what I mean." He winked.

*

Unbuckling her seatbelt, Carly twisted in her seat and glared at Asher. "I'm sorry you didn't get to finish your beer. If you're so thirsty, then run across the street and get a soda or something. I'm only going to be in here a few minutes."

"Fine," muttered Asher. He turned off the engine, hopped out and stuffed his keys in his pocket. "When I get back, I'll wait right here. But if you're not out of there in fifteen minutes, I'm coming after you."

Carly rolled her eyes. "Duh." He stared at her. Letting out an exasperated sigh, she jumped out of the old van, stomped to the front of the paint store and jerked the door open.

Asher was driving her crazy. If he wasn't nagging her about 'staying in his sight', he was staring at her and making her blush. If she didn't know any better, she might almost assume that he was developing a crush on her. But that was impossible. Men didn't get crushes on Carly Foster, she got crushes on them. Crushes that never, ever, resulted in anything except her own embarrassment and frustration.

Well, not this time. As much as she was attracted to Asher, she was not going to fall for him. She strolled down an aisle, absently plucking up a few paint samples. It was time to focus on work. The rest of the ceiling wasn't going to paint itself.

Grumbling, she dug around in her bag for her list. They had already hit the fabric store and the hardware store. All that was left were a few assorted cans of paint and some new brushes. It was a good thing the shopping trip was almost over, because she was developing a monster headache. Examining the shades of blue, she reached up to massage the back of her head.

Just as she started to relax, a strong hand gripped her own and squeezed firmly, the fingers pressing into the sides of her neck. Stiffening, Carly turned her head, fully expecting to snarl at Asher for the hundredth time that afternoon. Her stomach dropped like a rock when she found herself looking into Wheeler's menacing, narrowed eyes.

"Get your hands off me, you psycho," she demanded, jerking her body around. He released her, but placed both hands up against the shelf, backing her up to the paint cans and trapping her.

He cocked his head to the side and brought his lips close to her ear. "How's your new boyfriend?"

Carly shuddered and moved her bag up to her chest, hugging it. He wasn't going to intimidate her. That's all he wanted, and damned if she was going to give it to him. He deserved nothing from her but scorn. "I don't have a boyfriend, Wheeler, and I'm not looking for one right now, either. Work is keeping me pretty busy. I'm sure you can understand that, being a *dedicated* officer of the law, right?"

"Oh, I think you're lying," said Wheeler in a tight voice, running his hands down the shelves to rest on her shoulders.

Carly frowned and squeezed her bag. She took a deep breath and said, "If you don't take your hands off of me right this second, I'm going to knee you in the crotch again. Harder. Although you were shitfaced last time I did that, I'm pretty sure you remember how it felt."

Wheeler snatched his hands from her shoulders and stepped back. "I remember, and you're lucky. If I had thought about it then, I would have arrested you for assault. Touch me again, and it's gonna happen, Carly girl."

"Well, then, we're even. You don't want me to touch you, and I certainly don't want your revolting hands on me." Carly tossed her hair out of her eyes. "So, now that that's covered, just what the hell do you want, Wheeler?"

Wheeler stared at her stonily. "I think you can guess what I want."

"No, I can't. Please enlighten me."

"I want you to stay away from that Asher Day. You were my

girl first, and don't you forget it."

Alarmed, Carly glanced toward the entrance. This guy wasn't just an asshole. He was delusional. And dangerous. Suddenly, she knew Asher was right. She had to stay with him from now on, no matter what. Her mind racing, Carly tried to think of a response that wouldn't provoke Wheeler even further. Should she try to placate him? Just how did a girl deal with a stalker cop? There wasn't a clear solution, so she decided to go with logic.

Carly grimaced. "Wheeler, I hope you don't think that because we went out once, we have some kind of commitment. Let me make that very clear. I'm sorry we don't have anything in common, but that's just the way it is." She waited, her heart hammering for his response.

To her dismay, he immediately turned and walked away from her. This wasn't good. She had to make him see reason . . . maybe it would stop him from damaging things at the theater. "Wait!" she called, jogging after him. "Stop. Hold on a second, Wheeler. I really want to—"

"Shut up!" he yelled, rotating around to face her. "You don't fool me. I know you're lying. I saw you. I saw you with him. And you better stay away from him." Wheeler was so angry his eyes were bulging. Spit formed at the corners of his mouth and he jabbed a finger at her. "You're mine."

Carly's gaze darted around, checking for someone . . . anyone to walk by so she could escape. "I told you before, not that it's any of your business, but nothing is going on with Asher," she lied.

"Shut up!" he yelled again, and threw his hands in the air. "I don't believe you. What makes you think I'm so gullible? And what makes you think I can't do something about it? You better listen and listen good, Carly." He leaned in close and glared at her. "Think of this as your warning. Anything else happens up at Ruby Spring . . . you know it will be *your* fault."

Uttering a curse, he stalked off; punching a paint can on his way. It fell off the shelf with a thud and rolled to a stop at Carly's feet. In shock, she picked it up and set it back on the shelf. *Oh, hell.* What was she supposed to do? If she told Asher, he would probably go straight to the county sheriff's office. And from what Sophie had told her, that wouldn't be much help. The supervisor was also Wheeler's best friend.

Carly sighed and stuck her trembling hands in her pockets. It was best to say nothing for now. She couldn't bear the thought of being the cause of more injury at Ruby Spring. If she were careful to stay an arm's length from Asher when they were in town or outside, then maybe Wheeler would calm down.

It made her furious, though, to know he was watching. What gave him the right to intrude on her life like that? Well, she would think of something to put a stop to it. She was just too mad to do it right now. Carly stomped back up the aisle and grabbed two gallons of white primer and walked to the front of the store to plunk them on the counter.

The door jingled behind her and she jumped, dropping her bag on the floor. She reached down and scooped it up with shaking fingers. Asher ambled toward her, a frown on his face.

"What's wrong?" he demanded.

"Nothing. I'm just tired and I guess I'm not paying much attention to what I'm doing today." Carly forced a smile and shifted the paint cans on the counter.

"Are you sure?"

"Oh, absolutely. Don't worry about me. You know how I fret about deadlines. Sometimes it just wears me out," Carly dug in her bag again for the list. "I'm not quite ready. I got side tracked looking at paint samples. Would you help me pick out the rest of this?" She waved the list.

"I guess," he said, taking it from her hand. He looked at her, concern etching lines at the corners of his eyes. "I get a feeling there's something you're not telling me. But we can't stay here much longer. We still have to go by the hospital and pick up Daniel and company."

Carly smiled and crooked her hand through his arm. Her fingers still shook, so she squeezed his bicep to still them. "So how does it feel to be Uncle Asher?"

"Oh, don't say 'uncle.' It makes me feel so old," he groaned. "I guess we all have to grow up sometime, though, huh?"

Carly nodded. "No getting around it. So, why don't we start by being responsible and getting some work done?"

Asher winked and gestured with his free hand. "After you, madam."

A slow smile spread over Carly's face. God, she loved it when he winked at her. It made the rest of the world go away.

*

Outside the store, Wheeler stood with his hands cupped around his face, his nose pressed to the glass. He glared at Carly as she flirted with Asher. The bitch hadn't kept her promise more than a minute. He shook his head, and pushed back from the glass. "I fucking warned her," he muttered and strolled to the street, whistling.

Chapter Eleven

Marilyn stood with her feet planted in the center of the stage, her arms outstretched and her chin lifted. "My home is where I stand today. Men have tried to take it from me, but none have succeeded. So bring your best, Mr. Carson, bring your best. And be prepared for the worst you could possibly imagine."

Although Marilyn's voice was barely a whisper, it carried to the back rows of the theater and raised a chill up Carly's spine. She dropped her small paintbrush into the can and clapped along with her college student interns, who stood in amazement alongside her.

"She's a real star, isn't she?" breathed a petite pig-tailed girl, "Oh, how I wish that I could be that good someday. And she's so beautiful, too."

Carly chuckled and resumed painting the trim near the balcony steps. "So you're telling me you would rather be like Marilyn than a supermodel?"

The girl gasped. "Of course. Marilyn is a *real* star. Plus, look at her. Guys gravitate to her like bees to honey." She gestured toward the front row of the theater.

Marilyn was leaning over the front of the stage, listening to Ross. Although she was wearing a loud, loose, flowing top and faded black leggings, her hourglass shape was evident, and the top was cut low enough to reveal a lady-like hint of cleavage. Ross was oblivious to her physical appeal, but Carly noted the gleam in his eyes and he waved his hands as he spoke.

"I have to say again . . . good work, everyone. Marilyn, I like the change you made for that final line. You're right. The character wouldn't shout. It would be too common, and she's much too confident a person to do that."

Buddy, the hero and Jack, the villain, stood behind Marilyn and murmured in agreement. Carly could tell that as far as they were concerned, she could do no wrong. Jack eyed Marilyn with open admiration, and for once, Buddy was actually making notes in his script.

Marilyn smiled. "Excellent. Now that we've muddled our way through Act Two, is it possible to take ten?" she asked.

Parker, the stage manager, jumped up from his desk and checked his stop watch. "We're ahead of schedule by . . . wow . . . twenty minutes. We shaved twenty minutes off that act. How did that happen?"

"Because these three perform like clockwork together," Ross said with a chuckle.

Completely because of Marilyn, thought Carly, but it was just like her best friend Ross to massage actors' egos. Without kissing anyone's ass, of course. She winked at him.

Ross grinned and called back to Parker, "OK, if that's the case, then why don't we take thirty? If we run over on Act Three a little bit, I think Carly will forgive us . . . right, Carly?" He turned and peered toward the back row.

Carly raised an eyebrow and stuck a hand on her hip, feigning irritation. "I *suppose* so, Mr. Director. We're supposed to have the stage at four, but I *guess* we could wait a few extra minutes." She put down the paint can and walked up the center aisle, wiping her hands on the front of her paint-stained jeans shorts. "Seriously, we're ahead as well. I think I can give my helpers a thirty-minute break, too."

Cheers erupted from the back of the theater and Carly laughed again. She stopped in front of Ross and leaned in, lowering her voice. "I had almost forgotten what it was like to be so young and enthusiastic. These kids are so excited about their on-camera lessons with Nicky, and they are doing really careful work. To hear them talk, Nicky is a god, and this theater is his temple."

Ross plopped down in a new velvet-covered seat in the front row. "So, you're really ahead of schedule?"

"You know I wouldn't hide it from you if I was behind. Yes, we are, and because of that . . . I'm hoping to take . . . well . . . half a day off on my birthday." She sat down next to him and batted her eyelashes.

He shook his head and threw his hands in the air. "Oooh, an entire half day. Hmm, I don't know. I'm not sure I'm comfortable with that, partner."

Carly swatted at his shoulder. "You're supposed to be nice to a girl on her birthday."

"It's not your birthday until Monday. And I can't be nice to you, because I won't be around you. I'll be stuck in here . . . but I'm pretty sure that *Asher* would be very happy to be . . . nice to you. Although *nice* is not quite the word I'm searching for . . . " he trailed off.

Carly's smile narrowed into a frown. "Shut it, Ross. He's probably still up in the balcony," she whispered. Ross's head swiveled and his eyes searched the balcony area. She grabbed his head in her hands. "No. Don't look, you bonehead."

A polite cough echoed near the back of the theater. A blush spread across Carly's cheeks and she dropped her hands away from Ross's face. She peered over her shoulder, unable to stop herself. Asher was reclining on his elbows halfway down the balcony steps, grinning, his ankles crossed. He raised his hand and waved.

"Dammit," Carly whispered. She whipped back around and slid down in her seat.

Marilyn's booming laugh echoed through the building, and she swept down the front of stage steps, stopping before Carly. "You and I should take the break together, missy."

Grateful for the chance to escape, Carly jumped up. "Asher, Marilyn and I are going to go hang out in the saloon for a few minutes," she threw over her shoulder. Scrambling up on the stage, she headed for the backstage door.

"Hold on, Carly." She stopped short at Asher's outburst, but didn't turn around. He was so irritating, but just the sound of his deep voice sent a shock wave of pleasure through her stomach. She wanted that voice near her ear . . . whispering. And those strong arms around her . . . it had been days since he had hugged her or even taken her hand in his. Had she really pissed him off to the point that he found her unattractive?

She had not been pleasant to him very much in the past few days. In fact, she had been downright rude, cutting him off when all he was trying to do was engage in friendly conversation. But she was afraid the subject would turn to Wheeler, and Carly Foster was *not* a good liar. The asshole's warning to stay away from Asher was always at the front of her mind and if she broke down and told Asher about it, he'd go after Wheeler. And get hurt. And then Wheeler would turn his sights on Ruby Spring. She couldn't let that happen. For now, she was stuck.

But one thing she *could* do was avoid people like a true champ. And that's what she was going to do right this very minute, without Asher embarrassing her in the process.

Carly took a deep breath and turned to face Asher, who had jumped up on the stage and was walking toward her, frowning. She blocked his path and whispered, "We're only going to be in there for a little bit. If you'd like, you could sit on the bench out in front of the saloon and work on the color scheme for the oleo curtain."

Asher narrowed his eyes and glanced from Carly to Marilyn and back again. "I think you girls are up to something . . . but I guess so. Just let me check the saloon before you go in."

"Sure," Carly agreed quickly. She glanced down at Marilyn, who still stood in the front row, smirking up at them. "I'll grab a couple of sodas from the cooler stage left and meet you there, Marilyn." Grabbing Asher's hand, she pulled him into the stage left wing. "Could you please keep your voice down? I don't want the interns to know about . . . well . . . the sabotage. If they run away, I'm screwed," she said in a low voice.

Asher pulled his hand free and raised his eyebrows. "Don't worry, Carly. I wouldn't dream of scaring decent people off my own property." He glared and pushed past her, slamming open the backstage door and stomping down the old wooden steps to the dusty path behind the theater.

Carly stared after him and rolled her eyes. Who died and made him king of Ruby Spring? Oh, yeah, old "Aunt Ethel." She sighed and followed him up the path. She should be feeling more relaxed, because Wheeler seemed to have vanished. Two weeks had gone by without an incident.

Unfortunately, she couldn't seem to enjoy herself, despite the great strides she had made in the restoration. It was virtually completed, with the exception of a little paint here and there. She and Asher had finished the ceiling two days ago, and tomorrow she would set up her power tools in the saloon and turn it into a makeshift scene shop in order to build the set for the play. It wouldn't be that difficult. All she had to do, with the help of her interns, was move the tables and chairs up to the balcony and cover the bar area with protective sheets of plastic. Heavy-duty extension cords would be run around the stable to the costume shop next door, which was the closest building that had electricity.

Everything was shaping up, and she had nothing to worry about. Except that as of this minute, she hadn't come up with any realistic plan to beat Wheeler at his sick game. And she had to, soon. God knew when he would show up again. And if he did, it would be her fault.

Carly tried to shake off her apprehension as she scowled down at the dusty street. Unable to resist, she glanced up at Asher, who was walking ahead of her, his hands thrust in his pockets. Her expression softened. He was such a decent man. Infuriating and confusing and sometimes close to irresistible, but all in all, a really *good* man. Deep down, she knew that's why she was so attracted to him. And it was different from the other "summer crushes" she had had in the past. Those had been focused on men with authority . . . or pure sex appeal.

Asher had those things, too, but she knew that he could have been less attractive and she still would have fallen. Because of his good heart. He might have been attracted to her once, too, but she had pushed him away. Although she knew Asher thought of himself as the great protector, it was up to Carly to keep Ruby Spring, and all the people she had come to care about . . . safe.

*

Cracking open her soda can, Marilyn plunked it down and wiggled her way onto a stool in the saloon. "I wish I had a little something special to put in this soda," she declared, and winked at Carly. "Hey, is there any liquor back there?" She peered over the edge of the dusty bar.

Laughing, Carly wiped condensation from her soda and hopped up onto a stool next to her. "Nope. And if there really was . . . it would be over a hundred years old. Would you even want to touch it?"

"Damn straight I would. Well . . . I'd probably smell it first, but I think it would be a total kick to take a shot of authentic Wild West whiskey." Marilyn sighed and held out her soda can, swirling it. "But this is all we have for today, so bottoms up, Carly."

They touched their cans together and took long drinks, as if throwing back a shot. Marilyn promptly belched and plunked her can down on the bar in satisfaction. "OK, down to business, Carly. I want you to tell me exactly what's going on with this Wheeler fella."

Carly winced at the name and looked over her shoulder toward the dusty windows in the front of the saloon. Asher sat on the porch outside, a colored rendering of the oleo curtain spread out on his lap. "Do you think he can hear us?" she asked.

"I doubt it, but let's be as quiet as possible. If he gets wind of what I'm about to suggest, he won't like it." Marilyn replied.

"What do you mean?" Carly's eyes widened.

"Let me get this straight. When you first got to Ruby Spring, you had car trouble. A hot and sexy sheriff stopped and helped you, then came on to you. Am I right so far?"

Carly blushed and took a swig of her soda. "Pretty much."

"Then, he took you out on a date that same night, and he turned out to be a total loser. You kicked him in the balls and he took off. A few days later, Daniel broke his leg on a ladder . . . and then a costume was vandalized. But no one has reported anything because you all know it's Wheeler, and it wouldn't do any good because his boss is his best friend. Still correct?"

Carly nodded. "How did you know?"

"Ross and I had a talk."

Carly frowned.

Marilyn folded her arms and stared. "And there's more. So 'fess up . . . I want to help you nail this jerk."

Carly began to shake her head. "Oh, no . . . that's pretty much it. Really, I think he's not going to do anything more . . . it's been a couple of weeks . . . and I think it's going to be OK, because . . . " She trailed off and looked at Marilyn. "I'm dreaming, aren't I?"

"Not dreaming. Delusional, if you think Wheeler has just suddenly decided to turn into Mister Nice Guy. What else happened, Carly?"

Sighing, Carly relented and told her about the incident at the paint store. Marilyn listened in silence, frowning. When Carly stopped talking, she reached over suddenly and pulled her in for a hug.

"You poor girl. Although . . . I really think you should have told someone. But we can't change that now. What we *can* do is figure out how to trap that cowardly son of a bitch. If we catch him red-handed, we have proof. Do you have a video camera?"

"No," Carly said, "but the college does. Remember, they're using one for that on-camera class."

Marilyn snapped her fingers. "That's it. I think Nicky has a new job, in addition to being an acting teacher. He is now my personal private investigator . . . and a super-hot one, at that." She waggled her eyebrows and belched again.

Carly grinned and looked at Marilyn, who raised a manicured index finger and took another drink.

Marilyn's eyes sparkled as she wiped her mouth with the back of her hand and held the soda can out with a grand gesture. "Attention, please. I will now, for your listening pleasure, perform the entire alphabet."

Carly giggled and saluted Marilyn with a soda can. The door creaked open just as Marilyn ripped out an impressive "A."

*

"Are you two drinking something other than generic cherry cola?"

Both women looked at each other and then back at Asher. "No, Handsome, we don't drink on the job," replied Marilyn, all innocence.

Asher glanced at Carly. She was beaming, her pretty face lit up with happiness. It was a relief to see her this way. She had been beyond cranky for the better part of two weeks, and so cool to him that he had almost decided that she wasn't attracted to him anymore.

Well, who could blame her? He was, by general observation, a non-working artist, and a grumpy one at that. The only job he had right now was to follow after her, and sleep at her feet at night like a faithful dog. At least he *had* stuck to that plan. And it had almost kept him busy enough to keep his mind off of painting. Which, incredibly, he had actually wanted to do more and more of.

He had an idea for a new painting . . . an abstract of an angelic face. It first came from the cherubs on the theater ceiling, but soon turned to a likeness of a familiar woman. With soft gray eyes and a sweet smile. He wanted to paint Carly, but he was afraid. Of what, he couldn't tell, but that was reason enough to leave the canvas blank for now.

Asher smiled to cover his disturbing thoughts and walked over to the two women. Placing his hands on the bar between them, he joked, "I think you ladies have had enough. Last call is over. Now move it on out of here, before I have to throw you out."

"Mmm, that sounds tempting, but I have to go back to work now," replied Marilyn as she slipped off her stool. She left the saloon, closing the door behind her.

Carly's smile washed over Asher like a welcome sunbeam. "We should get back too, I guess. My busy little helpers will wonder where we are." She hesitated and then slipped her hand in his.

He paused for a brief second, and then squeezed it, a small smile playing around the corners of his mouth. "We wouldn't want that. May I have the honor of escorting you back?"

Carly gazed into his eyes with relief. "Of course. And Asher? I'm really sorry if I've been . . . well . . . "

He placed a palm on her cheek. "No explanation needed, Carly. To be honest, I know something's going on . . . but I'm not completely sure I want to hear about it just yet. And you wouldn't tell me anyway. Am I right?"

"You're right," she agreed. "I'm aware that we've only known each other a few weeks . . . and I know I've been awfully cranky. But could you just trust me on this? I'll get it sorted out." She gazed at him and reached up to curl her fingers around his warm hand.

Asher cleared his throat. "Yeah. But don't think that it's an excuse to wiggle away from me. You still need me, Carly."

*

Carly nodded and averted her gaze toward the doorway as his words hit home. Oh yes, she did need him. But not just for protection, that was abundantly clear. Her raging emotions were testament to that. She needed him for all the healthy reasons any woman needed a man she was in love with.

Her eyes widened in shock. In love with him. In love with him? No! She didn't want to be in love with him. Not in the summertime. Summertime was a curse. Any other time . . . like if she had met him in Chicago, around Christmastime. That would have been nice. Or at a New Year's Eve party. But not here. Not when she was leaving in a little over a month. Once the show was open, her job was over, and there would be no excuse to stay . . . even if her heart was bleeding all over the mountainside. It would be just like every other summer she'd driven away from a theater in tears.

Frustration seeped in. This wasn't fair. Why did this have to happen to her? She'd made herself a summer promise. But no matter what she did, or how hard she tried, she just couldn't seem to stop searching for love even though she failed every time. This summer, so quickly, so easily . . . love had sneaked in, finding her, not the other way around. She let out a ragged sigh.

"Carly?"

Asher's deep, soothing voice broke through her thoughts and she blinked to push back the tears forming at the corners of her eyes. She couldn't look him in the eyes. He would know . . . and that would be disaster. Taking a shaky breath, she forced a smile on her face, keeping her gaze fixed on the dusty window by the door. Quickly, she gave his shoulder a squeeze and stepped around him.

"Carly?" he asked again.

"I'm fine. I think I drank my soda too fast," she muttered, reaching for the old brass doorknob.

Before she could open it, Asher's arms slid around her middle and she felt her back bump against his broad chest. Goosebumps ran down her arms as his stubbly chin nestled in the crook of her bare neck.

"You're all tense," he whispered.

It was true. Her back was ramrod straight and her feet were planted as if she were on board a rocking ship in a storm. All she wanted was to not cry. All she wanted was to run like hell back to the hotel and lock herself in the tiny bathroom on the third floor, turn on the water and *then* cry. She had to force herself to relax, because she knew Asher would do everything he could to keep her from running off if he thought she was truly upset.

Upset. Ha. She was beyond upset. She was in love. And the most important man in the world was holding her close and safe, trying to comfort her. Oh, God. Why her? Why couldn't she have realized it when she was alone?

Carly's blurry eyes fluttered closed and she inhaled, drawing in Asher's clean, male scent. A burning tear escaped and slipped down her cheek. Then another. And another. Then a flood. Trying to suppress it was making it worse, and Asher's arms tightened around her as her body began to shake with sobs.

"Oh, sweetheart," he whispered, turning her around.

At the endearment, her troubled gaze sought his. For a full minute, she stared into his eyes, tears rolling down her face unheeded. He barely blinked. She barely breathed. Finally, he broke the spell and reached for her, his hands on the back of her head. A plaintive sob ripped out of her throat and he pulled her close, rocking.

Carly reached up and locked her arms around his neck and buried her face in his chest. She barely registered it when Asher's arms encircled her waist and lifted her off the ground.

Walking over to the bar, he lifted her higher and set her on top of it. Even though Carly was planted almost four feet off the ground, Asher was so tall that they were almost eye to eye. He cupped her tear-stained face. His gaze all compassion, he leaned closer, kissing her salty lips.

"You don't cry like that very often, Carly, do you?"

"No," she whispered, looking at her lap.

"I can tell."

"I'll bet you don't either," she countered.

"Almost never," he agreed. He placed his hands on her knees and a smile formed at the corners of his sculpted lips. The sexy laugh lines in his cheeks widened into deep dimples and he tipped his head to the side, observing her.

She glanced at him, then back down at her lap.

"Crying sucks," she declared.

"Yeah, sometimes it does. And sometimes it's an essential component of sanity."

The corners of her lips lifted and she blinked through the tears. She reached into a pocket, drew out a hair band, and then twisted her wavy hair quickly up and away from her face. She wiped the remainder of the tears away and shook her head at Asher, her smile growing.

"What?" he asked.

"I just think it's pretty amusing that an artist would have such a scientific explanation for going on an emotional crying jag."

Asher's palms squeezed her knees and he feigned irritation. "What do you mean? I *am* an artist, not a scientist."

"Crying is an essential component of sanity," she echoed back to him.

His hands slid farther up. "Oh, that."

"Yes, that," she countered, placing her palms on the back of his hands to halt them. She was beginning to get delicious shivers and she just didn't want to deal with them right now.

He looked to the rough-hewn ceiling, appearing to be in deep thought. "Well, now, here's the beauty of that remark. It would *seem* to be scientific because it is logical . . . but actually it is artistic." His hands wiggled under hers and gained a couple of inches.

"Oh, that's a load of crap," Carly retorted, pressing down on his roving hands.

"No, no . . . now hear me out. It clearly is a statement about emotions, and worded in a crafty way," he mused, his palms sliding upward. " . . . so the words in and of themselves are a creation . . . so they had to have come from an artist . . . therefore, my quote is artistic," he finished, his hands now on her hips.

Carly sucked in a breath and narrowed her eyes. She clapped her small hands over his wandering large ones and raised them to a safe distance. "So, now it's an actual quote? Like a Shakespeare quote? Or a Wordsworth quote?"

Asher snorted. "Yeah, right. More like an Oprah or Dr. Phil quote. Wouldn't I be great on a talk show? I could paint, and tell jokes and philosophize . . . all we need is a satellite dish and an audience of blue haired old ladies. Marilyn could be my first guest."

Carly released his hands and threw her head back, laughing. Asher didn't wait for a second. His hands were suddenly all over her middle, tickling her ribs.

"Oh!" She shrieked in laughter and slapped at his hands. "Quit it. *Quit it,*" she gasped, trying to grab his wrists.

Asher beamed like a little kid, his eyes sparkling as he went for her armpits.

"No," she wailed, "not there . . . anywhere but there!"

He reached up and grabbed her under the arms, pulling her off the bar toward him. Her body slid slowly against his before her feet landed on the floor.

"You did that on purpose," she accused, a rueful little smile playing across her lips.

"What else would you expect from me?" he retorted. Dipping his head, he kissed her soundly on the lips, and then pushed back, holding her at arm's length. "Are you happy again, Ms. Foster?"

Was she? Carly glanced at him. Well, if she had to go and fall in love with someone, at least it was someone as wonderful as Asher Day. And truth be told, he *did* make her happy. Even if she couldn't tell him that she loved him. Correction, wouldn't tell him. At least not anytime soon.

"Yes," she answered, "I'm happy."

Asher winked. "Good. I'm just happy that you're happy."

Carly winked back. "Can I quote you on that?"

Laughing and pulling her with him, he opened the old door to the saloon and walked out into the sunny afternoon.

Chapter Twelve

Sophie yawned and adjusted the tiny bundle in her arms. The baby eyed her and yawned in response, then smacked his lips in satisfaction before closing his dark eyes again. He wrinkled his little brow and began to move squirm.

"Is Daniel finished with his breakfast?" whispered Daniel.

"You never get tired of saying his name, do you?" asked Sophie, reaching up to stroke her husband's cheek.

"Nope. I have my very own little mini-me," he said and threw back the covers, swinging his long legs to the floor. He scratched near the top of his cast and then stretched, looking over his shoulder at his wife. "And mini-Soph, too," he added.

Sophie gestured toward the wall. "Danny, don't get up without those crutches. The doctor told you not to put any weight on your leg for at least another three weeks."

"Then why did she give me a walking cast?" he grumbled, reaching for the crutches propped up against the wall.

Sophie sighed and eased out of bed. "To irritate me, probably."

A thin wail broke through their friendly argument and Daniel abandoned the crutches, reaching out for the baby. "Go on, dearest. You need to get some breakfast so that you can feed Junior here in another hour or so."

Sophie chuckled and slipped on her bathrobe. "Thanks. Do you think you can reach the diaper bag from there?"

"What for?"

Sophie walked around the bed and folded back the blanket covering the baby. A pungent tell-tale odor wafted up and Daniel wrinkled his nose, holding the tiny bundle out.

"Mommy, he needs you."

"Oh, no. Fair is fair. Broken leg or not, you're changing that diaper." She grabbed the diaper bag and plunked it on the bed next to him, still chuckling.

Sophie belted her bathrobe and smoothed back her buttery blond hair. She grinned at her frowning husband and walked up the basement stairs, yawning. At the top she pushed open the old, wide door and entered the sunny lobby, a sleepy smile on her face.

"What's got you so happy, Sis?" Asher sat cross-legged on the front desk, a cup of coffee nestled in a large palm.

"Nothing much. Just simple things. I got to sleep most of the night through, and Daniel is on diaper duty today."

She stretched again and gave Asher a cautious glance. He had been so on edge lately, and she feared that he was slipping back into the moodiness that had a hold over him when he first came back to Ruby Spring. But today, there were no signs of it. His eyes were sparkling, and his smile was easy and warm.

"Better him than me," declared Asher as he hopped down from the desk. "How about I get you some eggs?"

"Sounds good. That's a pretty generous offer from a man who hates to cook. Where's Carly?"

"She's in the kitchen, fixing your eggs," he said with a laugh.

Sophie shook her head, grinning, and pushed open the kitchen door.

"Hey, Carly."

"Sophie, I was going to bring you down a tray to surprise you, but you beat me to it." Carly wiped her hands on a towel and reached into the refrigerator for the orange juice.

Taking the carton from her, Sophie sat at the table and poured a glass. "Now why would you want to surprise *me* today? You're the birthday girl."

The kitchen door swung open and Asher ambled in. He winked at Carly and sat on the edge of the table. She shooed him off.

"What is it about you and sitting on any kind of furniture *but* a chair?" she grumbled.

"Answer Sophie's question, sweetheart," he countered.

Carly shot him a look and cleared her throat. "I know I'm the birthday girl. I just figured that if I had the time off, I could do something special for someone else with it. We're in the sticks. It's not like being in a huge city where I can go power-shop."

She winced as soon as she said it. Why couldn't she keep her big mouth shut? She didn't want to come across as a snob. To her relief, Sophie laughed.

"No kidding. Only a few years ago, when I lived in L.A., I took shopping for granted," said Sophie, "but Albuquerque really isn't that bad. It's pretty fun, actually. If you wanted to go to the mall and the movies today, I'll bet that Asher wouldn't mind too much."

Carly glanced at him. He rolled his eyes and sighed.

"If it wasn't your birthday, you couldn't drag me into a mall, but seeing as how it is . . . " he trailed off.

Carly grinned and slipped her arm through his, looking up at his tanned, handsome face. A face that was becoming more and more handsome as each day passed. He was putting on some weight, and the exercise climbing all over ladders in the theater wasn't hurting him, either. Plus, since the day she had apologized to him, he had loosened up a lot and it was a relief to enjoy the tentative truce between them. As far as she could tell, he still had no clue that her feelings for him had deepened so much.

"I won't take you to a chick flick," she promised.

"Something tells me you're not too fond of them anyway," he countered.

"Yes I am." Carly wiggled free to stand next to Sophie, who had a mouthful of scrambled eggs.

Pausing to take a sip of coffee, Sophie rolled her eyes and glanced up at Carly. "*All* women love chick flicks, Ash. But most women don't *only* love them. Besides, I seriously doubt you two could have a bad time together if you tried to on purpose." She waved her hand in dismissal even as she smiled. "Go. Enjoy your day. Happy Birthday, Carly."

Asher reached out and tugged on Carly's hand. "C'mon. I'll buy you somethin' purty at the mall," he drawled.

"As long as it's not tacky, bright red, and from Victoria's Secret, you're on," she retorted, pushing open the kitchen door.

Asher followed her. "As much as I would like to see that, there is no way in *hell* I'm going in that store."

Sophie's hoot of laughter floated behind them and she called out, "Ha. That's what Daniel said a year before we were married. Now I have to steer him away from there every time we go into the mall."

Carly laughed, too, and shot a glance at Asher from beneath her lashes. He blushed and walked quickly past her to the front door.

*

Oh, hell. Asher set his mouth in a grim line. God, she looked pretty today. Her pale green sundress clung in all the right places and her wavy hair was caught back in a simple headband. Small pearl earrings dotted her delicate earlobes and she wore just a hint of makeup. Just enough to drive a man crazy.

With clumsy fingers, he dug keys out of his pocket and bounded down the front steps of the hotel. This friendly banter between them was getting ridiculous. He was too old to be playing flirting games. And both of them were too old to be dancing around romance as if they were frightened animals.

Why couldn't he just ask her out on a date like a normal man? If he wasn't such a coward, he would do it. But he was almost sure she would say no, because she was just as scared as he was. He knew her well enough to realize that.

He unlocked the van and pulled back the creaky, rusting door. Well, so what if she said no? Then he had the perfect opportunity to ask her why. But that would be a mistake. Carly Foster was a bad liar. So even if she *tried* to spare his feelings he would know . . . especially if she didn't feel the same way about him that he did about her.

He wouldn't do it. It was too risky. But he wasn't a coward, dammit . . . not with anything else in his life. So,why this? He *would* do it. He had to do it. Sighing, he rested his head on the doorframe. Maybe he would do it. Yeah. Maybe.

Asher jumped into the driver's seat and reached across to unlock her door, glancing over at her smiling face beyond the dusty window. She was so beautiful. He grinned and she winked at him, grabbing the outside handle. Quickly, he pushed the lock in and winked back.

Carly pulled up on the handle and then stomped her foot. *"Unlock it,"* she mouthed, smiling.

Asher did as commanded, and then snapped the lock down again, just as she moved the handle. Her mouth dropped open. Chuckling now, he leaned back and laced his hands behind his head. He closed his eyes and smiled as he heard her feet crunching on gravel.

As his door swung open, he casually opened his eyes and gazed at her. "Yes?"

Carly grabbed his arm and tugged. "I'm driving."

"But this is my van."

"So what? It's my birthday. I feel like driving. Scoot over."

Asher looked quickly into her smiling eyes. It was now or never. He swallowed and handed her the keys.

"I'll scoot over if you do me a favor."

"What's that?" There was suspicion in her eyes.

He blushed and forced himself to look at her. God, why did this have to be so hard? Clearing his throat, he began.

"Let me start over. I shouldn't be asking you for a favor on your birthday. I should be giving you a present. Well, actually, I have a present to give you . . . but I was going to do that later. So, this isn't really a present . . . I mean, it would be arrogant for me to assume that it is." He stopped short and drew in a deep breath.

"I'm not making any sense, am I?"

Carly tilted her head and gazed at him. "Nope. Not so far. But go on, I'm listening."

"OK. All right. What I am trying to say is . . . Carly, I want to go out with you. On a date. A real date. Today. May I take you on a date?"

A slow grin spread across her face. Leaning in to the van, she pulled him down for a soft kiss. "I'm sorry, but no . . . you're wrong, Asher."

His face fell almost as fast as his heart plummeted. What had he been thinking? Blinking, he looked away.

"You're wrong," she continued, "That is a good present. A *perfect* present. I would love to go out with you on a date . . . and I can't think of a better day than today."

Carly held out the keys and nudged his arm. "But I think I've changed my mind about driving. If you're taking me on a good old-fashioned date, then I guess I'll let you drive your own vehicle."

"You really want to go out with *me*?" Asher looked down at her in wonder, taking the keys.

Shaking her head, Carly beamed at him. "Of course I do, bonehead. Whatever did you think?"

They stared at each other for a few seconds, and then Asher smiled. "I'll unlock your door now."

"You better."

*

Carly bounded around the back of the van, hugging herself in happiness.

It was her birthday and the man she was in love with had just made a move. She giggled and hopped up and down behind the van. It seemed juvenile, but she didn't care. Today was her thirtieth birthday, not her thirteenth, but it just didn't matter . . . not where Asher was concerned.

She pulled open the passenger door and hopped up beside him. "So where are you taking me, handsome?"

Asher grinned and started the engine. "Not to the mall."

"No?"

"No. But I think you'll still have fun buying things."

"Curious. OK. I won't try to guess . . . I love surprises."

Leaning back in the comfy old seat, Carly gazed out the dusty window. She had an urge to reach out with her index finger and trace a heart with initials in it. But that would be ridiculous. Talk about a mood breaker. *Get a grip, Carly.*

But it was hard not to think like a love-struck teenager. Just as long as she didn't *act* like one and wear her heart on her sleeve, she would be safe.

*

Once in Albuquerque, Asher drove past the exit for the mall and continued on the interstate for a few more miles. At an exit for the downtown area, he slowed and moved the van off to a side street. Carly looked around, her head swiveling. "I've never seen this part of the city before."

"All it is is strip malls and box stores in this part. Don't you have those in Chicago?"

"Yes, but not like this. Everything is so open. And we certainly don't have cacti flanking the Arby's signs. This is cool."

Asher laughed. "It doesn't take much to amuse you, does it?"

"Not really. But don't forget . . . I am a complicated, mysterious woman," she said, batting her eyelashes and pursing her lips.

"Oh, I concur with you on that," he agreed, turning down another side street.

Carly flipped down the visor and pretended to check her lipstick in the mirror. "I'm not sure whether to be offended or be flattered by that."

"I think you should be flattered. Besides, doesn't being mysterious give you an edge?"

Carly flipped the visor back up and turned to him, frowning. "An edge in what? Why would I need an edge?"

He glanced at her and then quickly back at the road. "That didn't come out right. I just meant that mysterious women tend to drive a man crazy."

"Drive him crazy in a good way or a bad way?" She raised her eyebrows.

Asher continued to concentrate on driving, but a telltale blush crept into his cheeks. "What do you think?"

Carly stared at him, frozen. All she could envision was him poised above her, getting ready to give her the kiss of a lifetime.

"I'm thinking about you and me in the cabin," she blurted out. She clapped a hand over her mouth and peered at him. *Dammit!* Why couldn't she keep her big mouth shut?

He ran a hand through his dark hair and groaned. "Me, too, so there's your answer."

Now Carly was blushing, so she looked around for a distraction. Plucking her purse from the floorboard, she fished around in it for her digital camera. "I think I'll take a picture of a cactus."

Asher laughed, breaking the tension that had been mounting. "Well, if you can wait for a little while, that would be better. We're here," he announced as he swung the van into a parking space.

Carly looked up and grinned in delight. They were in famous old town Albuquerque, parked in a lot surrounded by small adobe buildings. Colorful signs for shops graced the store fronts and the sun glimmered off of the sandy pink walls. A few street vendors squatted here and there, hunched over blankets full of goods. A short way away, a quaint plaza spread out invitingly. At the end of it stood a large, sprawling old adobe church.

Sliding out of the van and slamming the door, Carly looped her purse strap over her shoulder and scampered to the edge of the parking lot. "That's San Felipe de Neri church, isn't it?" she asked and added, "Built in the late 1700s."

Asher chuckled and caught up with her. "Bingo."

"I want to go over there right now."

"I know you do. That's one of the reasons why we came here." He slipped his hand in hers and pulled her toward the plaza. "That and trinket shopping."

She frowned. "Trinkets? What makes you think I like trinkets?"

"Oh, please. Just try to tell me you can walk by hand-crafted silver jewelry and pottery and not even glance at it."

Carly stuck her nose in the air. "I can't. But so what?"

Chuckling, Asher led her across the plaza to the church. "Let's go on a tour first. This is the first thing I thought of today, anyway. I figured the architecture would be something you wanted to see."

"You had no intention of taking me to the mall, did you?" Carly clasped his large hand and smiled up at him.

"Nope."

"And you assumed that I would love to come here, didn't you?"

Asher shifted glanced at the ground. "Well . . . if you had really, really, truly had your heart set on going to the mall, sure, we would have done that. But I know me and I know you and this . . . date . . . just seems to fit." He cleared his throat and looked over at the sign in front of the church. "Look, the museum is open until four. That gives us plenty of time."

Not to be deterred, Carly tugged on his hand until he stopped. Although her mind told her to stop, her body had other ideas. She stepped closer and circled his neck with her arms. "This fits, too," she whispered, and pulled him in for a kiss.

*

Asher closed his eyes in pleasure as her soft lips met his own. What was this woman doing to him? A strand of her silky hair blew in the wind and brushed his cheek. He caught it in his hand, smelling the wildflower shampoo she used. Sighing, he deepened the kiss. This woman was perfect.

He had planned on buying her a silver bracelet or some other ornament today, but the way she was making him feel . . . in the very deepest part of his soul, a bracelet was not the jewelry he wanted to give her. It was something else.

Snapping open his eyes in alarm, he pulled away from the kiss. *Wow.* That was not where he wanted his thoughts to wander today. He needed to keep it light. Falling that hard for her was out of the question. At least right now. He would think about it later . . . when he was alone. How could he think when she was near him, anyway?

He wiggled his eyebrows at her and Carly chuckled. Her eyes were half closed and she placed a hand over her heart. "I . . ."

Asher grabbed her hand. "Yeah. All I can say is . . . thank you."

Chapter Thirteen

Nicky stood in the middle of Marilyn's room gazing into the full-length mirror. "I look ridiculous," he muttered, and then turned to the side to admire his butt.

"Oh, shut up. You couldn't look bad if I cut a hole in the bottom of a garbage can and stuck it over your head," Marilyn retorted. Lounging on the frilly pillows, she smoothed the satin bedspread and grinned at his reflection. "You have to be invisible, darling."

Nicky sighed. Dressed in camouflage pants and a tight black shirt and army boots, he had to admit he looked buff. But the black ski mask was going a bit too far. "Do I have to wear this thing?" he whined, tugging at his face.

"Do you want that psychopath sheriff to recognize you?" she countered, "If he caught you spying with a video camera, he could make up some excuse and throw you in the clink, Nicky. That would be awful."

"What if Asher sees me? What am I supposed to tell him . . . that I'm researching to be Rambo's understudy?" He sauntered over to the bed and plopped down beside her.

Marilyn reached out and massaged a giant bicep. "He won't see you. He and Carly are in Albuquerque celebrating her birthday all day long. All you have to do is get your camping gear and go up to that cliff we found yesterday before they come back. If he asks where you are, I'll just tell him you hitched a ride into town with one of the theater students. I'll say that you wanted to go to a movie."

Nicky sighed and flopped backward onto the mound of pillows. "I guess that sounds believable."

Marilyn chuckled and lifted the mask up to his eyebrows. "You'll be just fine. And if you catch him, use your cell phone to call the highway patrol or something. For God's sake, don't call the sheriff's office and don't say you caught Wheeler . . . just say it's a dangerous vandal. Make sure you tell the person who answers that you have it on tape, too."

Nicky frowned and pulled the mask back down. "Jeez, Marilyn. I know what to do. What are you, my mother?"

Reaching over, Marilyn pulled the mask back up and leaned in close. "I may be old enough to be your mother, but I'm sure glad that's not the case."

Grinning, Nicky pulled her in for a kiss.

"Marilyn?" The muffled male voice was followed by a soft knock on the door.

"Curses," whispered Marilyn as she rolled back over. "Get in the closet, Nicky, hurry!"

As he scrambled for the closet, the door creaked open an inch. The voice called again. "Marilyn, are you napping?"

"*Hurry up,*" she hissed at Nicky.

Rolling his eyes, he moved four large suitcases away from the closet door. "If you didn't have so much stuff, I'd be in there by now."

"Well, there's nothing I can do about that at the moment. Just get in there somehow."

Nicky pulled open the closet door and slipped inside. He poked his head back out and said, "You owe me, lady."

The knock sounded again. "Are you asleep?"

"No darling, come on in," Marilyn called.

Nicky cracked the closet door and grinned when Marilyn's eyes widened.

Poking his head into the room, Ross smiled. "Am I disturbing your beauty rest?"

Marilyn sat up and waved her hand in disgust. "Oh for God's sake, it's just Ross. Come on out, Nicky."

Ross snorted and stomped over to the bed. "Well, hello to you, too."

Ignoring his irritation, Marilyn grabbed his hand and pulled him down to the edge of the bed. "I have something to tell you. I planned to do it earlier, but there were too many people around."

"This better be good," Ross said.

"Oh, it is . . . I promise you that one." Nicky said as he emerged from the closet and walked to the rocking chair. He lowered himself into it and glared at Marilyn.

Ross stared at him, unblinking. "What the hell do you have on? What are you guys doing . . . playing some kinky burglar game?"

"No, but I'll have to take that into consideration." Marilyn said.

"We're going to catch Wheeler, Ross," explained Nicky, "I'm going to hide up a trail with a camera and a pair of binoculars and then if I see him, I'll sneak down and try to videotape him."

Ross frowned and scratched his head. "Why didn't I think of that? Damn."

"Well, it's not a foolproof plan, because there's a good chance that Wheeler won't even show up tonight. Or tomorrow night. Or the night after that." Marilyn sighed and reached for a tube of lipgloss on the bedside table. "Poor Nicky could be camping up there for a week before anything happens. If it happens."

Jumping up, Ross smoothed his shirt and walked to the door. "He won't have to. Just get me a sexy outfit like that one, and I'll take turns. Carly's so preoccupied with the show and Asher . . . even though she won't admit to that . . . she won't even realize that I'm not sleeping at the hotel every night."

"You know that it might be dangerous, don't you?" said Marilyn.

Ross looked at her. "Sure, but so is walking down the street in my neighborhood in Chicago half the time. I think it's worth it if my best friend is safe, and this show is a success."

Reaching out, he extended a hand to Nicky. "Deal?"

Nicky grasped it and shook. "Deal."

"I guess you should take first shift, Rambo, since you're already dressed up," Marilyn chuckled, waving her manicured hand toward Nicky.

"There you go again, trying to mother me." Nicky pulled the ski mask up and glared at her again, his hands on his hips.

Ross eyed Nicky up and down, and then shook his head. "I hate to break up your loving conversation here, but I actually came up to see if you could come down to the costume shop and get dressed up yourself, Marilyn. Remember the publicity photo this afternoon?"

"What? I thought that was tomorrow, darling." Marilyn jumped up and ran to the dresser, frowning. "Well, I'm glad you reminded me . . . it will take me at least an hour to put on my face."

Nicky rolled his eyes and gathered up his camping equipment. "Spare me. You already have ten pounds of makeup on. I'm leaving. See you in the morning, Marilyn."

As he stomped to the door, she caught his sleeve and whirled him around, whispering, "Sweetie, be very careful. And this is not your mommy talking." Pulling his head down, she planted a sizzling kiss on his lips.

"Whoa, there. I think I should be the one leaving now." Ross threw up his hands in mock defense and turned to the door, hesitating as he stepped through. "And Nick? She's right. Don't let that bastard see you."

*

Wheeler Barstow spat on the pavement and then leaned back into his cruiser, slamming the door shut. Shaking his head in disgust, he pulled out of the downtown parking lot and drove around the block before heading toward the interstate.

That had been Asher's van parked back there. With a lipstick sitting on the dashboard, melting in the sun. But what had he and that tramp been doing downtown? Any trips they had made into town lately had been to the hardware store. Or the paint store. Wheeler's eyes narrowed as he thought about the last time he had talked to Carly. It had been in a paint store.

Damn, but that woman infuriated him. It had been all he could do to keep himself from setting fire to every building in Ruby Spring . . . starting with that precious theater. But he had resisted. And resisting temptation would pay off in the end. Smiling in grim satisfaction, Wheeler swerved onto the interstate, unmindful of traffic, ignoring the angry honk of the car behind him.

Tonight, his wait was over. Tonight, he would teach her a lesson. And what a good day for it . . . a day she would never forget. People never forgot things that happened to them on their birthdays.

Swerving again, Wheeler exited the interstate and pointed the cruiser toward his house. He chuckled, thinking of the shock on sweet Carly's face when she discovered her precious painted theater ceiling covered in black spray paint. And if that wasn't enough to keep her away from Asher Day, he had another trick up his sleeve. And if he had to do it, it wouldn't be just Carly who got hurt. He almost wished she would defy him.

Pulling into his driveway, he growled as his radio crackled. He didn't want to answer it, he wanted to go in the house and get a drink. It had been hours. But he had been on duty, and he didn't want his boss all over his ass, friend or no.

Snatching up the radio, Wheeler kicked open the car door. "What do you want?"

"Jeez, buddy, what crawled under your saddle?" His boss and best friend, Joe Simmons, laughed and then let out a wheezing cough.

"Nothin'. I'm just tired today, is all. What do you want, Joe?"

The annoying laugh crackled through the speakers again. "You tie one on last night? Why didn't you invite me, huh?"

"I wasn't drunk last night. Just didn't sleep well." Wheeler sighed, closing his eyes. He let his sweaty head back against the cool vinyl headrest.

"Well, then, I hate to do this to you, but we really need to follow up on the vandalism report from Ruby Spring. It's been four weeks, and as much as I can't stand that clumsy dumbass Daniel Day, we have to serve and protect, ya know?"

Wheeler's eyes snapped open and he shifted in the seat, fully alert now. He had torn up the statement that the pansy Ross had made him take the day of the "accident." Who needed to know? As far what he had told the department, a stupid idiot had fallen off a ladder. End of story. "Someone filed a complaint? I'll be damned."

"Yeah, of all the nerve," Joe shot back. "Dang, Wheeler. People file complaints all the time. Anyway, I need you to go on up there tonight and check it out. I know you had to go last time when that fool fell off a ladder, but you were in the area then."

Wheeler opened his eyes and grinned. What a perfect cover. Good thing he wasn't having this conversation in person. Taking a deep breath, he summoned his acting skills. "Man, why me?" he whined.

"Oh, come on, buddy. I don't want to do it, and you're the only one with no overtime yet this month, you lazy ass. It won't take you that long."

Sighing again for effect, Wheeler gripped the radio in his sweaty palm. "I guess so. But you owe me, Joe."

Joe chortled again and Wheeler pictured him kicked back, feet on the desk, his pudgy hands clasped over his belly, a bag of French fries on the messy pile of papers in front of him.

"I don't owe you nothin', Wheeler. You owe me, still, you pretty boy son of a bitch." His laughter bellowed and Wheeler reached out to turn down the volume.

It was true. Joe had covered for him countless times when he had been drunk on the job, or found himself in a bar fight off duty.

"Yeah," Wheeler answered in a surly voice. "But I'm off duty until then, Joe. So don't call me." Sighing again, he turned off the ignition and heaved himself out of the car.

No matter how irritating Joe was, though, nothing could stop his excitement about tonight. And no one could possibly pin it on him. He was going to be up there on official business. Stretching,

Wheeler stomped to his front door. Damn, but he was tired. A little hair of the dog and a nap would take care of that, though. Then it would be time for some fun. He couldn't wait to give Carly her birthday present.

As the sun was setting that evening, Wheeler yawned as he turned off the hot shower and peered out the foggy bathroom window. Almost time.

He had had a hard time getting to sleep that afternoon, but finally was able to shelve his nervous, angry energy with a few stiff shots of liquor. Once asleep, though, his mind wouldn't shut off. He dreamed, and like most of his dreams these days, it was about Carly.

In this one, she was dressed in that cute sundress and tennis shoes . . . just like that night they had gone out together. The night she became his girlfriend. She had painted her face up like a hooker, though, and he hadn't liked that. And he especially hadn't liked how, in the dream, she had kept rubbing his back and calling him Asher.

The last person in the world he wanted to trade places with was that useless excuse for a man, Asher Day. As Wheeler combed back his wet blond hair he smirked, picturing that skinny fool acting as Carly's bodyguard. Like it was going to do any good. He doubted that Day could get one good punch in before he went down in a heap.

Cracking his knuckles, Wheeler flipped on the radio and hummed along to country music as he dressed in black jeans and a black sweater. He had almost decided to just go ahead and wear his uniform, but Joe would back him up if those whiners up in Ruby Spring found him where he shouldn't be. Joe always backed him up.

He looked into the mirror at his red-rimmed, bleary blue eyes and quit humming. It was Carly's fault that his handsome face looked like hell. Cursing, he crossed the bedroom and yanked out the drawer on his bedside table, dumping the contents on the bed.

A half a dozen or so crumpled computer-printed photos of Carly lay among empty pint bottles and match books. It was amazing what pictures a person could find on the Internet. Wheeler's laugh was brittle as he picked one up and smoothed it out. It was a printout from a two-year-old playbill from a theater in Minnesota. Her easy smile greeted him, welcomed him.

Didn't that woman realize that they were meant to be together? Well, she would soon. Still laughing, he walked outside and checked his trunk. A paper bag containing spray paint and a crow bar sat next to the spare tire. Chuckling, he slammed the trunk and got in the car. He patted his hip pocket for the flask. It was there, like an old friend.

*

"This sucks," Nicky muttered to himself as he draped a sleeping bag around his shivering shoulders. Although it had been hot all day long, he should have remembered how cold it got up at this elevation once the sun went down. And dark.

Pacing his campsite, he sighed. As much as he wanted to help Marilyn, he doubted whether anything would come of her "super sexy spy plan," as she called it. There just wasn't enough light down by the buildings in Ruby Spring. What he did have on his side, though, was the quiet. Any unusual noise would alert him, and he would start sneaking down the trail right away.

Almost as if on cue, the unmistakable noise of a car engine began to echo through the pass outside Ruby Spring. Nicky threw off the sleeping bag and ran to an outcropping in time to see dim headlights round a bend and then disappear again. He crouched and reached for the video camera to check the batteries.

The headlights appeared again, this time closer. The engine was louder, and with it was a faint pounding, like a deep bass. Frowning, Nicky scrambled to the edge and peered over. He couldn't see anything except for the shadowy outlines of bushes and the buildings far below. But the insistent throbbing noise grew clearer.

Music. Rap music . . . or some kind of driving rock. It was rock music. Heavy metal, actually. And though Nicky didn't know Asher and Carly very well, he seriously doubted that they listened to that type of music. It had to be Wheeler.

His stomach fluttering, he eased back from the outcropping and pulled the binoculars from the bag strapped around his waist. Suddenly, the faint echo of the pulsing bass ceased, and soon after it, so did the noise of the car engine.

Silence took hold for less than ten seconds, and his cell phone rang loudly. Startled, he fumbled for it in the deep pockets of his camouflage pants. It took him four rings to find it, and by the time he saw Marilyn's number on the screen, his apprehension had turned to annoyance.

"What?" he said with a hiss.

"Nicky, I think he's here."

"I know that," he answered, "but how do *you* know?"

Marilyn whispered, "Because I'm on the porch and I heard the music. Asher doesn't listen to that crap."

Nicky sighed in exasperation. "Woman, get back inside. That's all we need, for that freak show cop to find you all but waiting for him dressed in a black negligee with feathers and rhinestones . . . just sitting there."

"For your information, it's not black, it's emerald. But yes, rhinestones."

"Who cares what color it is . . . just go back inside. Now."

She grumbled, and then sighed, relenting. "Fine. I'll go. I just wanted to let you know, in case you didn't . . . "

She trailed off and Nicky rolled his eyes, waiting for her to flit back to her train of thought. When she didn't continue, he frowned.

"Marilyn?"

There was no answer.

"Marilyn, are you there?"

He stood up and brought the binoculars to his face, scanning for the shape of the hotel in the darkness. Damn, it was pitch black. This stakeout was a foolish idea. And now Marilyn could be in trouble, and he was all the way up here.

"Yeah. I'm here," she said in hushed tones, "Do you hear that, Nicky?"

He slumped in relief at the sound of her voice, but managed to keep calm. Getting Marilyn worked up would not help matters at all.

"Hear what, Baby?"

"Another car."

Nicky pulled the phone from his ear and looked over the outcropping again. Sure enough, he saw another pair of headlights . . . larger than the first. The engine belonging to them rattled a little as the vehicle slowed and turned a sharp curve.

"That's the van," he said, his tone matter-of-fact.

"Yeah, I know it. We have to tell them, Nicky. Asher would kick us into next week if we knew that Wheeler was up here and we didn't tell him."

He sighed. "I hate to do that to Carly on her birthday."

"Me, too, but unless I go back in right now and run up to my room . . . they're gonna know something is up, anyway."

Nicky shook his head. If Asher Day found out that Wheeler was anywhere near Ruby Spring, he would come unwound. It would probably get dangerous, and someone would probably get hurt. The safest thing was for Nicky to take care of the situation himself.

"Why don't you just go on inside and let me keep guard up here, Marilyn? I can hear everything. I can almost hear you talking all the way down there . . . but then you do have a big mouth," he joked.

"You're so mean to me," she gasped.

"I'm a lot of things to you, but I'll bet mean is not on top of the list," he shot back.

"OK. But if anything happens that you can't handle, you call me immediately, do you hear? I almost hate to agree to this . . ."

Nicky made soothing sounds. "It'll be fine. If anything happens, Ross will be out here like a shot."

"I'm going to wake him up right now," she said.

He heard the screen door slam and knew that it would be useless to argue with her.

"Yeah, do that. And turn the porch light on for them. Gotta go, now. I'll be careful." He hung up before she could say anything else and set the ringer on vibrate. He scrolled to Ross's number and slipped the phone back into a hip pocket.

Almost right away, the porch light illuminated the area in front of the hotel. "Good girl," he muttered, and tried the binoculars again. This time, he could make out more than shadowy shapes.

Nicky watched with the binoculars as Carly and Asher strolled toward the hotel. He had his arm around her shoulder and she looked happy. Nicky smiled as he witnessed them exchange a brief, but sweet kiss.

"Whatcha looking at, pervert?"

Nicky jumped at the gruff voice behind him and stumbled as he sprang up from his crouched position. A flashlight clicked on, flooding the rocky area with light, blinding him.

Instinctively, he threw his hands up to his mask-covered face. "Who the hell are you?" he grunted, even though he knew damned well that it was Wheeler.

"It doesn't matter who I am, son. What should matter to you is how you're going to explain yourself . . . squatting up here dressed like a commando, spying on those innocent people."

"I'm not spying on them, *Deputy*," retorted Nicky. He edged away from the cliff and shoved his hands into his pockets in what he hoped was a surly manner and reached for the cell phone. Praying that he was pressing the correct place on the screen, Nicky hit "call" and cocked his head to the side.

"How do you know I'm the law, boy?" Wheeler asked.

Nicky watched as Wheeler toyed with the weighty metal flashlight, slapping it in his palm. Powerful beams of light bounced off the mountainsides and Nicky barely held back his smirk. Not only was this guy crazy, but he was stupid too.

Wheeler advanced and poked Nicky in the chest several times with the flashlight. "I'll ask you again, surfer boy, in case you had trouble understanding me. How do you know I'm the law?"

Nicky knew it was foolish, but couldn't resist. Obviously, Wheeler knew who he was, anyway. He grinned and grabbed the end of the heavy flashlight. "Because I could smell you, pig."

Chapter Fourteen

"Aren't we going inside?"

Carly tried to keep her tone light, but she was a bit disappointed that Asher didn't want to go up to the room. Although she was nervous about it, she had been hoping that tonight . . . after the wonderful day they had shared . . . he would want to sleep in the bed instead of on the floor.

"We'll go inside in a little bit. Remember, I told you I have a present for you." Asher smiled and squeezed her hand as he led her past the hotel.

Carly smiled back and held up an arm. "But you already bought me a present. A beautiful present." She admired the delicate silver bracelet looped around her wrist, holding it out in the dim light.

"It's not as beautiful as you," he responded, wiggling his eyebrows.

Laughing, Carly reached up and pinched his cheek. "That's one of the lamest lines I've ever heard, Asher."

"Yeah, yeah. But it's not a line if it's the plain truth, now, is it?" His serious expression made the smile fade from her lips.

"You really think that, don't you?" she asked.

He answered her with a soulful kiss, and then buried his head in her shoulder. She closed her eyes in pleasure. Neither of them saw the light bouncing off the mountainsides above them.

"I love my bracelet, Asher," she whispered into his neck. It was the most she could muster, although in her head, she was chanting, "I love *you*, Asher." But she didn't want to tell him today. She wanted to remember this birthday with fondness . . . not as the day she declared her love for a man who didn't feel the same way.

"You'll love the next present even more . . . at least I hope you will," he said.

"You didn't spend more money on me, did you?" She pulled away and held him at arm's length.

"Kind of, but not really." His eyes twinkled.

"Another one of your guessing games, hmm?" Carly tugged on his hand. "Going to Old Town was perfect, so I'm holding high hopes for this one, too."

"Although it would be great fun, I won't keep you in suspense much longer," Asher said. He pulled free and stuffed his hands into his pockets, whistling. Stepping around her, he pulled out a small flashlight and headed for the theater.

Carly followed him, musing. Had he finished off the restoration without her knowing? Impossible. They had spent pretty much every waking moment together. So what could it be? Anticipation fluttered in her stomach as she followed the narrow beam of his tiny flashlight.

"No, I didn't finish the theater for you." Asher laughed.

"That's not what I was thinking," Carly lied.

"Okay, Beautiful, whatever you say." Asher pulled his keys out of his pocket and unlocked the backstage door, reaching past her to pull the switch for a spotlight.

On stage, in the pool of light, stood a table she had built for the set, covered in a snowy white cloth. Two empty wine glasses and a bottle chilling in a bucket caught her eye and she moved forward, her hands clasped in front of her.

"Oh, Asher. This is great. What a wonderful way to end the day."

Behind her, she heard him rummaging in the darkness. On instinct, she opened her mouth to ask him what he was doing, but shut it again. *Don't let your nerves ruin the moment, Carly.*

Walking to the table, she trailed her hands over the cloth, and then crossed to the old-fashioned settee sitting stage right. The same settee where the hero and the heroine shared a passionate kiss in the play. Shivering, she wondered if she and Asher would be doing the same . . . and more . . . tonight. She sat down and folded her hands.

"Close your eyes." Asher's warm breath tickled her neck and she shivered again.

"I'm closing them."

Carly heard a rustle of paper and then the thrill of contact as his muscular body sank down next to her. All of her nerves were on end, but she willed herself to keep her eyes shut.

He cleared his throat and took one of her hands, guiding it to what felt like a thin edge . . . a book? She felt along the object. No, it felt like wood. A mirror? She reached down and brushed lower with the back of her hand. No, it wasn't smooth.

"Careful now," Asher whispered.

"May I look?" she asked.

"Guess first," he answered.

"It's a painting," she said, smiling.

"Not just a painting, a masterpiece."

Carly's eyes flew open and she found herself staring, unblinking . . . into her own eyes. Dimly, she sensed Asher shift next to her.

He coughed. "I almost hate to ask ..but what do you think?"

Carly's eyes welled up as she gazed at the painting. A glorious, complex tumble of blues and purples, it was a perfect, dark image of a starry night sky in the mountains. The peaks were barely visible on the horizon, but next to one of them, in a sheer silver wisp, floated an angel. Though the entire painting was abstract, the single image of the luminescent angel was realistic. And it was her.

"It's . . . it . . . " she began, before her voice broke, and she reached out, trembling to grasp the painting in both hands.

"It doesn't freak you out that I painted you, does it?" Asher asked, looking at the floor.

"Oh, of course not," she answered. "I'm just speechless, that's all. I . . . I ..don't even know where to start . . . to describe how beautiful it is. No, not beautiful. That's not good enough."

She turned to him, her eyes bright with love. Now she had the courage. Now she could tell him. She propped the painting next to the settee and reached up, locking her hands behind his neck. His eyes widened and he dipped his head to kiss her.

She pulled back and shook her head. "I have something to tell you, Asher. Something I will never say to anyone else but you."

He stared at her for a few long seconds and then heaved a nervous sigh. Reaching down, he placed a palm on her chest. "Your heart is going a million miles an hour."

"And so should it be. You make it do that," she said, her eyes never leaving his face.

"Do you want some champagne first?" He slid his warm hand from her chest up to her face. "You look pretty tense."

Carly nearly lost her nerve. It was almost as if he knew what she was going to say. As if he knew how hard it was for her, and how important. Nervously, she shook her head.

"Okay, then," he whispered, stroking her cheek with his long, tapered fingers.

"Asher," she began, and then stopped, frowning.

Faint voices floated somewhere outside the theater. And they sounded angry.

"What's that?" she whispered.

He frowned too, and moved his hand to her shoulder. "More like who's that."

The voices grew louder as the argument escalated, but Carly couldn't make out who was yelling. Closing her eyes in a mixture of relief and frustration, she slid off the settee and tiptoed to the backstage door, cracking it open.

Asher was close behind her, a hand on her arm. "Don't go out there, Carly," he said softly.

She nodded and leaned closer to the crack. The chilly mountain breeze blew in, and with it, more distinct voices.

"I said go to hell." One of the voices sounded familiar, but she couldn't place it.

"Is that Buddy?" she asked.

"Who, the actor? No, I don't think so."

"*You* go to hell, Surfer Boy!" The other voice was louder, and meaner. *Wheeler.*

Carly felt her heart plummet and she reached back for Asher. "Oh my God," she whispered.

Asher gritted his teeth. "That son of a bitch."

Before she could stop him, he was around her, out the door and down the wooden steps.

"No, Asher, don't," she hissed.

He ignored her plea and reached up to grip her hand. "I want you to kill the lights in here and go down to the dressing rooms. Do you have your cell phone?"

Carly nodded and swallowed. She took a deep breath and pulled it out of her dress pocket.

"Call Ross. Now. And I swear I'll be back to get you. Just don't move. Promise me you won't come after me."

How could she let him go after Wheeler alone with nothing more than an attitude and a flashlight? Wheeler was dangerous and probably armed. Looking deep into his eyes, Carly nodded again, and then lied. "I promise."

*

Nicky took a step backward as the butt of the flashlight viciously slammed into his ribs again. The pain of being hit a second time turned his initial shock to anger. He stomped forward and shoved Wheeler in the chest. Although Wheeler was taller and bigger, Nicky was quicker, sober, and in good shape. He knew he could hold his own.

"What are you doing up here, Wheeler?"

"I'm up here on official business . . . which is none of *your* business," retorted Wheeler as he twirled the flashlight in his hands.

"I seriously doubt that."

Revulsion curled in Nicky's stomach as he stared at Wheeler. The man sighed and wiped sweat from his forehead. Weaving where he stood, he blinked at Nicky. What a loser.

"We'll see about that when I book you. You're under arrest for assaulting an officer of the law . . . and for being a creepy Peeping Tom asshole." With a mean smile, Wheeler jerked his thumb in the direction he had come from. "Now, let's get this over with. I'll do you a favor, even if you don't deserve it. The trail is steep and I won't handcuff you until we get back to the car."

Nicky folded his arms and stood his ground, thinking of a way to buy some time until Ross got up the trail.

"I'm not going anywhere . . . and neither are you. You have some explaining to do, Wheeler."

"Oh, Yeah? About what?" Taking the bait, Wheeler spit on the ground and raised the flashlight to his shoulder, playing the beam into Nicky's face.

"About a broken leg. About a ripped up, ruined costume. About threats painted on that costume. And about verbal threats delivered in a paint store a few weeks ago. Just stuff that your employer would probably be interested in." Nicky shrugged and averted his eyes from the light, smirking. *Where the hell was Ross?*

Sucking in a breath, Wheeler weaved again and almost lost his balance.

"I don't know what the hell you're talking about, boy," Wheeler sneered, "unless you're talking about yourself. Sounds like something a Peeping Tom would do to me."

"Maybe. Except that I'm not spying on Carly. I'm up here to catch the psycho who's been bothering her and trying to wreck this theater. I'm up here to catch *you* and hand your pathetic, drunk ass over to your boss."

Nicky advanced and shoved at Wheeler again. This time the man did lose his balance and he fell sideways, his hip colliding with a boulder. There was a crunch of glass and the sour stench of cheap whiskey floated up to Nicky's nostrils. Wheeler scrambled up and his arms flailed through the air, but he couldn't regain control. He fell again, sprawling in a heap of thorny shrubs.

"Ow! Damn you!" he howled.

Nicky chuckled and reached into his pocket, pulling out the phone. He pressed the menu button to light up the display. Sure enough, his call had gone through to Ross. But it was disconnected. Could Ross have heard part of the conversation? The phone had been in Nicky's pocket the entire time.

"Just stay right there, Wheeler," he commanded, redialing Ross's number. It rang once and was answered quickly.

"Nearly there," said Ross, panting. "Only a few more hundred feet or so. You okay?"

"Oh, absolutely. But our inebriated friend here isn't faring so well."

Picking up the flashlight, Nicky trained it on the bushes and laughed as Wheeler rolled to the side moaning, grabbing at the thorns protruding from his hip. The front of his pants was soaked and he stared down at the crotch in disbelief.

"Damn," Wheeler whined. "That was my last pint."

As Ross scrambled up to the top of the trail, Nicky threw his head back, hooting with laughter.

"Sounds like you really do have it under control," Ross said. Walking over to Wheeler, he kicked at the man's boot. "Get up, and then get the hell out of here."

Glaring up at him, Wheeler spit near Ross's foot and shifted again. "I'm gonna arrest both of you for assaulting an officer of the law," he muttered.

Ross and Nicky looked at each other, grinning. Wheeler was barely in shape to stand up, much less make an arrest.

Ross circled behind Wheeler and stood over him, pursing his lips. "My, my, that sounds like fun. You're such a big, strong man. Would you promise to pat me down when we get to the station?"

At that, Wheeler growled and scrambled to his feet. He stumbled again and grabbed at a rock for support. "You stay away from me, homo."

Nicky slapped Ross on the back and then swung an arm over his shoulder. He pointed at Wheeler. "You're awfully insecure for such a handsome man," he said, "Although I might feel a bit foolish, too, if my ass was covered with thorns and I had peed my pants right out in the open."

Anger replaced the pain in Wheeler's puffy, watering eyes. He leaned forward, jabbing a shaking finger at the pair of chuckling men. "I changed my mind. I'm too tired to deal with you assholes tonight. But just wait . . . your time is coming. And jail is no picnic, boys." He backed toward the trail, pointing at Ross. "Especially for you, sweet cheeks."

"You scare the shit out of me," Ross retorted, rolling his eyes.

*

Grumbling, Wheeler turned his back on them and began to pick his way down the trail. This was not how it was supposed to have gone down tonight. Seething with pain and fury, he tripped over a boulder. Where the fuck was his flashlight?

He willed his foggy mind to swim through the fog of alcohol. How the hell had that surfer boy known about his activities in Ruby Spring? Probably his fat bitch of a girlfriend had told him. Made sense. But who had told her? Well, women gossiped, didn't they? Carly had sobbed on her shoulder for sure. He'd bet his badge on it.

It was on to the next plan, then. The big one. And Carly and her useless, clueless friends would never see it coming.

*

Keeping his breathing even, Asher ran up the familiar trail. He had taken the long way around instead of climbing up the path behind the theater. He was hoping that the element of surprise would be in his favor. Ahead of him, he heard an engine rumble to life. It had to be Wheeler. Picking up the pace, he gritted his teeth and dodged a boulder in his path.

Who exactly was up there, though? He thought he had heard Nicky, but the voices had been so faint that it had been hard to tell. Grimacing as he stumbled over a fallen tree branch, Asher rounded a bend, just in time to see the headlights of a car backing up in the small clearing ahead. Sprinting now, he turned off the trail and ran straight for the car.

"Hey, Wheeler," Asher shouted, "Stop right there."

The car stopped for a few seconds, and then the engine roared as Wheeler gunned the accelerator. Suddenly, the car lurched forward, heading straight for Asher. Asher stood his ground and held out his hands in front of him.

"Get out of the way or I'll mow you down, son," Wheeler screamed over the noise of the car. He jerked to a stop and revved the engine again.

"I'm not playing chicken with you, Barstow. But we do need to have a serious conversation," Asher yelled as he trudged closer to the headlights pointing at him.

Wheeler's eyes narrowed and he inched forward. "Are you deaf, Art Boy?"

Asher answered by planting his feet and folding his arms. Though the clearing was lit only by the car's headlights, he was close enough now to see the fury in Wheeler's red-rimmed eyes. And the drunkenness. Playing the tough guy was starting to seem like a foolish idea, but it was too late now to back off. Willing his hands not to shake, Asher lifted them as if in surrender.

Smiling in triumph, Wheeler put the car in park and sat back. A second later, Asher's palms came slamming down on the hood of the car. "I'm not giving up, Barstow, just making a point. We need to talk. Man to man. Get your drunk ass out of the car."

"Make me."

Without hesitating, Asher bounded around the car, jerked open the door and dragged Wheeler out by the front of his shirt. "Listen up, loser. I'm on to you. You leave Carly Foster and my property alone or there will be hell to pay," he said between his teeth.

Pulling himself loose, Wheeler clutched at the doorframe, panting. "You don't own Carly." he spat.

"Neither do you. *Especially* not you. And I'm sure she would tell you just that if she was face to face with you, asshole." Asher nudged him. "Now turn around and face me."

The radio crackled to life inside the car. "Hey, hey, hey. Wheeler, you up at Ruby Spring? Copy."

Sighing, Wheeler ducked into the car to grab the radio. "Shit, you have bad timing. What'ya want, Joe? I'm busy here."

Joe Simmons' voice sounded again. "If you're all done up there, swing on by the bar and we'll have a couple. That is, if you're not still in a nasty mood."

"Well, I am in a nasty mood. A hell of a mood," Wheeler yelled into the radio. Glancing back at Asher, he glared and spit on the ground.

"Oh, hell. What did you do now? You got trouble up there?" asked Joe.

Slowly, a malicious grin spread over Wheeler's face and he hesitated, still staring at Asher, who shook his head.

"Not a good idea, Barstow. Your boss might overlook it, but the rest of the sheriff's department would certainly wonder why you hauled me in while you were on duty and drunk off your ass."

"I don't have to be the one. All I have to do is radio for backup and *your* ass is grass, Day," Wheeler muttered, fumbling on his belt for handcuffs that weren't there.

"What's that? You need backup?" Joe's wheezy voice crackled again, "What's going on? Talk to me, Wheeler, you dumbass."

"You'd never pull it off," said Asher. Advancing, he stopped for a second in front of Wheeler, looked him in the eye, and then matter-of-factly punched him in the gut. Wheeler collapsed to the ground, the breath knocked out of him.

God that felt good.

Pulling the radio from Wheeler's hand, Asher depressed the talk button. "Hey Joe. This is Asher Day. Hey, listen. Old Barstow seems to be a little under the weather here, if you know what I mean. But everything's okay here. Nothing to worry about."

Joe answered with his characteristic raspy laugh. "Yeah, I know what you mean. Under the weather. That's a good one. Well, tell him to walk it off, and then go home."

"No problem, Joe." Asher looked down at Wheeler and indeed, he was under the weather, puking all over his own shoes. Asher smiled and reached into the car to put the radio away. "Damn, Barstow, you're a mess. Peed your pants, it looks like, and now your dinner is all over the ground. Seems to me like you've had a pretty rough day."

Taking a few gulps of air, Wheeler pulled himself to his feet eased into the driver's seat. "You're gonna regret touching me, Art Boy."

"Yeah, yeah, yeah, you'll threaten to arrest me for assaulting an officer. What man in this county haven't you said that to?" Asher shoved Wheeler over until he was sprawled in the passenger seat. "You just shut your mouth and I won't drive you to headquarters." Asher slid into the driver's seat and strapped on the seat belt.

"Where are we going?" whined Wheeler. "Oh, I think I'm gonna be sick again." He rolled down the window and laid his cheek against the cool metal of the doorframe.

"I thought I told you to shut it. You're lucky I didn't just take your wheels and leave you in the woods," said Asher, his eyes flashing. Putting the car in drive, he angled it over the uneven ground toward the gravel road that led back to the main highway.

It was over now. Carly would be safe.

Chapter Fifteen

Carly waited until she was sure Asher had gone before pushing open the backstage door. The welcome cool night air blew across her face, but she sighed in frustration all the same.

Two seconds from being able to say the three most important words she would utter in a lifetime and it was interrupted by the biggest loser she had ever encountered. Well, it fit her track record with men. Although the way she felt about Asher was different. It was thrilling. And beyond scary.

And it overwhelmed the fear she felt about her own safety. Glancing over her shoulder, she took another look at the painting. It was exquisite, and it was still sinking in that it was painted for her. That it *was* her. He eyes flew to the unopened bottle and the untouched glasses. There was Asher's cell phone, sitting next to the wine bucket, forgotten. A frown creased her forehead. Well, now she had no choice. She had to find him.

Easing open the stage door, she ran toward the path that led to the clearing, wishing for hiking boots and a flashlight. A sundress and sandals were less than ideal for a rescue mission, but fueled by fear, she managed to scramble up the mountainside pulling on rocks and exposed tree roots. She took a deep breath. Almost there. Getting down the other side would be the real challenge.

As she reached the top, she hit a patch of loose dirt and pitched forward, biting back a shriek. A branch caught her hair and she gritted her teeth. As she slid on her belly, she clawed in desperation at rocks and tree trunks, her mouth wide open in a silent scream. Sharp pain ricocheted through her legs as they slammed into the uneven ground and she ducked her head, tensing. It would smash into a boulder any second now. But it didn't. The ground began to even out and her body slid sideways, coming to a rest half under a bush. She lay on her side, panting. As her heart slowed, she stared in the darkness.

Far above her she heard angry voices again, but this time she recognized both of them. It was Asher and Wheeler. At the sound of the car engine starting up, her eyes widened and she pushed herself to her feet, wincing at the sting from the scrapes on her legs. Can't stop now. She stumbled toward the noise and frustrated tears welled in her eyes. Maybe she should just stay put and call Ross. By the time he found her, though, something terrible could have happened to Asher. She had to get to where he was, and soon. It didn't sound that far away.

As Carly climbed, she soon discovered that she wasn't on a trail at all. Thick fallen trees and big boulders blocked her way, and it was all she could do to forge ahead without stumbling again. In the distance below her, she saw light bouncing around. A flashlight. She gathered her courage and pulled herself up to a crest, where she stood panting, gripping the trunk of a tall pine tree.

Far below her in a clearing, a pair of headlights swung toward the edge of a clearing. Slowly, the car moved over the rocky ground and she sucked in a breath. It was Wheeler's cruiser. What if he had Asher? There was no way she could make it down there in time to find out.

Throwing her head back, Carly shrieked in frustration.

*

Asher slowed the cruiser at the faint sound. What was that a scream? He leaned toward the open window on the passenger side, but recoiled at the stench emanating from Wheeler. He stopped the car, rolled down his window and listened. There it was again, a high-pitched shrill sound. A hawk?

Turning off the engine, Asher opened his door and leaned out, cocking his head toward the sky. Once more, the sharp noise pierced the thin mountain air. It wasn't a hawk. It sounded too human. Human . . . and female . . . .that was weird. He hadn't heard any feminine voices up here earlier.

Realization hit him and he slammed his fist down on the steering wheel. *Carly.*

He had told her to stay put. Sighing, he patted his chest pocket for his phone. It was flat. "Dammit," he muttered as he searched his jeans. Shaking his head, he realized where it was; sitting next to the bottle of champagne in the bucket of ice all the way back at the theater.

"Well, she's just gonna have to trust me on this one," he said to himself, and leaned out the window. Taking a deep breath, he shouted, "Carly!" He waited. "Carly!" No answer. He tried again. "Go on back to the hotel. Everything is *fine.*" There was still no answer, but he heard a rustling noise and an answering yell high above. Satisfied, he started the car again.

Glancing over at Wheeler, his lip curled in disgust. Because of this dimwit, his evening with Carly had been ruined. He had had such great plans, too. If they'd only had a little more time . . .

*

"Carly!"

It Asher's his voice. She closed her eyes in relief and swayed backward, catching onto a tree branch. She heard it again, but this time it sounded more urgent. "Carly!" Her eyes snapped open. Oh my God. What if he was hurt?

She gripped the branch and yanked on it to pull herself upward. It was not a wise decision. Brittle and dead, the branch snapped and she lost her balance, tumbling forward. *Fuck!* Not again. As she slid toward the clearing, she heard yelling again. Taking a deep breath, she screamed once more and flailed for something, anything to grab on to.

Hitting the bottom of the incline, Carly lay face down in the dirt, shaking. She raised her head just in time to see tail lights disappear on the other side of the clearing. Wincing, she sat up and covered her face with her hands as tears welled up. Some birthday. Reaching in her sundress pocket, she knew it was time to give up and call Ross.

Her heart sank. It wasn't there. She patted the ground around herself, but she knew it was hopeless. It could have fallen out anywhere along the way. Grabbing the rock that was digging into her thigh, Carly gave it a violent throw. It connected with a boulder, making a hollow, echoing sound. How ironic. It sounded a lot like the time Wheeler had grabbed her cell phone and thrown it in the roadhouse parking lot a few weeks ago.

Had it only been a few weeks? It seemed like a year. Life was like that sometimes, though. At times, it moved so fast that a person could barely blink before months had gone by. Other times, it seemed so slow that a single hour seemed like a week. That's how it was with Asher. Both ways. They had moved fast in slow motion.

Carly shook her head. Now was not the time for crazy thoughts. She had to get back to the hotel and find Ross. But she didn't seem to have the energy. Sinking down onto the cold ground, she laid her head on the dirt and shivered.

*

Ross held out a hand for Nicky, who swung over the last boulder and down onto solid ground. Pulling Wheeler's flashlight out of his cargo pants pocket, Nicky switched it back on and nodded.

"Let's go."

"You did a really good job up there, man," Ross said as they jogged toward the hotel. He pulled his cell phone out and scrolled to Carly's number.

"Yeah, it wasn't that tough. The guy was drunker than a skunk."

Ross slowed down and then stopped, the phone to his ear. "She's not answering, Nicky."

Without breaking stride, Nicky turned and started running for the theater. Ross pocketed the phone and followed close behind.

"Shit," they uttered in unison as they approached the backstage door. It was hanging wide open, swinging in the breeze.

"Do we even bother to go inside?" Nicky asked.

"Just for a second," Ross answered as he stepped through the doorway. He whistled when he saw the champagne and glasses. "Looks like Asher was planning a very memorable evening. Jeez, Nick, do you think they went after Wheeler?" He frowned.

"I hope not. What's this?" Nicky walked across the stage and lifted the painting from where it was propped next to the settee.

"I have no idea, but it looks really cool. Bring it over here."

Nicky brought it over to the soft circle of light created by the spotlight. He whistled, too. Tracing the angel with his fingertip, he stopped near one of the tiny, delicate hands and peered closer. "I would say that memorable would be an understatement, bro. Take a look at this."

Ross leaned in and his frown softened. He reached out and traced the angel with a fingertip. "He's in love with her, isn't he?" A slow grin spread over his face.

Nicky laughed. "Oh, hell yes. Absolutely."

Ross nodded. "Finally. No one deserves happiness more than Carly. And I must say, it's a big relief after witnessing her past relationships. I was worried, though. Ready to kick Asher's ass if he'd hurt her."

Nicky grabbed his shoulder. "Don't mean to spoil your moment, Ross, but the question remains: where the hell are they?"

Ross glanced around and his gaze rested on the round table. "Holy shit," he muttered.

"What?"

"Asher's phone. He left it here."

Ross and Nicky looked at each other for a few seconds, and then bolted for the door.

*

"I thought I told you to shut your face," Asher said between his teeth. It was all he could do not to reach over and pop Wheeler in the mouth.

"But where are we going?" whimpered Wheeler, "I need to lay down, man. My ass is covered with thorns and I feel like I'm gonna hurl again."

Asher thought a minute. "Give me your cell phone," he answered.

"Why don't you just use yours?"

There was no way Asher was going to tell him he had left it back at the theater. "Because I don't want to waste minutes on anything having to do with you. You're pathetic. Now hand it over."

Tentatively, Wheeler glanced out his window, reached into his shirt pocket and pulled it out. "Ow, that hurts," he muttered.

"Shut up," commanded Asher, holding his hand out for the phone. "Give it to me."

"Could you please pull over for a second? I really need to throw up again," Wheeler whined, looking at Asher out of the corner of his eye.

"God, you're useless," Asher snorted, "How did you even make it through law enforcement training?" He slowed the car and stopped in the middle of the gravel road. "Go ahead, loser. Puke your guts out. Just hand me the damned phone first."

Wheeler heaved a sigh and reached for the door handle. "Could you get out, too? I'm so bad off, man. I think I need someone to hold me up," he moaned

"Oh, for God's sake," Asher muttered as he unfastened his seatbelt.

At this rate, it would be daybreak before he could get back to Carly. Just as he reached for the door handle, Wheeler slammed his fist into Asher's jaw. Asher's head snapped back and he gasped in shock. *Fuck.*

"Who's the loser now?" Wheeler said with a snort. "I'm such a good actor. I'd be great up at your theater, wouldn't I? Too bad for you I don't want to have anything to do with that pansy-assed shit."

Pocketing the phone, he punched Asher again, and then reached across to shove open the driver's side door. With a giant heave, he propelled Asher out onto the rocky ground.

"So long, asshole," Wheeler yelled, spit flying onto the dashboard. Climbing into the driver's seat, he gunned the engine and started forward with a jerk.

Asher lay on the ground for a few seconds, willing his head to clear. It felt as if someone had hit him with a sack full of bricks. He heard the car back up, heard the door open again and then felt a booted foot on his chest.

Wheeler leaned out and surveyed Asher with amusement. "One more thing, Art Boy. Just wanted to remind you that it's not over. Not by a long shot. This is your final warning. Either you stay away from my girlfriend, or both of you will regret it for the rest of your lives."

Wheeler stomped down on Asher's chest, got back in the car, gunned the engine again, and then drove off in a cloud of dusty smoke.

Asher stared after the fading tail lights, coughing, and then the dark enveloped him once more. Groaning, he turned onto his stomach and laid his throbbing cheek against the cool earth. As the shock subsided, coherent thought returned. God, he was tired. It had been very late when he and Carly had come back from Albuquerque. Now it had to be the middle of the night or later. It was hard to tell. All he needed was a few minutes rest, and then he would make his way back to the hotel. He had to. Carly would be worried.

Asher closed his eyes and shifted his body to a more comfortable position.

*

A short time later, he opened his eyes. Where the hell was he? Panicked for a minute, Asher laid still as memory flooded back. That's right; he was lying in a ditch by the side of the road after being beaten up by the biggest loser in all of New Mexico. *Great.*

Anger rushing into his gut, Asher rolled onto his side and sat up, wincing. How could he have let that asshole get away? How could he have let his guard down like that? There was going to be hell to pay when he finally got hold of Wheeler Barstow. But in order to do that, he had to get back to the hotel first.

He shoved himself to his feet and peered into the darkness. Best way back is the way I came, he thought to himself as he rubbed his throbbing jaw. He climbed back onto the gravel road and started walking uphill. He could barely see his hand in front of his face. Just his luck for it to be clouded over. Now, it would probably rain, too. Sighing, Asher felt his way into the clearing. He stopped for a second to catch his breath and froze when heard a noise close by.

He crouched. There it was again. A sniffling, moaning sound. It was probably Wheeler, that devious son of a bitch. Trying to trap him again. Asher felt along the ground for a weapon, and came up with a solid tree branch. Narrowing his mouth in satisfaction, he stayed hunched, moving closer to the noise.

*

Carly's head snapped up when she heard a sound. Someone was here, very close by. Oh God, what if it was Wheeler? She closed her eyes and pressed her fist against her mouth. Whatever it was, it was too close for her to chance running. She stayed motionless, trying to breathe quietly.

A few seconds later, she heard a twig snap. It was dangerously close this time. A moan escaped her lips. She was trapped now. All she could do was fight back as best as she could. And she would fight. Whoever was out there was going to have hell to pay because she was pissed.

"Get out here in the open, Barstow. We're not finished."

Carly's eyes widened and she stopped short. "Asher? Oh please, is that you?" She scrambled up and peered into the darkness.

"Thank God," he answered. "Keep talking, my love. Tell me

where you are."

"Over here," she yelled, standing up.

"Please tell me you're not hurt," he said.

"I'm fine, Asher. Just a few scrapes and bruises. I think. Are you okay?" She moved forward, feeling for solid ground.

"I'm fine. Dammit, where are you? I can't see a thing. Can you see me?"

Carly stared into the darkness. In the corner of her vision, she saw a moving shape near the tree line. Her heart in her throat, she ran forward, a sob escaping her lips. "Asher, I was so worried."

He held out his arms and she ran into them, weeping. Clasping her hands around his neck, she sank down, and he let her pull both of them to the ground.

"Shhh," he soothed. "We're both fine. Nothing broken, no harm done."

Too upset to respond, Carly burrowed deeper into his embrace. Asher laid his cheek on her soft hair and gathered her closer. He rocked her for a few minutes, letting her cries subside until they were just sniffles.

"I was so afraid you were going to get hurt. I just couldn't stay back there, Asher."

She could hear the frown in his voice. "I can take care of myself, Carly."

She pulled away and cupped his face in her hands. "Oh, I know that. But he's crazy, Asher. And he owns a gun. Probably lots of guns." She sank down to the ground.

Asher eased himself down next to her. "I'm well aware of that," he said with a sigh. "It was kind of foolish to set out after him alone. I know it. But it's my job to protect you, Carly. And part of that, I guess, seems to be taking risks."

Carly's heart plummeted. His job. Yes, that was true. Daniel had asked Asher to be her bodyguard, but she had hoped that after tonight he would be concerned for more than just her safety. She pulled away from his arms and lay down on her back.

"I know you don't like it, and never have, but that's the way it has to be, my love," he continued.

Carly squeezed her eyes shut. Why did he have to call her that? It just made a horrible evening that much worse. Sighing, she folded her arms around herself in protection. "You're right, I don't like it," she replied.

"We'll get him soon, I promise. He got away tonight, I'm ashamed to admit, but it won't take long. I'm so pissed off now that all it will take is a tiny mistake on his part and I'll make sure he ends up in jail." Asher lay down beside her and placed a large, warm palm on her shoulder.

At his touch, Carly closed her eyes. No. She didn't want to feel this way anymore. Being in love with this man was torture. It was making her crazy, and it was making her sad. Enough was enough. She reached up and removed his hand.

"Carly?" he asked in confusion.

"Just don't, Asher."

"Carly, love," he said in surprise.

"Please don't call me that, Asher," she said in a small voice, "It drives me crazy."

He was silent for a few seconds and then cleared his throat. "In a good way or a bad way?"

Carly couldn't help but smile as she recalled their conversation earlier that day. God, that seemed like months ago. She was exhausted. And she didn't want to deal with this.

"I think you know what way I mean," she replied in a weary voice.

Asher put his hand back on her shoulder and inched closer. "Were you thinking about the cabin?"

"Yes . . . partly," she answered.

"And?"

"And, I was thinking about earlier tonight. In the theater."

Asher's hand began to caress her shoulder, and he shifted his body so that he was above her. "I figured that. Weren't you going to tell me something?" His hand moved down her arm and rested on her stomach. His lips hovered near her face.

She swallowed and closed her eyes. Against her will, her arm came up and brought his face closer to hers. "Why don't you just kiss me?"

Asher shifted again so that he was laying on top of her, his strong arms supporting his weight. She drew in a ragged breath. "Why don't you just *kiss* me?" she whispered.

"Why don't you just tell me?" he countered. He leaned in closer and reached down to caress her knee. When he shifted, she felt his hardness push into one of her hips and she opened her mouth in surprised pleasure. Asher's hand continued, teasing. It ran up her thigh, taking the sundress with it. At the top of her leg, he stopped, kneading her other hip.

"Tell me," he whispered again.

She couldn't take the teasing anymore. Her heart hammering, Carly slid her legs apart and reached for him. She pulled him in so that his entire body was pressed against hers, hardness and all.

"Oh my God," she said in a choked voice, "Asher, please."

He answered by nestling closer and moving his hand slowly on her hip. Gently, he gripped it and lifted her up, running his palms up her smooth skin. The sundress and his hands inched farther up . . . over her waist . . . over her ribcage . . . and as she gasped, over her bra. The cool air was a shock to her skin, but his warm hands were even more so. He grasped the front of her bra, unsnapped it and lowered his lips to her breasts.

She threw her head back as his mouth closed over a nipple. She stared up at the sky. It was beginning to lighten, but she was practically blind with desire. As his mouth dragged across her breasts, she reached for him again and slipped her palms under his shirt to caress his broad back.

He lifted his head and gazed at her. In the pre-dawn light, the planes of his face were beautiful. She reached up to caress his cheek.

"Tell me," he repeated, and began to rock slowly between her thighs.

Carly's eyes flew shut. Her breath came in jerky gasps and her body throbbed. She lifted her face to his. He stopped moving and lowered his head.

"Trust me," he whispered against her mouth.

Opening her eyes, Carly glanced up at him. A surge of panic surfaced, but she tamped it back down. It was now or never.

"I love you, Asher."

He let his breath out in a sigh. "Thank God. I am the luckiest man in the world." His eyes suddenly filled with tears and he caressed her cheek with his thumb. He moved his palm to the back of her head and pulled her in, still looking into her eyes. Her soul. "And I love you, Carly."

Before she could suck in a breath, his lips were on hers, strong, insistent, and searching. She opened her mouth and kissed him back, deepening the passion.

Without a word, he pulled the sundress and bra over her head. She unbuttoned his shirt and smoothed it back over his muscular chest. Drinking the sight in with her eyes, she pulled him down for another kiss.

Taking the shirt off, Asher balled it up and placed it behind her head. He stared at her for a few seconds, his eyes traveling down her body. "You're beautiful," he whispered.

She could feel herself blushing as she reached for the front of his jeans. She watched as he closed his eyes in pleasure while she unbuttoned them, taking her time. Slipping a hand inside, she gasped at the sensation of him large and thick against her palm.

Suddenly, Asher growled and pushed her backward. He kissed her again, this time with more urgency. Never breaking stride, he shrugged out of his jeans, kicked off his shoes and slid her panties off. He hovered above her for an instant and she smiled.

"Asher, I love you."

He smiled back, and then brought his mouth down for another

searing kiss. "And I love you . . . with all my heart." He raised an eyebrow. "And with other parts of me, too."

Carly grinned and a bubble of laughter rose in her throat. "Oh, yeah?"

"Mmm." He leaned over her and brushed a kiss over her forehead. And onto her shoulder.

Carly pressed her lips to his throat and thrust her hips upwards in welcome. He entered her with a slow groan. She shut her eyes and rocked forward, moaning, but he held back, stilling himself inside her while he claimed her mouth again.

When he tore his mouth away hips thrust forward, and he stopped again, buried within her. Her eyes fluttered open when she heard him moan.

"My God, Carly . . . you feel amazing. I feel so deep . . . "

Her breathing ragged, she shifted her hips and clutched at his back. "Deeper," she gasped. He moaned and complied, and then thrust again, setting a steady rhythm. She ran her hands up his muscled back to cup his face. Asher gazed into her eyes and increased the pace.

A coiling pressure built higher and higher and she gripped his taut biceps. "Asher . . . Oh God, Asher . . . "

"My love," he answered with a kiss. His firm lips trailed across her cheek; his breath was hot on her neck and he thrust deeper and deeper, lifting her hips from the ground.

Her moans became staccato and she wrapped her legs around his back. Black spots danced in front of her eyes, and seconds later, the climax ripped through her.

When she whimpered, he collapsed on top of her, shuddering. Her trembling arms lay at her sides and she drew in a gulp of air. "Asher."

Asher lifted himself off her and rolled onto his side, cradling her next to him. They lay together, not speaking, as the sun crept over the mountains. He brushed her tangled hair out of her eyes and smiled tenderly. "Pretty Carly."

She blushed and smiled. "I'll bet I don't really look that pretty right now," she replied.

He surveyed her with mock appraisal. "No. You look like hell. And I like it that way."

Throwing her head back, Carly laughed in delight. "And you look like you've been in a prize fight, Mister."

Asher placed a strong palm on his swollen jaw. "Yeah. But the other guy feels worse. He peed his pants and puked on his shoes," he said with a chuckle.

Carly stared at him for a few seconds, her eyes sparkling. "Really?"

"Sure enough. Plus, he fell into a thorn bush and has stickers all over his ass."

At that, she burst into gales of laughter. "Oh, God," she gasped, "I wish I had a video."

Asher chuckled in agreement. "So do I, Carly. That would really be a bargaining tool. I'll have to think about that when I go hunt the son of a bitch down."

She stopped laughing and sat up. "What do you mean, Asher?"

"Nothing, nothing, forget I mentioned it." He threw his hands up and winked at her.

She opened her mouth to argue, but at the mischievous look in his eyes, she shut it again. Gathering up her dress, she shook her head. "You're going to do something, Asher Day. I just know it. But I don't want to think about it right now. I want to enjoy perfection as long as it lasts."

Asher slipped his hands behind her head and lowered his forehead to hers. "Happy Birthday, Carly love."

Chapter Sixteen

Hand in hand, Carly and Asher picked their way back down the trail to the main street of Ruby Spring. The sun was bright in the sky, but the chill breeze still swept through the mountains.

Shivering in her sundress, Carly started to trot when the hotel came into view. "Hurry up. I'm freezing," she exclaimed, even as she beamed.

Chuckling, Asher put an arm around her shoulders and began to run with her. "Don't worry, love. As soon as we get back to the hotel, I'll warm you up again."

Although her teeth were chattering, Carly managed a short laugh. "You're so bad."

Suddenly, Asher gripped her hand and jerked them both to a stop. "Oh, hell."

"What?"

Slowly, he lifted an arm and pointed to the hotel. Shading her eyes, Carly peered down the street. "What? It's just Ross and Nicky. Sitting in the rocking chairs." She waved at them. They didn't wave back.

Without warning, Asher jerked his hand away from hers and took off at a dead run for the hotel. He scrambled up the porch and stopped short. Nicky and Ross were in the rockers, but not by choice. Each man's hands were bound to the back slats, and each man's feet were bound in front of them. Their eyes were closed. And they weren't moving.

"Oh, hell," Asher repeated.

Behind him, Carly sucked in a breath as she came up the steps. "Oh, God, are they okay?"

Asher reached out to Ross and shook his shoulder. "Hey Buddy."

Ross moaned and cracked open an eye. "What the hell is going on? Why am I so cold?" he mumbled.

Gasping in relief, Carly knelt beside him and instantly began to work at the knots around his ankles. "Ross, what happened?" she asked.

Ross groaned and shut his eyes again. "That bastard was waiting for us, that's what happened," he retorted as he struggled to get loose. Giving up, he sighed. "I kind of remember being hit over the head, but that's the last thing I can recall before you two woke me up. Damn, my head hurts. Hey, Asher, be a good friend and get this crap off of me."

Without responding, Asher pulled back the screen door and went inside. Within seconds, Carly heard the sounds of cabinet doors and drawers slamming open and closed.

Nicky slowly opened his eyes and then turned to Carly. "Who's making all that noise?" He raised an eyebrow.

Carly sighed and gave him a wan smile. "Asher's pissed," she said.

"He's going to kill Wheeler," sighed Ross.

"Oh no, he's not. I refuse to be in love with a prison inmate," Carly retorted as she stood and folded her arms. "He's going to catch him. And we're all going to help."

"I don't need any help," Asher said as he returned with a butcher knife. Squatting, he quickly sliced through the cords binding Ross, and then turned his attention to Nicky.

Ross stretched and stood up, wincing. He sat back down. "Look, Man, Wheeler is beyond dangerous. I know you could handle it, but why risk it? You have a lot at stake right now."

Asher stared at him for a few seconds, anger clouding his eyes. He muttered an oath and then turned and flung the butcher knife off the porch. It landed with a thunk in the dusty ground. He shook his head and then glanced at Carly. "I want to hurt him," he muttered.

"That's what he's hoping for," she answered, and reached out to hug him to her. "He's practically begging you to come after him. So don't."

"Well, I tried the 'come and get me' method and we all know how that worked out," Nicky mumbled as he stood up on shaky legs.

Asher sighed and went down the porch steps to retrieve the knife. As he pulled it out of the ground, his eyes narrowed. "What's Nicky talking about, Ross? And why are you both wearing camouflage?"

"Promise you won't be mad," said Ross, as he flashed his killer grin.

"No, I'm not promising anything. Just tell me, Ross."

Gripping the arms of the rocking chair, Ross heaved himself out of it and weaved a bit, moaning. "I'm dizzy," he murmured.

"Then sit back down. Tell me," Asher repeated.

Nicky stepped forward. "Ross didn't come up with this plan. If you want to be mad at anyone, it should be Marilyn and me. Actually, she thought of it first. It didn't seem like a bad idea at the time, but I wasn't bargaining for . . . " He stopped and clapped a tanned hand over his mouth and his eyes widened. "Marilyn!" he exclaimed. Without a word, he stumbled into the hotel and pulled himself up the stairs. Carly and Asher followed. Ross stopped in the lobby for a brief second and then made for the basement door. "I'm checking on Sophie and the Daniels."

On the third floor, Nicky flung open Marilyn's door and then gasped.

Lying in her green satin negligee on her frilly pink pillows, Marilyn's eyes flashed fire. She struggled furiously against the cords binding her hands and feet to the four-poster bed. Through the duct tape over her mouth, she mumbled.

Asher walked around the bed and sliced the cords, and then dropped into the rocking chair near the window. Marilyn sat up and flexed her hands, staring daggers at Nicky.

"Marilyn!" Nicky rushed forward and pulled the tape from her lips.

"You idiot," she gasped in a croak, "For the last ten minutes I've been listening to you shoot your mouth off down there through the open window and it takes you that long to figure out that *maybe* poor old Marilyn might *possibly* need some help. What did you think I was doing up here, my nails?"

Glancing down at her hands, she shrieked. "My nails. Oh, my beautiful nails. They look like pink corn chips." She groaned and flopped backward onto her pillows again.

Sinking down beside her, Nicky took one of her hands with its ragged and broken nails, and brought it to his lips. "What did that bastard do to you, Marilyn?"

She closed her eyes and shook her head. "If I'd been just a little more alert. If I'd quit playing with the damned cell phone, trying to contact you. If I'd just quit struggling to get loose, my nails would be fine."

Carly sat on her other side. "What happened?" she asked.

"Well, last night after I turned on the porch light and you and Asher showed up, I hid here in the lobby and waited. It was pretty quiet for a little while, but then I started to hear shouting. I knew Wheeler had found Nicky, just like we figured would happen. But then, well . . . I guess I started to panic a little bit. What if Nicky needed help? What if Ross couldn't find him?" Marilyn shifted to a more comfortable position and looked up as Ross came through the doorway. He stopped and leaned against the doorjamb, raking his hands through disheveled hair.

"They're fast asleep," he muttered.

Carly breathed a sigh of relief. "Thank God. I'll bet they didn't hear a thing last night."

Ross reached up and touched the back of his head, scowling. "Yeah, small miracles."

Marilyn patted the bed beside her. "Come here, darling. Don't just stand there in the doorway."

Obliging her, he walked over to join the rest of Marilyn's audience. She smiled as he sat cautiously on the edge of the bed, and then continued. "Well, I tried to call Nicky, but something was messed up in my contact list and it kept dialing his home number in L.A. I guess I was flustered and that's when I realized that I needed to scroll down to the . . ."

"Marilyn," Nicky cut her off, "just get to what happened."

"That *is* what happened," she snapped, "and every part of the story is important."

Nicky sighed and slid down to lay beside her, crowding the bed even more. "Go on," he said.

"Okay. So, I was trying to dial your number, but I had the wrong one and couldn't get through. Then I heard a car start up. Well, that really put me into a tizzy. I mean, what if Wheeler had hurt you or something and then left you lying in the dirt?" She glanced at Ross. "You too, honey."

Ross smiled weakly. "Sure, of course."

Marilyn raised a hand to examine her nails again and frowned. "So, I decided to go outside and take a look. I could still hear the car, ever so faintly, and then it went away. I stood out there in the street, freezing, and listened. A few minutes later I heard the car again, and this time, it was coming right down the ridge and right into town."

Asher raised an eyebrow. "He came back to town?"

"Oh yes, he did. But me, stupid idiot, thought I could hold my own and I stood in the street like a gunslinger in a nightgown waiting for him. His car was weaving all over the place. Anyway, when he got to the hotel, he stopped and got out and fell right on his face. He hit that ground hard. I couldn't help but laugh . . . and that's what did it." She sighed.

"That asshole absolutely doesn't like to be laughed at," Ross added.

"No kidding. He picked himself up and stumbled over to me. He had his hand over his mouth. It was hard to see in the porch light, but it looked like it was bleeding. Maybe the bastard cut his lip. We can only hope," Marilyn scoffed. "So, I yelled at him, something like: *Where the hell is my boyfriend!*"

She sat up all of a sudden, tumbling Ross off the bed. "And you know what he said to me? He called me a fat bitch. Can you believe that? I hauled off and slapped him right across his bleeding mouth. Well, it felt good, but it was a mistake. Quicker than anything, he had me in a death grip and had slapped tape over my mouth. Next thing you know, he was wrapping cords around my hands. Should have realized the bulge in his pockets wasn't anything interesting. It was just stuff to tie me up with."

Ross peered up over the edge of the bed. "Did he say anything else to you?"

"Oh, yeah. He wouldn't shut up. After he pushed me upstairs and tied me to the bed, he sat over there in the rocking chair and whispered in this creepy voice. I was half afraid he was going to try something on me, but I knew he was too drunk to really do anything awful."

Asher shot up out of the rocking chair as if it had stung him and began pacing, the butcher knife still clutched in a hand. Carly heaved a sigh and then patted Marilyn's hand. "I would have been scared, too. What did he talk about, Marilyn?"

Marilyn glanced at her, and then over at Asher. He shook his head silently and she swallowed. "Well, it wasn't anything important. Just a bunch of crap, really."

Asher walked over and gave Carly's arm a squeeze. "Carly, love, could you go downstairs and get a pitcher of water? I think all of us could use some."

Carly rolled her eyes. "No way. I need to hear this, too. Especially if it's about me."

Marilyn's eyes filled with tears. "Oh, Carly. It's not good."

"I don't care. Out with it."

Sighing, Marilyn wiped her cheeks as the tears fell. "He told me that he was going to grab you and take you away from here. Somewhere where none of us could ever find you. Then he proceeded to describe how he was going to make you love him. In detail." Her breath caught in a hiccough. "And then in even greater detail, he told me how he was going to . . . to . . . murder you. Then he got up and left."

Carly looked down at her tightly clasped hands. "Thanks for telling me. I'm going to get the water now." She rose from the bed and slipped through the doorway.

Asher went to the window and leaned his forehead heavily against it. His eyes were full of pain and his mouth was a grim, taut line. "I'm calling the FBI," he said.

"Do it, bro. It's for the best," Nicky muttered.

*

Ross paced the stage, clipboard in hand, as he wound up his speech. "So you see, that's why we didn't make this public until now, folks." He sank down on the edge and dangled his legs over the side. "Any questions?"

He was met by the stony gaze of a handful of college students sitting in the house. The professional actors, Buddy and Jack, shifted in their seats. No one spoke.

Finally, one of the college students, a dark-haired girl named Anne, raised her hand from the seats out in the house. "When did this happen exactly?"

"About a week ago." Ross answered. He glanced at her and then down at his feet.

"What?" Anne retorted. "Why did you wait so long to tell us? Do they really have him in custody?"

Ross was silent for a moment and the students frowned, looking at each other.

"No," he finally answered, "But the FBI is taking care of things."

"Does that mean he's in jail?" asked Parker, the stage manager. He sat behind his desk, a neat row of pencils and scripts in front of him.

"Good question, Parker," Ross answered. "Unfortunately, no. Because Sheriff Barstow told his colleagues that he had been in a bar fight, they have no solid proof that he incurred his injuries when he was up here that night. So, no, he's not in jail."

A shocked gasp rippled through the seats in front of him. Ross jumped down from the stage and raised a hand. "Now, don't get panicked. They are watching him like a hawk. He's been relieved of duty pending investigation, and his house is being monitored. He's not going to come back up here. We're pretty sure about that."

"I don't know, Ross," Parker said, "I don't think any of us would be safe here until that psycho is in jail." Assenting voices murmured from the seats around him. He continued, "I'm sorry, but that's just the way I feel."

Sophie nodded from the front row and stood, cradling her baby. "Well, I'm sorry you feel that way, but it is true that Wheeler is being monitored. Danny and I will understand if you don't want to be here anymore, but please remember how close we are to opening this show, folks. Every performance is sold out, but we still need your help."

Her plea was met by silence, and then everyone began talking at once. As the clamor got louder, Sophie's eyes widened. Finally, she sat back down.

In the third row, Jack, the actor playing the villain, rose. He cleared his throat and raised a self-conscious hand to his white ponytail. "Uh, despite being an actor, I'm no good at speeches, but I think I'll give it a go." His deep voice resonated in the near-empty theater, drowning out the voices of the excited students.

He cleared his throat again when the house fell silent. "Well, what I mean to say is this. Daniel and Sophie have worked very hard to make this place a success. They've also been through a lot in the last few weeks, what with the broken leg and the new baby . . . and somehow, they've managed to get us to this point. And we're in pretty good shape if you ask me. And I've done lots of shows in lots of places, by the way." He turned around to face the students and continued, "They've pretty much done all the background work themselves, from doing the publicity to giving all of you an opportunity to work in a professional theater. Look around you. This theater is not only beautiful; it's a piece of history." He shoved his hands into his pockets. "That's pretty much all I've got to say on the matter."

Half-hearted claps broke out, and then faded away. Jack scratched his head and shrugged. Next to him, Buddy, the leading man, stood and faced the students with Jack. "I think you guys can do better than that. Who's with us?" He smiled and winked at Anne, who blushed.

"I'm with you, Buddy," she said in a loud voice.

"Who else?" he demanded.

Parker stood up and sighed. "Me," he muttered, staring at the floor.

"You don't sound very sure about that," Buddy continued to prod.

"I don't want to lose my job," said Parker, "and I don't want Sophie and Daniel and Ross to think I'm a loser."

Ross smiled at him. "You're not a loser, Parker. You may just make a professional stage manager someday."

Parker gulped, and then beamed. "Really?"

Ross laughed. "Sure. Same goes for the rest of you. This is your first professional theater job. You want to finish it, don't you?"

"Yes!" the students chorused.

"Then get back over to the scene shop. Carly needs your help," he ordered.

Quickly, the students scrambled out of their seats and ran up the aisles.

Chuckling, Ross went to shake hands with Buddy and Jack. "Thanks, guys."

Buddy shuffled his feet and tightened the bandanna covering his head. "No prob, man. I really want this show to succeed, but it's not just that. Dude, I gots to get paid."

"No kidding." Jack chortled and slapped Ross on the back. Ross gave them a quick smile and then sighed. He rubbed his hand across his forehead.

"You OK, man?" Buddy leaned in and put a hand on Ross's shoulder. "Usually you are, like, always joking and stuff."

Ross slumped into a seat in the front row and laced his fingers around the back of his neck. "Yeah, I'm fine. I just wish they really *had* put him in jail. I think we'd all feel a lot better then." Suddenly, he sat up straight. "Hey, you guys are living in Albuquerque for the summer. Whereabouts is the apartment Sophie and Daniel rented for you?"

Jack replied, "It's right on the northern end of the city, near the interstate. What does that have to do with anything?"

"Nothing, except for the fact that I have an idea. How would you guys like to give up all that comfort . . . you know, things like running water and television, and come sleep in here on the stage for the next couple of weeks?"

"Huh?" Buddy stared at Ross. "No offense, dude, but that's crazy."

Jack gave Buddy an impatient look. "I used to have a day job as a security guard, and Buddy here knows tai kwon do. He practices *all* the time, don't you, pal?"

"What are you trying to say? I thought you liked martial arts," Buddy retorted, "I don't see what any of that has to do with . . . oh." He smiled and began to bob his head. "Right on, Ross dude. Sure, man. We'll protect the assets. No prob."

Ross sighed in relief. "Good. And I doubt if you guys will mind if we moved Sophie and Daniel and the baby into your apartment for the time being."

Jack cleared his throat. "Absolutely not. We'll be happy to have our stuff up here by this evening."

"Yeah, dude. This is going to kick ass," Buddy exclaimed as he struck a fighting pose.

"I really owe you guys one. Remind me when this show closes to keep you in mind for the next show I direct, wherever that might be," Ross said. He rose and stretched. "I gotta go down to the costume shop and see how Marilyn's fitting is going," he said with a yawn.

Jack jumped up beside him, suddenly spry for his age. "Need some company?" he asked.

Ross shook his head. "Taken, man. The lady's taken."

"Yeah, yeah. But a man can always dream," Jack said with a chuckle.

Chapter Seventeen

"Heads!" Carly shouted as she began to pull the ropes that lowered the oleo curtain into place. Nine students stopped pounding nails and screwing together platforms and looked upward as the curtain drifted to the stage floor.

"Can we go out into the house and look at it, Carly?" asked Anne.

"Sure. Just let me see it first to make sure it's straight." Carly smiled as she locked the ropes into place and removed her rawhide gloves. She walked to the outside right edge of the curtain, pulled it back and then slipped to the other side.

A low whistle sounded from the back of the house. "Looking good, Good Looking," Asher shouted.

Carly beamed and shaded her eyes from the stage lights. She bounded down the front of stage steps, adjusting the waistband of her jeans shorts and smoothing her tank top self-consciously. "Really?"

"Don't look yet. Come on back here and see it."

Carly's gaze flew to him as her eyes adjusted in the dark house, and she gave a whistle, too. "Wow. I don't think I've ever seen you dressed up, Asher. You're hot."

It was his turn to be self-conscious. He ran a hand over his head, smoothing back his soft, wavy hair. Grabbing a lapel of his tan linen suit coat with one hand, he adjusted his tie with the other. "Why thank you, ma'am," he drawled.

The curtain forgotten now, Carly drank him in. "You should always dress like that," she murmured, clasping her hands behind his neck.

"What, you don't like me in paint-stained overalls and ripped old T-shirts?"

Carly pulled herself up to her tiptoes and whispered against his mouth, "I like you any way I can get you."

For a second, Asher's eyes darkened with lust, and then he pulled back. "Oh, no. You're not going to distract me now. I told Danny I'd be at the TV station in one hour, and that's where I'm going to be. Marilyn is already in the van, all dolled up. It took half the morning just to get her going, so I would be a fool if I made her wait now."

Carly sighed in regret and released him with a kiss on the cheek. "I wish we had TV up here. I would love to see the publicity interview."

"It's just for the twelve o'clock news . . . no big thing," said Asher, walking toward the front door and opening it.

"That doesn't matter to me. I would want to cheer you on even if it was just on the radio."

Asher winked. "It will be. Simultaneous broadcast. Tune in at noon, Carly love. You know which station is the local NBC?"

Carly nodded. "I can't wait, sexy," she countered, and then walked over and placed a hand on his chest.

He sighed and looked down at her. "Just one kiss, then." She smiled and raised her face, but before their lips could meet, a car horn blared outside, making both of them jump.

"Asher Day, get your bony ass out here. I'm the *star* and I don't like to be kept waiting." Marilyn's booming voice floated through the open doorway.

"Carly? Can't we come out and look now? Is there something wrong with the curtain?" Anne's muffled shout carried across the rows of seats to the back of the theater.

At the same time, Carly and Asher sighed, and then pecked each other on the lips like an old couple.

"Love you."

"Love you, too."

Carly slipped outside to wave goodbye, and then came back in the dark, cool, house. She gasped in delight when she saw the curtain. It hung, shimmering in the stage light, the intricate gold scrolled paint glittering on the edges. All of the sponsors' logos covering the rest of the giant canvas were painted in neat sections, all fifty of them. She couldn't have done that much work in such a short amount of time without Asher's help. The man was talented; there was no getting around that. Carly hugged herself and grinned in satisfaction.

"Come on out. You guys need to see this," she yelled.

Slowly, the students emerged and climbed down the steps. One by one, they sat down in seats and stared in silence. After a moment, claps and cheers broke out. When it was quiet again, Parker stood up and faced the back of the theater. "Carly, you rock," he blurted out.

"Thank you, thank you." Carly bowed and then walked to the front door. "Who wants to help me strip and then repaint some wooden chairs?"

Groans rose from the seats and Parker piped up again. "I think I have some stage manager stuff to take care of."

"No, you don't," chorused a group of girls.

Laughing, Carly pushed the door open and blinked in the sunlight. Suddenly, she felt a hand lightly grip her arm and she stiffened, whirling around.

"I'm so sorry, Carly. I didn't mean to scare you," said Anne. She pushed her long fall of dark hair over her shoulder. "I just wanted to ask you a question."

Carly lifted a hand to her fluttering heart and breathed out. "That's okay. I'm just a little keyed up right now." Pushing the door open again, she motioned for Anne to follow her.

They walked around the theater toward the saloon, their feet crunching on gravel. "What is it, Anne?" Carly glanced at the girl, whose face was turning red.

"How do you know if a guy really wants you?" she blurted out.

"Um . . . what?" Carly stopped and stared at her in surprise.

Anne pressed her small, delicate lips together and then raised a hand to her dusky cheek. "It's Buddy," she said.

"Buddy? But he's way too old for you, isn't he?" Anne gave her a sharp look and Carly closed her mouth. As usual, she had spoken without thinking.

"I don't know," Anne said miserably, "Why, do you know how old he is? What, is he, like, thirty or something?"

Throwing her head back, Carly laughed. "Yeah, that's ancient. Thirty . . . then I guess that makes me ready for social security and a walker, huh?"

Anne winced. "I'm sorry. You don't look that old. I didn't know . . . God; I have this bad habit of not being able to keep my big fat mouth shut sometimes."

Carly put an arm around the younger girl's shoulders. "So do I. Well, then, how old do you think he is?"

Anne shrugged. "Younger than thirty?"

"Try twenty-six." Carly said as she winked.

Anne's dark eyes sparkled. "That's not too old. I'm twenty-two."

"Really? I would have pegged you for eighteen. That's interesting."

Anne's mouth dropped open. "No. I'm a senior. Plus I took a year off before I went to college. Jeez, Carly, do I act like I'm eighteen?"

Carly winked again. "The question is, do you act like you're eighteen when you're around Buddy?"

Anne closed her mouth and stared up at the sky for a moment. She smiled again, and then reached out to hug Carly. "That's it. You're so smart, Carly. That's probably why you've found the love of your life. I hope you realize how absolutely lucky you are."

It was Carly's turn to blush. She had never heard anyone mention her relationship that way before, and it really did hit home just how lucky she was. Tears sprang to her eyes and she cleared her throat. "We better get down to the saloon and get to work, then."

Anne squeezed her arm and they walked the short distance to the saloon. Several students were already inside, surrounding Parker, who had an open can of paint thinner in one hand, a rag in the other. He surveyed a dusty old rocking chair with disdain.

"This stuff stinks, Carly," he complained.

"It would stink a lot less . . . and poison us a lot less if you took that project outside, Parker. That stuff is toxic," she answered. "And wear a mask. I bought a whole package of them."

Giggling, a girl lifted the rocking chair and headed for the door. "C'mon, loser, I'll help you." Grumbling, Parker followed her outside.

Carly turned to the rest of the students. "In fact, why don't all of you go outside? We have three pieces of furniture left, and you can work in pairs. The sooner it's finished, the sooner you can get fitted for your opening night costumes." The students nodded in agreement, picked up the furniture and made their way outside. Anne lingered behind, smiling.

"So . . . if we are staying to help run the show once it opens, we get to wear costumes?"

Carly chuckled. "Sure. Danny and Sophie thought it would be fun. If all of you are working as ushers, wouldn't it be cool if you were dressed in period clothing just like the actors?" Carly grinned in return.

"Won't that put Nancy in a bind? She still has all the costumes for the show to finish up." Anne walked around some sawhorses and began to untangle power cords from a pile on the floor.

Carly slipped behind the bar and rummaged for her old paint-splattered radio. "Nancy's a whiz. She finished the show costumes three days ago, and we don't even open for another week. Plus, we got this costume donation from an old-timey photography studio up in Colorado. Danny and Asher's cousins, I think. They must have needed some new ones. So, Nancy's turning those into costumes for all of the theater staff. I guess she's bored."

"Well, then. I'm going to go over and talk to Nancy on a break, if you don't mind," said Anne. Her eyes sparkled with mischief.

Carly set the radio on the bar and unwound the cord. "Uh, oh, Miss Anne is up to something."

"Maybe. And if Nancy can help me out with a corset, my breasts will be up to something. Try *pushed* up . . . to the bottom of my neck. And we'll see if Buddy can take his eyes off me on opening night. Care to make a bet?"

Carly shook her head as she eyed Anne's well-endowed chest. "No thanks. I need all the money I can get."

Anne detangled an orange cord and handed it over the bar to Carly. "Yeah, I guess you do. Wedding dresses can get expensive," she teased.

"What makes you think I'm getting married?" asked Carly, even as she grinned. She shook her head again, took the cord and plugged in the radio. Raising the antenna, she looked over the bar at Anne, who sat cross-legged on the floor, smirking.

"Please, Carly. I'm surprised he hasn't asked you yet." She stood up and dusted off her shorts. "It's none of my business, though. Now, which project do you want me to get started on?"

Carly eyed her with amusement. "Your 'make Buddy melt into his shoes project' would be just fine with me."

Anne clapped her hands in delight. "Thanks, Carly. Just leave something boring for me and I'll do it after lunch." She scampered to the door and was gone before Carly could answer.

Reaching into her pocket, Carly pulled out a barrette and began twisting her hair into a loose bun. It felt good to do Anne a favor, but it was a favor for herself as well. She didn't want to be interrupted when the radio show came on. She couldn't wait to hear what Asher had to say. Smiling, she tuned in the station and set the radio on the far end of the bar with careful hands.

What Anne had said sent butterflies careening around in her stomach. Proposal. Wedding dress. It was almost too overwhelming to think about right now. Usually, when a show was a week away from opening, Carly had little else on her mind. Right now, her mind was almost unbearably crowded. But in a good way.

She sighed and reached for a jar of paintbrushes. Carefully, she laid out pieces of wooden trim and mixed up some gold paint. For a half an hour, she painted and tried to make mental notes about the project, but her thoughts strayed to Asher constantly.

As hard as she tried to concentrate, her mind kept slipping into fantasyland. Finally, she gave up and began to clean the brushes. It was almost time for the interview, anyway.

She smiled when a love song came on the radio. What would it be like to finally plan her wedding? She hadn't fantasized about wedding dresses for years ..and now it looked as if she might need to actually be picking up some bridal magazines. She turned and grabbed a rag to dust off the clouded old mirror set into the carved woodwork behind the bar.

Humming along to the song, she reached up and released the barrette to let her wavy hair tumble down. It was almost past her shoulders now. She looked into the mirror more closely and surveyed her face. Her cheeks were pink, and her soft gray eyes were full of life. She batted them at her reflection and then laughed out loud. Maybe she needed some fake lashes for a wedding day. But would Asher view that as silly? He seemed to like her with no makeup at all.

She stuck her tongue out at the mirror and twisted her hair back up. He hadn't asked her yet. So she didn't need to think about details until he did. It would jinx it. Marilyn's booming laugh broke through her thoughts and she gasped, running over to the radio. Grabbing a high stool, she slid onto it and turned the volume up.

"It certainly seems as if you are enjoying yourself here in our sunny state, Ms. Masters," the female announcer said with a hoarse chuckle.

"Absolutely, darling," Marilyn cooed, "This theater has been a joy. Thanks to the wonderful skills of the producers, the show is going to be first-rate, I promise."

"Isn't it a culture shock, though, to go from your penthouse in L.A. to a ghost town in New Mexico?" the announcer continued in her brash voice.

Marilyn laughed again, lower this time. "I like to be shocked, darling . . . it gives me a thrill," she answered.

In the background, Carly heard Asher clear his throat, and she grinned. She wished that she could see him on TV, but this was better than nothing.

The announcer snickered. "Speaking of thrills, it seems that we have quite a few people lined up outside the studio wanting your autograph, Marilyn. Do you get that type of attention everywhere you go?"

"Oh, I don't *go* anywhere, really. Ruby Spring Theater is the first summer stock job I have accepted in years. I was terribly busy with television, you know."

"So what's so special about this place that made you come all the way out here?"

Marilyn laughed again. "Why don't you ask my boss that question, darling?"

"All right," the announcer agreed, "So, Mr. Day, what is so special about Ruby Spring Theater?"

"Ruby Spring itself is a very special place," Asher began in his smooth voice, "The town itself, although small, is quite well-preserved. And the theater, thanks to an expert, is now the only restored, fully operational, Victorian theater between here and southern Colorado."

Carly sighed and closed her eyes. Asher was such a wonderful man. He had managed to mention her almost right away. He was thinking about her. He was in love with her. She had to keep reminding herself, because it was true.

"That's very interesting. I read something about the fact that your family owns the entire town?" the announcer asked.

Asher chuckled. "That's right. Ethel Crabtree won it in a bet many years ago, and after she passed away, our family has had it ever since. My brother Danny . . . "

"But you don't live there. You live in New York, right?" the announcer interrupted.

Asher paused for a second, but then went on. "I have lived in New York on and off. Like I was saying, my brother . . . "

"But out here, no one really knows who you are, right? Since you've been out here, you haven't been going by your professional name. Why don't you want people to know that you are Frederick Day?"

Carly opened her eyes.

"My real name isn't Frederick Day. That's the name I sign to my paintings. Let's get back to the theater, please. If you want an interview about my work, we can arrange that another time," he said in irritation.

Carly's eyebrows rose when she heard that. Well, well. So Asher was more famous than he had let on. She had heard of *Frederick* Day. Critics said that he was an up-and-coming modern-day Chagall. No wonder he wanted to get away from the city; the art world in New York probably had a field day with his recent problems. Traitorous girlfriend, stolen paintings. But still, keeping her in the dark was pretty sneaky, and why? Carly frowned. She should have put two and two together. Just because she was in a different profession didn't mean she was totally ignorant about contemporary art and painters. Now was not the time to worry about it, though. She gripped the bar and turned her attention back to the interview.

" . . . sure, sure," the announcer said. "I appreciate your insight, Marilyn. But I really would appreciate it if you would just answer my question, Mr. Day. Do you know where your paintings are right now?"

"No," Asher answered in a flat voice.

"And your wife? That must have been simply awful to be betrayed like that. You have no idea where she is?"

His what? Carly's heart plummeted. She grabbed the radio and stared at it. That couldn't be right. Asher wasn't married. The stupid announcer must have made a mistake in her research.

"I'm just not going to dignify that with a response. Now, if you're not going to ask me questions about the theater, I'm leaving. I don't appreciate being blindsided like this," Asher responded in a clipped tone.

"I'm sorry, Mr. Day. It's just that your hometown is very interested in one of its most famous sons. Do you think you'll ever paint again after your tragedy?"

"What kind of question is that?" Asher retorted, "Of course I will. Miranda means nothing to me now. What I mean is . . . " He caught himself and groaned. "Dammit. Look, finish up with Marilyn. I'm outta here."

The announcer gave a trilling laugh. "But Mr. Day. We have a surprise. There's someone on the phone who has been waiting to speak with you."

"Oh, no, Carly," Asher whispered.

At the sound of her voice, Carly raised her swimming head and blinked. "Asher, why?" she whispered in return.

"No, sir. I don't know who Carly is, but this voice is one you'll be familiar with. Ladies and gentlemen, please stand by for Mrs. Miranda Day."

"What?" Asher gasped.

"Hello, Freddie." A low, melodious female voice wafted through the radio and clenched icy fingers around Carly's heart.

"Hello, Miranda. Where are you?" Asher answered.

"In Paris. The Hotel de Grace. When are you going to come and get me?"

Asher sighed heavily. "I'll be on the next flight out. And you better be there. I don't care about the paintings. You know all I want from you is . . . "

The announcer cut him off. "Well, well, now we have that mystery cleared up. So what are you going to do when you reunite with your wife, Mr. Day?"

"The real issue is what's going to happen to this studio if you ask me one more fucking question about her?" Asher countered.

"Mr. Day, we're live! You can't say that on live television," the announcer said with a titter. "Mr. Day. Mr. Day? Where are you going? Ah, ladies and gentlemen, it looks as if our famous painter is living up to his classic artistic temperament and has left us. But don't worry; we'll keep you informed when . . . "

"Ma'am?" Marilyn asked.

"Yes, Ms. Masters."

"I would like to demonstrate, if I may, what a true artistic temperament is like. Darling, could you bring that camera closer? That's right. Okay, here goes."

Carly heard the sharp crack as Marilyn slapped the announcer with all her might. She heard shrieking and scuffling. And then silence. And then static. And then her head dropped down to the bar and she let the burning tears slide down her face.

Chapter Eighteen

Daniel ran a hand through his hair and whistled. "Well, I'll be damned. My brother is married?" He turned to Sophie, who stood next to the kitchen table in shock.

She shook her head and reached over to the counter to turn off the radio. "I guess so. Danny, this is not good. He simply can't go running off again. Especially not to Europe. The show opens in one week."

"I know that. But what do you expect me to do?" he countered.

"Talk to him. Tell him that whatever is wrong with his life can wait one week. You'd do the same for him, and you know it."

Daniel sighed. "Of course I would, but I'm not the man who is in love with one woman and married to another." He shifted in his chair and scratched at the top of his cast with a spatula.

Sophie frowned and chewed on a fingernail. "God, he pisses me off sometimes. I can't believe he didn't tell us. Well, it's out of the question now to ask Carly to talk to him. Even if she didn't hear the interview."

"Oh, she heard it, all right."

Sophie and Daniel looked up as Ross came through the kitchen door. He pulled out a chair and sat down, cradling his head in his hands. "It's pretty bad. She ran into the theater, crying, and asked me for my car keys."

"Did you give them to her?" Sophie asked in alarm.

"No. I took her outside and made her talk." Ross looked up and his tired, red eyes spoke volumes. "She's heartbroken, guys. She kept telling me over and over that she has to leave. She's actually ready to pack up her stuff and drive back to Chicago. Today."

Daniel groaned. "Where is she right now?"

"Over in the saloon. When I told her she couldn't have my car, she got really pissed and ran in and locked the door. I told the college kids to go back to Albuquerque. She's mad at me, but I'm not going to let her leave. We can't be sure where Wheeler is . . . even if he is being watched." Ross looked up, his expression grim.

"Good man," replied Sophie, "We'll get to the bottom of this. And if I can help it, nobody is leaving Ruby Spring until the show opens."

Ross cocked his head to the side. "About that. I have a favor to ask you two that would help set my mind at ease."

"Sure buddy," said Daniel, "What do you need? You've done so much for us; it's the least we can do."

Ross rubbed his forehead. "Even if you don't want to do it?"

"What are you getting at, Ross?" Sophie asked.

"I've made arrangements for you and the Daniels to move down to Albuquerque temporarily. Buddy and Jack agreed to give up their apartment and come up here. Not only will they guard the theater, but you guys will be much safer. The apartment complex has a security system, and you have to admit, you're pretty vulnerable up here . . . what with a newborn and Danny's broken leg."

Sophie frowned at Ross, but said nothing. She turned to Daniel, who opened his mouth to retort. Before he could speak, she squeezed his arm in warning.

"You're a sweet man, Ross," she said in a quiet voice. "We'll do it."

Daniel heaved himself up from the chair and opened his mouth again. "But this is my property. I can take care of it and my family."

"Look man, no one said that you can't. But it's kind of a strain with your leg, isn't it?" Ross stood to face him.

"I'll manage," Daniel grunted. "Thanks for the offer. But we're staying right here."

Ross glanced at Sophie. She rolled her eyes. "Danny, we're going. And I know just how to get you to agree."

Daniel snorted. "I doubt it." He leaned over and scratched at his ankle with the spatula.

Sophie whipped it out of his hand and threw it in the sink.

"Two words. Cable television." She grinned.

He reached out a hand. "Give me my crutches, woman. I have to start packing."

Ross chuckled and rose from the table. "Thanks, you two. It's for the best, and it's only temporary. Do you need help getting stuff to the car?"

Sophie grabbed him in a heartfelt hug. "Go see about your best friend, Ross. She's the one who needs you now."

Ross nodded and sighed. "Yeah. I may need a good bottle of something to get that job done, though. Do you have anything?"

Sophie pulled a chair over to the cabinets and stood on it. She opened a door and surveyed the contents. "Gin? How about some vodka? Oh, here's a bottle of red wine." She blew the dust off of it and handed it to Ross. "Good luck."

He shook his head in despair. "Luck's not going to help this problem, but thanks anyway."

He left the hotel and trudged down the street to the saloon. Trying the front door again, he frowned. Still locked. He peered in a window and knocked. "Carly?"

"Go away," she answered. Her stuffy nose made her voice sound odd.

He sighed and tried again. "Let me in, sweetie. I brought you some wine."

"Fine," she answered, "I'll drink it and then break the bottle over *Freddie's* head." She hiccoughed and then began to cry.

Ross knocked on the window again. "I'd love to see that, but you have to let me in first, Carly." He waited another minute and the knob finally turned. The old door creaked as she opened it. Carly stood before him, her eyes swollen and red. Ross cocked his head to the side and surveyed her, compassion in his eyes. "Oh, sweetie. I'm really sorry."

She reached out and grabbed the bottle from his hand. "I know you are," she said in a tired voice. "Now let's get this open."

"I forgot a cork screw." Ross slapped a hand to his forehead and turned to go back to the hotel.

"That's what power drills are for," Carly replied as she walked to the bar.

"You can do that?" Ross asked.

"Sure, why not? I'll be very careful and just pretend that it's *Freddie's* ear canal."

Ross bit back a laugh and held the bottle while she drilled the cork. "You're a funny woman. And multi-talented as usual, Carly," he commented.

"Oh, absolutely. It seems that my talents don't extend to holding onto a man, though." She pulled the cork off the drill bit and threw it over her shoulder. "For luck. Yeah, right." She grabbed the bottle from his hand and tipped it to her lips, draining a third of it.

"Carly," Ross began cautiously, "You don't know the whole story. There's a reason Asher didn't tell you."

"I can't think of any." She wiped her mouth and tipped the bottle for a second pull.

"May I have a sip of that?" Ross tugged the bottle from her hands. "Don't you think you should at least talk to him?"

"Never," she replied matter-of-factly. "Besides, I'll be halfway to Chicago by this time tomorrow."

Ross sighed. "No you won't. Think about it, sweetie. I know you, and no matter how bad a situation is—and admittedly, this is pretty bad—you don't quit before a job is over. You can go home in a week. But for now, you've somehow got to pull it together, be professional, and finish this up."

"Damn, Ross." Carly blinked at him. "Thanks for the sympathy."

He placed the wine bottle on the bar and put his arms around her. "Like I said, I know you. Sympathy won't work for long. But what I will do is take you into Albuquerque and buy you something fun. And then tonight, you'll talk to Asher. Deal?"

Carly snorted. "No deal. I'll go with you, but I don't want to ever set eyes on him again as long as I live."

"That's good enough for now, I guess," Ross replied.

"It better be. Now give me back the wine." Carly reached around him for the bottle, but he was quicker that her. Deftly, he grabbed it and ran out of the saloon to pour the rest onto the dusty ground.

She followed him outside and then gasped. "What are you doing?"

"I'm not taking a drunk shopping. Now wipe your eyes and comb your hair. Momma needs a new pair of shoes." He winked at her, and she smiled in spite of herself.

"It will help a little, but only for a few minutes, Ross," she said.

"I know that." He kissed her cheek and held out his hand. "Let's go, buddy."

She sighed and allowed herself to be led toward the parking lot. "What would I do without you, Ross?"

"You'd manage just fine. You're stronger than you think you are, Carly."

She smiled up at him fondly, her eyes sad. "So are you, Ross."

*

Ross kissed her forehead and opened the car door for her. Carly sighed and climbed in. She buckled the seat belt and leaned her head back to stare out the window as they began the drive down to Albuquerque. Although she tried to keep her mind blank, pain and anger bubbled below the surface. How could she have let this happen? After all the promises she had made to herself. And who was she kidding . . . she had been nothing more than a diversion. Asher was famous. And intoxicatingly handsome. And most likely rich. This Miranda was probably some kind of supermodel.

Before she could stop herself, she blurted out her thoughts. "I think it's safe to assume that his *wife* looks like a model," she said.

"Now Carly," Ross returned, "It doesn't matter. What matters is that you talk to him before he leaves."

"I'm not going to talk to him," she shot back, tears welling in her eyes. "But I have to know . . . somehow I have to find out about why he did this to me or I'll never be able to forget about it. Or forgive myself."

Ross looked at her in shock. "Why in the hell do you think you have to forgive yourself?"

"I made a promise to myself before the summer started, Ross. I wasn't going to get caught up in some stupid crush . . . it's not like I'm twenty anymore. I just wanted this summer to be different . . . to be something other than me, *driving* away from a job, completely pissed off at myself." The tears began in earnest now, and she sobbed into her hands.

"And this summer has been awful? Every part of it?" Ross reached out and stroked her back soothingly.

"Y-y-y-essss," she managed, "It's sucked. And I . . . I . . . am never going to do another show or go to another art gallery or another museum ever again as long as I live. I'm going to go back to Chicago and I'm going to eat and eat until I get so fat that I have to live in a wheelchair. And I'll let my fingernails grow into claws. And . . . and I'll get a cat . . . then another one . . . and another one . . . until the entire apartment is full and the neighbors start complaining about the smell and call animal control and they haul me away with the cats and throw me in the loony bin." She finished on a hiccough and squinted up at Ross. He was shaking in silent laughter, barely able to keep his eyes on the road.

"*Hey.*" Carly's eyes narrowed in accusation. "Are you making fun of my pain?"

"No, sweetie . . . it's just that you are brilliant, even when you're at your worst."

Carly frowned and folded her arms. "Humph." She glanced out the window as they began the descent toward the interstate. She saw a sign for the airport and winced. Her eyes filled again.

Ross observed her in silence for a few more minutes, and then tried again. "Carly, I know I just told you a while ago, but you're a strong woman. I'm going to take the airport exit so that you can talk to Asher. His first flight leaves in a couple of hours, and he'd be checking in about now."

"Do it and die, Ross," Carly gasped, "And how do you know when his flight leaves?"

"Because I talked to him."

"Traitor," she screeched. "Why would you do that?"

Ross sighed. "He called me, not the other way around. He knows you, sweetie. And he knows that you wouldn't talk to him for all the money in the world right now. He wants me to bring you to him so he can do it in person."

"Do what? Rub in the fact that he lied to me, betrayed me, and used me all summer long until he could get back with Ms. Model?" Her eyes glittered with anger.

"It's not like that. Just trust me that he isn't screwing you over, OK?"

Carly studied her best friend in silence. He had bags under his eyes, and his hair was a mess. Two earrings were missing from the collection that usually adorned his ears, and his usually immaculate, tight black T-shirt had a big rip at the neck. Definitely not the Ross she knew. Her expression softened. "I'm sorry. And I appreciate everything you're trying to do for me, Ross. You know I'd do the same for you," she said.

"Then you'll talk to him?"

"No. I simply can't," she whispered, "Not right now. But . . . I'll try to believe you."

Ross sighed and reached in a pocket for his phone. "Then I gotta tell him that I failed."

Carly watched as they zoomed by the exit to the airport. She pressed her lips together and closed her eyes. It was too late now. And in a way, it was too late the day she met Asher. "No, don't tell him that. Just tell him that it wasn't meant to be . . . not today . . . not ever, I guess."

*

Wheeler Barstow hooted with laughter, crushed his beer can in one fist and then threw it at the trash can in the kitchen. He missed by three feet and it rolled across the linoleum to rest next to a stack of empty pizza boxes. Still chuckling, he turned down the TV and staggered up to get another beer.

Asher Day was married. Well, it served Carly right. Now she would know just who was who. Now was the time for her to apologize and come back to him. He knew it would happen all along . . . it was just a matter of being patient. He belched and walked over to peer out the window. Good. Somehow Joe had gotten rid of those loser FBI agents that were watching the place.

What a pain in the ass that had been. And embarrassing. He clenched his teeth. No sooner than he had gotten to sleep the morning after the night of Carly's birthday . . . there was a knock at his door. And he was in bad shape, too. Still a little drunk and cut up and bruised all to hell and back. The least Joe could have done was call and warn him that the FBI had been contacted. And that Wheeler himself was going to get hauled down to the station. But no . . . . Joe had gotten scared. Well, at least he was helping now. Wheeler chuckled. God help him, Joe was stupid. All Wheeler had to do was complain about needing some space, and Joe had ponied right up.

He thought of the story he had concocted for Joe to tell and chuckled again. Old Coach Bentley up at the high school should have kept his mouth shut when he had told Wheeler a couple of months ago about his pot farm thirty miles south of Albuquerque. It had been so simple to just elaborate a bit . . . throw in some south of the border trafficking, some heavier drugs, and pronto . . . get those agents off his ass and onto Bentley.

They wouldn't be back until tomorrow, if he was lucky. Just enough time to go and get his girl. And then he'd have her in Mexico by sundown. Wheeler yawned and shuffled to the bedroom to take a nap.

*

Three hours later, he woke with a smile on his face. He showered and pulled on his jeans, scratched at his scruffy face and posed for the mirror. No woman could resist a man with stubble . . . and Carly would fall for him all over again . . . he just knew it. He grabbed for his gun belt and then frowned, remembering. The bastards had taken it from him. Well, it was good that he had a shotgun hidden inside his truck.

Grabbing his car keys, Wheeler eased through the front door and looked up and down the street. Nobody but a couple of kids playing ball. Good. He got in his truck and left for Ruby Spring. Four miles onto the interstate, the light traffic became congested. He sighed as he slowed down to a crawl, and then a stop. Damn, it must be a wreck. Straining his neck, he peered around the car in front of him, but couldn't see anything . . . it must be too far ahead.

Cursing, Wheeler veered onto the shoulder and drove ahead, ignoring the honking behind him. He cursed again when he saw the eighteen-wheeler jack-knifed across two lanes of traffic. Well, he didn't have time to wait for the accident to be cleared. He'd just have to take a back road. With a reckless maneuver, he drove down the embankment to the service road below and turned into an apartment complex.

Pulling into an empty space, he let out an irritated sigh and reached for the county map stuck up in the visor. He should know the roads like the back of his hand, but lately, he'd been so drunk that he couldn't remember his own name half the time. Wheeler rolled down the window to let some fresh air in and flipped the map open. He was tracing the route with a finger when he heard a familiar female voice whining across the parking lot.

"Do we need anything else, Danny? How many diapers do we have left?"

His head snapped up and he looked over at a tall, blonde woman standing in the doorway of one of the apartments. It was Sophie Day. What the hell was she doing here? For that matter, what the hell were she *and* her husband doing here? Had they moved into town again? Wheeler frowned and hunched into his seat to listen.

"We have plenty of diapers. Just go, woman . . . you're interrupting my precious TV viewing time."

"Danny Day, you can watch TV all night long. I have to go get groceries for at least two weeks . . . well, at least until they lock up Wheeler Barstow and we can move back up home. Pay attention."

"Soph, they may never lock him up. And I am paying attention. I said . . . we don't need any diapers."

"Fine!"

"Fine."

"I'll be back as soon as I get finished at the store."

"That's what I assumed."

"Don't start with the sarcasm, Mister. It's been a long day already."

"Then don't start with the nagging, Missy . . . it's not helping."

"Oooooh, you drive me nuts. I'm glad I'm going to the store. I need to escape for a little while."

"You'll be missed."

"Danny, that wasn't funny."

"I wasn't trying to be funny . . . I meant it sincerely. Now come here and give your studly husband a kiss."

Wheeler winced as he listened to the soft laughter and kissing. Disgusting. That man didn't know how to handle a woman. But the Days were the least of his concerns right now. He had to get out of here without them seeing him. But how? Maybe he could just lie down on the floorboards for a few minutes until she left. That was probably the best idea. He turned off the engine, heaved himself to the floor and waited until her car was gone. After another few seconds, he sat up again and sighed. What a meddling woman. He was half-tempted to barge right in and tell Danny Day to quit being such a sissy, but what would that accomplish?

Nothing, other than seeing the look on his face. Wheeler chuckled. Danny Day would piss his pants if Wheeler walked into his little 'safe' house. It was almost worth it. Hell, it was early. Wheeler licked his lips and climbed out of the truck. It would be fun to get the baby riled up, too. Then Danny would be left humiliated with a crying brat on his hands. Grinning, he stopped in front of the apartment door. The brat was already crying. *Perfect.*

Suddenly, his head snapped up. The brat! That was it. There was one sure way to get Carly to come to him, and it would be easy. Take the baby. His eyes glinted with determination as he reached for the doorknob.

Chapter Nineteen

Stifling his laughter, Wheeler turned the front door knob and walked quietly into the room. He stood for a minute and observed father and son. What a ridiculous pair. That long-legged idiot asleep on the couch, foot resting on the baby's cradle. The little bundle of drool was asleep too, his mouth open just like his dad's. Well, it was time for wakey-wakey. Stealthily, he took one of Daniel's crutches and reached with it to turn the television volume up as loud as it would go.

Daniel's eyes quickly snapped open and he sat up in confusion. "What the hell?" he mumbled. Just as quickly, he spotted Wheeler and scrambled to his feet. "What are you doing in my apartment, Barstow?"

He hopped in place and Wheeler glanced at the man's leg cast. This was going to be easy.

"Just paying a friendly visit to see how you're getting on," Wheeler drawled.

"Well, I'm fine. Now get the hell out before I call the cops."

"I am the cops, idiot. And anyway, what are you going to call them with? I don't see a phone here and something tells me that your wife has your cell, huh?"

Daniel moved his body protectively in front of the cradle and reached out to turn off the television, his eyes never leaving Wheeler. "Get out, now. Or you'll be sorry," he said between his teeth.

Chuckling, Wheeler grabbed the other crutch and threw it at Daniel. "Why don't you try to make me, cripple boy."

Daniel growled as the crutch bounced off his chest and tumbled to the floor. Not taking his eyes off Wheeler, he bent and fumbled for it. When his hands grasped it, he waited a few seconds, motionless. Wheeler chuckled again in derision, watching as Daniel's anger rose to the surface.

"Like I said, Barstow, leave, or you'll pay for this. In blood."

"What a cute little baby. It's a little girl, isn't it? Sure looks like a little girl to me . . . all cute and cuddly." Wheeler moved closer.

Daniel let out a loud howl and swung the crutch with all of his might. It connected with the side of Wheeler's face and sent him stumbling backward. He yelped as he crashed into the blinds covering the window by the front door. God damn that hurt!

Daniel nodded. "Now get out or there's more."

Oh, hell, no. He was not going to be beat up by a guy in a cast. Wheeler shook his head to clear it and leaned against the wall, his chest heaving. Slowly, his face contorted into a red, beefy mask of anger. He narrowed his eyes and opened his mouth. A thin stream of blood slipped from his lips and ran down his chin. He reached inside his mouth and pulled out a tooth. Trembling, he cupped it in his hands and stared at it. "You son of a bitch! That was one of my front teeth!"

"I wish it was all of your ugly-assed teeth, Barstow. And unless you want the rest of them knocked out, too, do what I told you to a few minutes ago. Get the hell out!" Daniel yelled.

Wheeler glanced down at the brat, who had fallen quiet when the fight began. The little baby's face was screwing up again and in a matter of seconds, impressive wails burst out of his tiny mouth.

Wheeler shoved his tooth in a pocket and covered his ears. "Shut that little monster up!" he yelled, "Dammit, my head hurts!"

Daniel looked at him and smiled in derision. "You're a pathetic excuse for a man, Barstow. You couldn't beat up a ten year old," he said in a deliberate voice.

Slowly removing his hands from his ears, Wheeler narrowed his bloodshot eyes. "What did you just say to me, boy?"

"Let me translate for you since you seem to be somewhat challenged. I said you're a fucking sissy. That's what I said." Daniel gave him a cold smile, reached back and rocked the cradle. "So now that we're finished here, you can leave."

Wheeler stared at him for a few seconds, and then suddenly lurched forward. "I'll kill you," he screamed as he knocked Daniel backward onto the floor in a frenzy of fury. Wheeler found himself at an immediate advantage because of Daniel's leg, and he soon had him straddled with one of the crutches pressed against the other man's throat. "I'll kill you," Wheeler repeated, spitting saliva and blood into Daniel's eyes.

Wheeler tightened his grip and pushed down, and watched with an impassive stare as panic mounted in Daniel's eyes. The baby wailed at the top of its lungs.

He watched with wonder as Daniel's eyes went wild and began to get large. And then snorted in satisfaction as his eyes fluttered and then closed. *Good.* Almost finished.

He let up pressure on Daniel's neck and waited. Well hell. The man was still breathing. Too bad, but then again, Wheeler didn't relish the thought of being wanted for murder. Throwing the crutch onto the sofa, he heaved himself up and wiped his bloody hands on the cushions.

"Sweet dreams, fucking sissy," Wheeler muttered.

Little Daniel Day had stopped screaming and his breath came in short hiccoughs. He raised his little arms and whimpered. Wheeler snickered and reached down. "You don't know a thing, do ya, pal. All you want is someone to take care of you. Well, I have a perfect new mommy for the job. Carly Foster. You already know her, don'tcha, pal?" He lifted the baby out of the cradle and held him against his bloody chest.

Looking around the room, he spied a diaper bag and a can of baby formula on the kitchen table. He grabbed them, hooking the bag over his aching shoulder. Better be safe about it; Carly would not like it if he neglected the little shit. It was already bad enough that he was missing a front tooth. She wouldn't like that for sure, but he could make it up to her in other ways.

Walking back to the living room area, Wheeler reached out and kicked Daniel square in his cast. "So long, asshole. And you should be thanking me. I've just granted you a lifetime of peace and quiet." Daniel grunted, but didn't open his eyes. Grinning, Wheeler slipped out of the front door and swaggered to his truck.

*

Carly chewed on a thumbnail as she surveyed the shoes through the display window. Her head hurt, and she was exhausted. It was taking all of her energy not to burst into tears yet again. The mall was crowded, and incredibly loud. Wincing, she hugged her purse to her chest and glanced up at Ross.

"Do you like any of these, sweetie?" he asked in a patronizing tone.

Carly pointed to a pair of bright red spike heels. "Those. I think I'll buy those and wear them every day for the rest of my life. That way, if I ever run into *Freddie* I can kick him in the crotch with every ounce of strength I possess." She gave a bitter and walked into the store.

Ross sighed and followed her. "Carly Foster. My little vigilante."

"I like that one, Ross. *Vigilante.* Has a nice ring to it. I'll have to consider changing my middle name." Carly wandered around the store, her fingers brushing over the display shoes.

"Come on, sweetie. You don't really want spike heels. In fact, I don't think you're going to buy anything today. Let's just go. We could still make it to the airport . . ."

"*No*," Carly shouted. The tears she had held in check sparkled in her hollow eyes. "So quit trying to convince me."

Ross sighed in exasperation and raised his hands. "Fine. I give up. Let's just get out of here, then, before you make a scene." He grabbed Carly's arm and began to haul her back to the entrance. They had barely made it ten feet out of the store when his phone rang.

"Better answer that," Carly muttered and shrugged free of his grasp.

"This is Ross," he answered. "What? Slow down, Sophie, you're not making a bit of sense. Danny said what? Are you sure?" Ross gasped and sank down on a bench in the long, wide mall corridor.

Carly paced and frowned. "What's wrong now?"

Ross waved her away impatiently. "Just hang on. We'll be there as fast as we can. Have you called the FBI yet? Uh-huh. Does Danny need an ambulance?"

Carly stopped in her tracks and lifted her hand to her mouth. "Oh my God," she whispered, "Wheeler."

Ross glanced up at her and nodded. "Just stay there, Soph," he said into the phone. He hung up and reached for Carly's hand. "We've gotta go. Now. That bastard has the baby. And he hurt Danny."

Carly's face turned white and she gripped Ross's arm. "Please tell me this is just a bad dream."

"I wish I could. We have to get over to the apartment." He started running. "This is my fault. All my fault."

"No. Don't blame yourself, Ross," Carly jerked on his arm until he stopped. "There's no way you could have prevented this. And I know why Wheeler did it. There's only one thing he wants. Me. And the way I feel right now . . . well, let's just say that I am primed and ready to go after him. I'm so angry I could tear someone's face off right now. And all the better if it is him."

Ross began to run again. "We can't use you as bait, Carly. That's stupid. And besides, Asher would kill me."

She jogged beside him, reaching her hand into his pocket for the car keys. "I could care less what he thinks, frankly. I'm doing it, Ross. Even if the FBI doesn't want me to, I'm doing it."

Ross frowned, but said nothing. They ran to the parking lot and stopped by the car, panting. "Fine," he said finally. "But I won't let you do it unless the FBI handles it."

Carly jumped into the car and started it. "Get in. The sooner we get to the apartment, the sooner all of this will be over with, and the sooner Wheeler Barstow will be in jail."

*

During the drive, Carly felt Ross glancing at her, but he held his tongue. That was probably because she did look angry enough to rip someone's face off. She was going to tear Wheeler to pieces. Carly pulled into the parking lot, spraying gravel and screeching tires. She unsnapped her seat belt and jumped out of the car.

The apartment door swung open and Sophie ran out sobbing, tears streaming down her face. "He took my baby! He took my baby, Ross," she screamed as she threw herself into his arms. Ross held her tight and glanced at Carly. She knew her face was a mask of fury.

"Calm down," he mouthed. Carly nodded.

"He won't have him for long, Sophie," she said in an even tone. "Have the FBI arrived yet?"

"Yes," Sophie answered, her voice trembling, "They're in there with Danny."

Ross took Sophie's hand and led her back to the apartment. Inside, Danny sat on the sofa, his head in his hands. Three FBI agents stood in front of him, frowning.

"And then what did he say, Mr. Day? Did he give you any idea where he was going?" one of the agents asked.

"No," Daniel answered in a hoarse voice, "I blacked out. Dammit!" Suddenly Daniel stood up and raked his hands through his hair. He stumbled on his broken leg and sat back down. His eyes were wild, and an angry welt covered the front of his swollen neck. He raised his hand to it and croaked, "If he does anything to hurt my boy, I swear to God, I'll kill him."

"He won't hurt him Danny," Carly said. She leaned against the door frame, her arms crossed. "All he wants is me. And I'm going after him." She braced herself for the protest.

"Oh, God, Carly, no," said Sophie. She grabbed Carly's arms. "You can't do that. What if he got you, too? What then?"

"He's not going to. And besides, using me is the quickest way to find him." Carly narrowed her eyes and glanced at the FBI agents. "Your best chance is to send me after him."

The agents looked at each other and nodded in silent agreement. "Fine. Let's set up the equipment and we'll let you call him," said an agent. "But you can't go in without a wire," added another.

Ross cleared his throat and hugged Sophie to him. "It's settled, then. If you will all excuse me, I have to make a phone call myself." He slipped out into the parking lot.

"Who's he calling?" Daniel asked.

Carly sighed. "Your wonderful brother, I suspect," she retorted. "But I don't want Asher anywhere nearby when we catch Wheeler. It'll just complicate things. And he won't follow orders." She shot a determined glance around the room. One of the FBI agents nodded and followed Ross out to the parking lot.

*

"What's this about his brother?" asked the agent.

Ross sighed and shoved his hands into his jeans pockets. "He's in love with Carly. Man, the entire situation is ridiculous. This is going to sound like a soap opera. I doubt you'll believe me."

"Try me," the agent said, "All situations like this sound like a soap opera. That's why so many of them end up as tragic TV movies of the week."

"Well, this is not going to end up as a tragedy. We've worked too hard this summer for everything to turn to shit." Ross cleared his throat and filled the agent in on the details.

*

Asher sat in a window seat, staring out at the heat waves rising from the tarmac. Carly hadn't called him. No doubt Ross couldn't convince her to because she was the most stubborn woman on the face of the planet. And the most angry. Asher slid down the window shade and reached for his phone again. Glancing around to make sure there weren't flight attendants nearby, he turned it on to check for messages one last time before the plane took off.

The phone came to life with a little chime and he scrolled to his voice mail. There were six new messages. His eyes widened in surprise. Just then, the plane lurched forward and began to taxi. He groaned with frustration. It was too late to go back to the terminal, even if he wanted to. He glanced up. A flight attendant was beginning her safety demonstration. Asher hunched in his seat and began to play the messages.

Ross's voice was tired and full of trepidation. "Hey buddy. I hope you're not in the air yet, because we have a situation here. Now don't freak out, but I've gotta let you know that Wheeler really has done it this time. Um . . . how do I say this? Okay, there is no easy way. He took the baby, Asher. Kidnapped him." Ross paused. "Hang on, buddy. I have to go for a second. Hopefully next time I call, you'll pick up the phone."

Asher's stomach sank as he closed his eyes and brought the phone to his forehead. *Why? Why was this happening now?* The minute he left for the airport, he knew that he was leaving his family . . . . and the love of his life unprotected. It was selfish. Purely selfish. He groaned again and looked at the phone. He had to hear the rest of the messages, no matter how horrible they were.

"Sir? You have to turn that phone off right away. I made the announcement about that fifteen minutes ago." The frowning flight attendant stood in front of Asher, her arms crossed.

Asher opened his mouth to argue, but decided against it when he saw the resolute set of her mouth. He leaned back instead, his gaze flicking over her determined expression. He gave a low chuckle and then winked at her. "No problem, Miss. Sorry about that." He flipped the phone shut and slipped it into his pocket.

She blushed. Wagging a finger at him, she replied, "Charm will get you pretty far, but I'll be watching you. Keep that phone off."

Still grinning, Asher waited for her to walk down the aisle, and then flipped the phone open again. The next message was worse than the one that preceded it.

"Hey Buddy. Why is your phone off? You must be on your way. Well, then, this isn't gonna do any good, but if I don't tell you, you'll rip my legs off when you get back." Ross sighed. "God, you're gonna be pissed. Okay . . . Carly is going after Wheeler. The FBI has it all set up, and she's wearing a wire. They know what they're doing, Asher, and it will probably be all over by early this evening. Stay on the plane and do what you need to do, okay? It's really important for you to clear all that up. You owe it to Carly, buddy. All right. I'll call again in a few minutes just in case you answer. Bye."

Asher listened to the remaining messages. All of them were Ross, wondering why he didn't pick up. He turned off the phone and opened the window shade again. The Albuquerque airport flew by and soon they were airborne. He was exhausted, but half tempted to get off the plane the minute it landed in Dallas and turn right around and book another flight straight back to Albuquerque. But Ross was right. He had to trust the FBI. It was vitally important to his and Carly's future that he make it to Paris by tomorrow morning. He folded his arms and willed the international flight out of Dallas to be on time.

Somehow, he was able to fall asleep for the two-hour flight, but it was restless slumber, plagued with disturbing dreams. He woke with a start as the plane bounced down on the tarmac. "Ladies and Gentlemen, welcome to Dallas-Fort Worth International. The local time is 7:24 Central and the temperature outside of your window is an impressive 102 degrees. Please remain in your seats until the captain has turned off the fasten seatbelt signs and . . ."

Asher rubbed his eyes, ignored the rest of the speech coming over the loudspeaker and pulled out his phone. He dialed Ross. There was no answer. He cursed under his breath, scrolled to Sophie and

Danny's number and then hesitated. Should he? Maybe it would just upset them. They had to be pissed that he'd left right as he was needed most. Well, at this point, he didn't care. He had to know what was going on. Carly answered on the first ring.

"Asher, don't call this number."

His eyes widened in surprise. "Carly? Thank God. What are you doing with Sophie's phone?" He frowned. "Never mind. I'm just making sure you're okay. Ross told me what's going on, and I have to say . . ."

"I *know* what you're going to say and I don't have the time to deal with it right now," she cut him off. "Besides, this line has to remain clear. I'm waiting for Wheeler to take the bait and I'm expecting this phone to ring any minute."

"Fine. I'll get off. But please promise me you'll let me know the second it's over. Okay?" Asher rubbed his aching forehead and waited. "Carly?"

"I'm not going to promise you anything, Asher. Promises and you are like oil and water. They do not mix." She blew out a breath. "Ross will call you."

He flinched, stung by her words. "I'll be looking forward to it," he said, "and Carly, for what it's worth . . . I still love you. You have to trust me on that. Because I trust you and I know you're going to handle Wheeler like a champ." He stared unseeing at the seat pocket in front of him and paused. "Carly?"

"Asher, I have to go now," she said. And then she hung up.

Chapter Twenty

Carly stared at the phone in her hand as tears began to well. She shook her head and wiped them away with her sleeve. Now was not the time. Now she had to focus and will herself to be tough. It was getting near dusk, and she didn't want to face Wheeler in the darkness of night.

Turning, she glanced at one of the FBI agents, a young man with auburn hair and freckles who looked like he was about twelve. He made some adjustments on his mobile surveillance equipment and grinned at her. "Let's test this thing. Say something. Are you feeling like Lara Croft yet?"

Carly smiled back at him in confusion. "Who? What are you talking about, Bruce?"

He walked over and deftly turned her around to check the wire under the back of the waistband on her jeans. "You know . . . the kick-ass character from the movie 'Tomb Raider.' She's really awesome."

Carly chuckled. "Oh, of course. I saw those movies. Oh, yeah. Sure . . . that's me. I rappel upside down from cliffs every day of the week. With an impossibly handsome ex-lover bad boy who wants me back . . . dangling right next to me for moral support." She snorted and raised her arms as Bruce fiddled with the microphone cord.

"Well, I'd be your Terry Sheridan any day. He's hot." He winked at her.

"Who?" Carly laughed.

Bruce grinned. "You know . . . the impossibly handsome ex-lover bad boy who wants you back."

"She already has one of those, guy. You're out of luck." Ross folded his arms and leaned on a huge boulder, his eyes twinkling.

"He's not the only one out of luck," Carly muttered under her breath, "so is Freddie."

Bruce laughed and pulled the back of her T-shirt down gently. Shrugging, he walked back to his equipment. "Hey, I don't want to get in your business, Carly, but the offer still stands if you change your mind."

"Thanks, Bruce," she replied, "You really know how to cheer a girl up. I just hope I do a good job today."

Ross patted her shoulder. "Come on, now Carly. You're going to be great. The plan is foolproof. We will be right over there hiding in the trees." He pointed to a wooded area at the edge of the clearing. "Wheeler will be like a lamb led to the slaughter. A really stupid lamb. You're not nervous, are you?"

Carly gaze followed his hand and she winced. It was right next to where she and Asher had made love. Against will, powerful, sexy images from that night flashed into her mind and she blushed, her heart beating faster. Asher rising rhythmically above her, fire in his eyes. Asher's hands gripping her hips . . . his mouth moving on her throat, leaving a burning trail.

With a jerk Carly shook her head and, clearing her throat, she managed to answer Ross. "I'm not nervous in the least. I just want that loser Wheeler to call me back so we can get this over with."

Ross walked over and squeezed her arm. "Look at me, Carly."

She tipped her head up and smiled into his familiar, caring eyes. "I know how you feel, Ross. You don't need to say anything else. I'll be fine, especially knowing that you are going to be nearby." Reaching out, she pulled him in for a hug and then kissed him on the cheek. "Now go. And summon up your inner butch bad-ass just in case."

Throwing back his head, Ross hooted. He struck a feminine pose and batted his eyelashes. "I'm scared. Ooooh, if that mean old policeman got near me, I would run away . . . simply run away." He minced and paraded around her in a circle.

"Shut up. You're a black belt in karate. Now, GO." She pushed him toward the woods. He skipped off, swishing his hips and making her laugh.

The phone in her hand buzzed to life. She swallowed and glanced at Bruce. He already had his headphones on and his joking expression was gone; replaced by an impassive mask of concentration. He held up a finger, signaling her to wait.

The phone rang again. And then a third time. She lifted her arms and burst out, "What the hell? I need to . . . "

"Shhhhhh! Carly! Hang on a sec." Bruce fiddled with his equipment, and then lowered his finger and motioned for her to answer.

Taking a deep breath, she put the phone to her ear. "Hello?"

"I knew you would call me, Carly girl." Wheeler said in a thick voice. "I just knew it. It's time for us to be together now. You had your little side-trip with Asher Day, and I'll forgive you for it. I really will. But it's OUR time now. No more excuses."

The sound of his hateful voice made her tense up. Carly pressed her lips together and willed herself to be casual. "Thank you, Wheeler. I knew you would understand. Can you come get me . . . now?"

He ignored her question. "How do you feel about being a mommy, Carly? Because I have the baby right here beside me. We would make a good family. You, me and our kid . . . living by the beach in Mexico. What do you think of that?"

"Sounds really lovely, Wheeler," Carly managed, choking back revulsion. "And I'm sorry. Again . . . I really mean it. I've learned my lesson and all I want is you. When can you come and get me?"

"Right now, girl. Hell, tell me where you are and I'll be there as fast as I can," Wheeler slurred. He belched. "Sorry 'bout that. My stomach hurts and I've had a rough day. Spent most of it in the bathroom."

Carly just managed not to make a sound of disgust. She forced a giggle. "That's OK, lover boy. Come to the clearing above town. You know . . . the one next to the cliff directly above the hotel. There's a back road leading right to me."

"I know exactly where it is," he grunted. "And you better be alone. I don't want sissy boy director there. I know he's your best friend and all, but you've gotta say goodbye to him . . . and hello to a *real* man."

"Oh, I'm all alone, baby. Just little ol' me waiting here for you." Carly looked up at Bruce who nodded in encouragement. "Hurry up, now. It's going to be dark soon, and I can't wait to see your handsome face."

"I'll just bet you can't. You always were one to be clawing all over me. That's okay, though. I'll let you claw all you want as soon as I get there. I'll see you in a bit, Carly girl . . . I'm only about thirty minutes away. Get your lips ready for some lovin'."

"Can't wait. Bye-bye, now!" Carly shuddered as she ended the call. "Nasty. The man is just foul." Walking over to Bruce, she scanned the tree line. Ross stood at the edge, waving. "At least I have moral support. How'd I do?"

"Fantastic. I have to move to Ross's location now. You'll be fine, Carly." Bruce winked at her and began to gather up his equipment. "Don't forget, there are six more agents surrounding the location. And let's see the distress signal one more time."

Carly raised her left arm as if stretching and pointed toward the sky. "Okay?"

"Yep. Good luck, good lookin'." Bruce winked and started jogging for the trees.

She shivered a little and sat down on a large, flat rock. This was going to be nerve-wracking, but at least she was safe. She took several deep breaths and looked up at the pink-tinged horizon. Above it, dusky clouds loomed. The sun was setting in the darkening sky and up there, hundreds of miles away, Asher was in a plane, flying to his wife.

*

Marilyn let out a shriek. "*Nicky.* You mean to tell me all this happened while I was in my costume fitting?" She gave his face a light smack.

"Look, woman. I didn't know, either. Ross just called me. And you were down at the costume shop for hours. I just assumed that you and Nancy were dishing dirt."

"We were," Marilyn retorted, waving her ruby red nails in the air. "Little Anne needed some pointers on how to reel Buddy in and we got sidetracked adjusting her corset. Then we worked on Carly's dress for opening night. God, it's gorgeous. I guess I lost track of time."

Nicky shook his head and sat down on the bed. "Women," he muttered. "Well, what are we going to do now?"

"Help, of course," Marilyn answered as she perched her negligee-clad hip next to him. "I don't care if the FBI thinks they have it under control . . . this Wheeler is a slimy, sneaky son of a bitch. They need backup."

Nicky snorted. "Backup from us? The queen of melodrama and her toothpaste commercial boyfriend?"

"You did not just say that." Marilyn widened her eyes and shoved Nicky back on the pillows. She climbed on top of him and shook a finger in his face. "We are very helpful. You kicked his ass last time. And I have a brilliant plan. So we're going to do our duty. No more arguing, young man."

Nicky looked up at her and sighed. "Yes, ma'am."

"Now give me a kiss and put your camouflage back on," Marilyn commanded.

"Aww, do I have to wear that again? I looked like a stalker," he complained even as he gave a suggestive shift underneath her.

Marilyn threw her head back and laughed. "You might have, but it was sexy. And you know it was sexy. Now hurry up. I have to change, too." She leaned down and fastened her mouth to his. Nicky's hands slid up her ample hips and she smacked at them, ending the kiss. "NO. Not right now. Good Lord, Nicky . . . at a time like this." She frowned.

Nicky ran long fingers through his hair. "Then why do you tempt me like that? Get up," he grunted, shoving her to the side. He walked to a dresser, stripped his shirt off and began rummaging for the camouflage clothing. "So tell me about this plan, woman."

Lounging on the pillows, Marilyn examined her nails. "Here's the deal. You go and sneak up to the woods where Ross is. But you should probably call him and tell him first so that the FBI doesn't shoot you by accident." She gave a deep laugh as Nicky raised an eyebrow. "Okay, okay, that wasn't funny. Anyway, I will stay here. As soon as you get up there and you see Wheeler pull into the clearing, text me so I will know. Then I'll call him to distract him."

Nicky shrugged out of his jeans and put a hand on a muscular hip. "Huh? If you're staying here, why do you need to change clothes? And what are you going to say to him, anyway?"

"Darling. You know I need a new outfit for each new occasion," she said answered, "And I'm going to whisper sweet nothings in his ear . . . Marilyn style." She chuckled and struck a pose.

"You mean it's going to be X-rated," Nicky muttered. "So, what am I supposed to do . . . just hang out in the woods?"

"Yes. Unless it gets out of hand . . . and then you and Ross can decide what you want to do, I guess." She waved her hand in the air.

Nicky pulled on his camo pants and swaggered toward the bed. "I actually get to make up my own mind?"

Marilyn grinned. "Of course, sexy. Now put a shirt on before you get me all distracted."

Nicky placed a hand on one of her thighs and leaned in. "Here's the real deal, then. I will call Ross and tell him about your plan, but don't expect him to go for it. This is the FBI's operation and I really don't think that our last minute help is going to be wanted."

"Why do you constantly have to suck the adventure right out of my life, Nicky?" Marilyn pouted.

"Because one of us has to be the adult in this relationship, darling," Nicky replied with authority. His hand slid farther up her thigh and she gasped, grasping him by the belt buckle. He chuckled and lowered his face to hers, stopping right before their lips touched. "NO. Not right now. Good Lord, Marilyn . . . at a time like this," he said.

Chuckling again at her frustrated shriek, he pulled on a shirt, sat on the edge of the bed and dialed Ross's number. As it rung through, he glanced over at Marilyn. "I'm only doing this for you so you won't cut me off later."

"Cut you off? Why, whatever do you mean, sweetie?" Marilyn batted her eyes.

"You know good and well what I mean, woman. Leave me all frustrated. It's not like you've never done it before and each time I'm forced to—Hello? Ross. How's it going? Uh-huh. Yep. We're fine here; I'm just checking in to see if you need my help. No? Okay then, that's cool . . . "

Marilyn sat up and punched his shoulder. "*Ow*. Damn, woman. Look Ross, Marilyn has a plan. Yeah, I know . . . but I think it might actually help."

Marilyn rolled her eyes and flopped back on the pillows. Nicky winked at her as he continued to talk. "This is it. I will go up and stick with you, and she's gonna stay down here. Yeah, I know. Good thing. Anyway, her plan is for me to text her when Wheeler gets there. Then she's gonna call him and distract him with . . . um . . . trash talk. No, not insults. That would just piss him off. The *other* kind of trash talk." Nicky chuckled and reached out to massage Marilyn's foot. "She's good at it, believe me. So you think they'll go for it? Sure, I'll hang on."

Marilyn sat up and looked at him. "Does he like my plan?"

"Hold you horses, woman!" He glared at her, but continued to rub her foot, his hand sliding up the calf. She chortled and wiggled her bright red toenails.

Nicky's face broke into a grin. "That's great. Yep. I'll be up there as fast as I can climb. And for God's sake, Ross, make sure the agents know I'm on my way. Getting picked off by a sniper is not how I plan to spend my evening." He licked his lips and glanced at Marilyn. "I have better things to do."

*

Carly gave a worried glance to the sky as the sun slipped past the horizon. It was almost completely dark now and she was having trouble controlling the panicky feeling in her stomach. Forcing herself to stand still, she clasped her shaking hands over her middle and closed her eyes. But her mind wouldn't obey. What if he tried to kiss her? Or worse, what if he hit her? She knew that physically, she was no match for Wheeler's strength. Even if he was a slobbering drunk, he still outweighed her by a good fifty pounds and was a foot taller, too.

The wind picked up and blew her hair around her face. She batted it away, but it flew back and landed in her open mouth. This was not good. She needed to be able to see, dammit. Irritated, she stood up and began searching her pockets for a barrette. The wind was blowing harder now and what she could see of the sky looked ominous. Great. Not only was her hair flying around like snakes on Medusa's head, but it was going to storm, too.

She bent over, grabbed her hair and separated it into two sections, tying them in a tight knot at the back. It hurt and it wouldn't stay for long, but at least she had to try. A rumble in the distance made head snap up. A truck. She could hear a truck approaching. Quickly, she drew in a deep breath and whispered to the microphone, "He's here. Oh, God. I hope you can see me, Bruce. It's dark. And Wheeler's here."

The sound grew louder and it was accompanied by the blare of heavy metal music. A glow of light seeped through the tree line and seconds later, headlights bounced over the clearing just as the first fat drops of rain began to fall. Carly moaned as she watched the truck swerve into the clearing. Wheeler was smashed, no question about it. Well, she would just have to use that to her advantage as much as possible. She straightened her spine and waved at him, shading her eyes from the glare of the headlights.

The truck stopped with a jerk and Wheeler slowly folded

himself out, staggering as he stepped onto the rocky ground. Carly sighed in relief when she realized he didn't intend to turn off the headlights. With the truck door still open, the dome light on the inside was on as well. "Hey, lover boy," she called out. "It just started raining. You have excellent timing. My hero."

Hitching up his belt, Wheeler stumbled toward her, a pint bottle in his hand. "Of course I'm your hero. I rescued you once before. Although I was beginnin' to think you'd forgot all about that day." He frowned and belched a cloud of alcoholic fumes into Carly's face. She flinched just a little, but managed to paste a smile on her face and wink at him.

"Wheeler, you'll always be my hero, honey." She tugged at his sleeve and motioned to the truck. "I want to go see the baby you brought for me. Is it cute?"

He pulled his arm away with a jerk. "I'm not stupid, Carly girl. You know 'xactly who the baby is. It's your baby. I was just keepin' it for you, like you asked me to. And you know that I know that it's the only way I could get you to come to me," he muttered and then staggered again. "I'm not stupid." He stared at her and then raised the bottle to his lips, draining it. He threw the bottle and it shattered on a rock, making popping sounds that echoed through the clearing. Narrowing his eyes, he drew closer to her and grabbed her rain-slicked arms.

Carly gulped back the fear rising in her throat. This was going to be harder than she thought. Not only did she have to stall him, but she had to get him to admit out loud that he had kidnapped the child. And terrorized and vandalized Ruby Spring. Pressing her lips together, she gently loosened her arms and wiped the rain out of her eyes. She leaned into him. "Oh, honey. The baby doesn't matter to me. Only you do. The way you've fought for me these past few weeks has been so . . . well . . . so romantic," she said with a forced sigh.

He continued to stare. "Whatta ya mean, fought for you?"

"You know . . . doing things to make people around here mad . . . " she trailed off, and ran a hand down his damp shirt.

"You're up to something, girl. I don't know what it is, but I definitely don't like it." Wheeler grabbed her wrist and jerked it away from his body. His face split into a menacing grin, revealing the jagged stump of his broken front tooth. Carly recoiled before she could stop herself, but not before Wheeler saw her reaction. His grip tightened on her wrist and he narrowed his eyes. "Yeah, I'm real pretty. I know it. But you'll get used to it, girl. You have no choice."

"Who did this to you, baby? Who did this?" Carly wailed, summoning any convincing acting skills that inhabited her shaking body. She reached up with her free hand and touched his cracked, blood-dried lips. "My poor baby."

Confusion flashed through Wheeler's glazed eyes and he loosened his hold on her wrist. "Yeah, well . . . the other guy looks pretty bad, too," he said, relenting. "Do you think I'm ugly now, Carly?"

The ugliest, nastiest, most repulsive human being on the face of the planet, she thought as she opened her mouth to make soothing sounds. "No. No, of course not, Wheeler. You're still my hot cop, right?" She forced herself to giggle.

He let go of her wrist and leaned on the hood of the truck. "Okay. I believe you."

Carly breathed out and relaxed her body. This wasn't so bad. She'd have his confession in a matter of minutes. Her confidence gaining, she squeezed his shoulder and stepped around him to peer in the passenger side window. *Please let the baby be okay.* She pressed her face to the steamed-up glass. It was hard to see, but she spied the edge of a car seat, new, with tags still attached. She leaned closer and breathed out. He was in there, a little sleeping angel. So sweet. She just had to figure out a way to get him away from here and back to safety.

All of a sudden, she shrieked as Wheeler's rough arms grabbed her around the middle. He jerked her backward against his chest and fisted his hand in her hair. She gasped and he whispered, his bloody lips on her ear, "I changed my mind. I don't trust you for one second, bitch."

Still holding her, he stumbled to the back of his truck and pulled out a crowbar. Chuckling, he gave her a vicious squeeze. "You're not going anywhere, Carly girl. Not 'till you explain some things to me."

Pushing her in front of him, he grabbed the back of her neck and marched her to the front of the truck. Rain ran in rivulets down Carly's face, blurring her vision. Breath seared in her lungs.

Wheeler shook her. "Who's the boss?" he demanded.

"You are," she whispered.

"Damn straight," he retorted, and then swung the crowbar at the headlights. With two crunches of breaking plastic, the clearing plummeted into darkness.

"Now nobody can see us. It's just you and me, Carly."

She screamed.

Chapter Twenty-One

"What's Carly saying, Nicky?" Marilyn demanded.

"Marilyn, I'm trying to concentrate. It's hard to hear out here . . . it is raining, you know. And I don't have time to give you a play by play. Just hang up the damn phone and call Wheeler, for God's sake," Nicky retorted as he squatted in the underbrush. The wind was howling now and he could barely make out the dim shapes up ahead in the clearing. Carly was in trouble; he had seen Wheeler smash out the headlights . . . he had heard her scream. But he wasn't about to let Marilyn know that. Nicky glanced over at Ross, who stood stock still, his face frozen in fear.

"Is she hurt? Did he hit her?" Marilyn continued, "If he did then, by God, I'll rip that son of a bitch a new . . . "

"Marilyn, hang up the phone and call Wheeler *right now*," Nicky commanded through gritted teeth. He heard her gasp and then the call ended. Not ten seconds later, the faint, shrill sound of a phone ringing echoed through the clearing.

*

Wheeler cursed and loosened his hold on Carly's neck. "Dammit," he whined, fumbling for his phone. "Who is this?" His head snapped back. "Ow! God damn, you have a loud voice. I'm puttin' you on speaker. Hang on." He squinted at the brightly lit screen and pushed a button.

Carly's eyes widened when she heard Marilyn's characteristic deep laugh rumble out of the device. She swallowed and willed herself to remain still.

"Mmmmm, ees this Wheeler Barstow?" Marilyn purred in a

French accent.

He sighed. "Yes, it is. I'm busy. Who is this and whadda ya want, bitch?"

"I want lots of things . . . but most of all, I want a date with vous," she said with a moan.

"Huh?" Wheeler let Carly go and leaned on the truck. "Who the hell are you?"

"I am your deepest fan-ta-see come true," Marilyn answered. "Let me just tell you zis . . . your boss . . . hees name is . . . ah, Joe, right? Well, zis Joe knows that you have been going through a hard time lately and he wants you to have a *good* time instead. A very good time. Let me show you a good time, Wheeler. Please? I want to soooo badly." Marilyn panted.

Carly saw the confusion on Wheeler's face. It was her opportunity, and she sneaked around the back of the truck on shaking legs. If she could just make it into the driver's seat without Wheeler seeing . . .

After a long wheezing pause, Wheeler spoke up. "You're a whore? Joe ordered me a hooker?" He giggled. "Unbelievable. That asshole has the worst timing in the world. Believe me, baby . . . if this was any other night I'd meet you and we could do something about it, but I'm kinda busy right now."

"Aw, come on ba-bee . . . you have me for zee entire night . . . and I can do things that will make your toes simp-lee curl. Mmmmmm."

Pressing her lips together, Carly slid into the cracked, old driver's seat of the idling truck. Glancing at Wheeler through the windshield, she reached back and touched little Daniel's face. He was warm and breathing. She sighed in relief and reached for the ignition. The truck jolted as Wheeler slumped backward onto the hood. She sucked in a breath, listening, although she couldn't hear well over the rumble of the engine.

Wheeler let out an abrasive laugh. "You sound like you could show me a good time, so . . . well, I have to do something first . . . get rid of some people and then I'll meet you. But you better be damn good, lady. Real good. Or else you'll be sorry. Where are we gonna meet?"

"How about zee bar at zee base of the road to Ruby Spring, sexy monsieur?"

"Fine," Wheeler said with a grunt, "And you better be there or I'll be pissed. Just wait for me . . . it might take a while."

"That's okay, dahling. I can't wait to touch you. Au revoir!"

*

In the dim light, Carly's heart sank as she saw Wheeler snap his phone shut. Should she just put the truck in reverse and back up? He would probably fall. But what if he didn't and she couldn't get the door closed and he grabbed her as the truck was moving? She wasn't stupid or cruel enough to just put the truck in drive and step on the gas.

Behind her, the baby started to fuss. She shushed him in a quiet voice and stared at Wheeler. To her horror, he turned around. Stared at her. Then slammed his fist on the hood of the truck. Eyes wide, Carly gripped the gear shifter and froze. Oh God. She had to make a decision.

Why hadn't she sent the distress signal? It was too late now, though, and her mind went blank as Wheeler lurched forward. He gripped the hood with one hand and pulled himself toward the driver's side of the truck. *Shit!* She couldn't run him over. Could she? She slammed the door closed. It was then that she realized the window was rolled down.

Wheeler's cell phone rang again. "What?" he yelled into it, slapping his hand down on the hood for balance. "Look, whore, I told you I'd meet you in a little while. What the hell do you want now?" Wheeler answered.

Carly eased the gearshift into reverse. Her heart hammered in her chest. Wheeler was only inches from the driver side window, leaned over the hood, his head turned away from her. The baby let out a whimper. And then began to cry in earnest. She reached for the handle to roll up the window. It stuck halfway up and her slippery fingers yanked in desperation. Wheeler took a step closer and wrapped his free hand around the side mirror on the door.

He chuckled into the phone. "Look, hon, I can't believe I'm saying this . . . but tell Joe I'm gonna have to take a rain check on your . . . uh . . . services. I've got too much shit to deal with right now and on top of it my mouth hurts like a son of a bitch."

Wheeler turned and touched his upper lip. Carly's breath caught as he stared straight into her eyes. She had to do it. The fact that he hadn't actually admitted to kidnapping was pointless now. If she didn't get out of there soon, he'd hurt her. And the baby.

Gritting her teeth, she slammed down on the gas. The truck lurched backward and instantly stalled. Carly's heart sank as Wheeler, who had been knocked to the ground by the sudden movement, scrambled to his feet, growling. Lightning flashed and in that instant she saw a thin line of red spittle hanging from his lips. His eyes were crazy. Absolutely crazy.

Just as he reached for the driver's side door, Carly's fingers reached the lock button. He pulled up on the door handle repeatedly.

"Bitch. Bitch!" he screamed, reaching over the top of the half-open window.

Carly leaned away from his clutching fingers and tried the ignition again. A crack of thunder sounded and another burst of lightning illuminated the sky. And then Wheeler disappeared. She peered into the driving rain, hoping for one more flash in sky. It didn't happen. Where the hell had he gone?

In the back, little Daniel wailed. Carly reached back and gently squeezed his tiny foot. The truck engine wouldn't turn over. And she couldn't make the distress signal without rolling down the window all the way. In fact . . . how would the agents see her anyway? It was dark now, and the rain was beating down in earnest.

Her thoughts flickered to Asher. Both anger and love swelled within her. Would she see him again? Did she want to? The only thing she was certain of was that it couldn't end like this between them. And it would kill him if something happened to the baby. She simply had to get out of there. She gritted her teeth once more and turned the key. *Nothing.* Raking her fingers through her damp hair, she cursed and pounded on the steering wheel. She must have flooded the truck when she tried to back up.

In a panic, Carly yanked down the neck of her shirt and spoke into the microphone attached to her bra strap. "I need help. It's out of control. He's out of control. Come get me." She waited for what seemed like forever. There was no sound aside from the crying baby and the driving rain.

"Ross? Guys, *please.* Hurry!" She looked out of the window, trying in vain to see any moving shape coming from the trees. *Nothing.*

Suddenly, a tree branch crashed through the passenger window. Carly screamed as it slammed into her right arm and scraped alongside her neck. She watched in horror as Wheeler's hand reached into the gaping hole of the window to unlock the door. *Oh my God.*

Acting on instinct, Carly wrenched the tree branch away and began to beat his hand with it as hard as she could. He howled, but didn't give up. Pain, sharp and terrible, seared through her injured arm. The branch began to slip away. Jerking it from her grasp, Wheeler reached farther into the truck and grabbed her hurt arm and twisted. With his other hand, he unlocked the door.

Carly screamed and reached for her own door. She couldn't leave the baby. But she couldn't let Wheeler get into the truck, either. Leaning down, she bit into his hand as hard as she could. Gasping, he let go of her arm and with shaking, fumbling hands, she tried the key again.

The engine roared to life and Carly stepped on the gas. A sickening thud sounded outside the window as she backed up over the rain-slick mud and grass. *Oh hell.* She had hit him. Not stopping to see if it was true, she threw the truck into drive, fishtailing in the muddy earth.

She drove for the trees, wind and rain whipping through the broken window; little Daniel howling in the back seat. *Please, please,* she thought as she peered through the dark. *Please let them be there.* Why hadn't they come for her? What the hell was going on? Carly accelerated the truck and forced herself to concentrate on the tree line. It was a smudge of gray on the horizon. She was driving blind with no headlights.

The trees should be closer. Carly frowned. The guys weren't that far away. Maybe she'd misjudged it. Carly craned her neck and peered out the passenger window. Dark rain. She looked out of her own window. Nothing but blackness. Training her eyes on the windshield again, she screamed as realization hit her. She was headed for the cliff.

*

Asher gritted his teeth as he unfolded his tall frame from the airplane seat. Stretching, he reached into the overhead compartment and grabbed his old leather traveling bag. Jet lag was already beginning to take hold of him, but he had to remain alert until he dealt with Miranda. After stumbling through the line at customs, he walked outside and breathed in the foggy Parisian air.

A cab idling nearby caught his attention and he raised his hand to hail it. Easing into the backseat, he threw his bag on the seat and cleared his throat. "L'hotel De Grace, sil-vous plâit." The car lurched forward and Asher leaned his head back, closing his eyes. He awoke at the sound of the driver's hoarse voice.

"We are here, Monsieur."

"Merci," Asher replied, shoving three twenty dollar bills at the man.

"But Monsieur . . . "

"I didn't have time to stop at the currency exchange. Please just deal with it," Asher mumbled as he grabbed his bag, jumped out and slammed the door.

He squinted up at the hotel in the early morning light. Miranda was in there. He sighed in resolution and then pushed open the heavy front door. After stopping to get her room number, he stepped on the elevator and fumbled in his bag. Pulling out the divorce papers, he clenched them in his hands, his stomach plummeting at the thought of facing his wife again.

Asher assumed it had all been over months ago, but right after leaving New York for Ruby Spring, his lawyers had notified him that Miranda hadn't signed the papers after all. Instead, she had emptied their bank account and shipped all of his newest paintings, the ones intended for his upcoming gallery show, out of the country. Only hours later, she boarded a plane and followed them. And then disappeared. Until the phone call from Paris during the publicity interview in Albuquerque, he hadn't known where she was.

He stepped off the elevator and walked down the hall to her room, and then rapped on the door sharply. Nobody answered. Growling, Asher pounded on the door. Just like her to keep him waiting. She *knew* he was out there.

"Miranda. Open the damn door," he bellowed.

The door swung open, and there she stood, all slutty five-feet-eleven inches of her . . . clad only in a pair of sheer black panties. Her hipbones jutted above them and her ribs were visible. She raised her thin arms to push back a long fall of brassy red hair.

"Hello, husband," she said, her glance flicking over his wrinkled linen suit. "Dressed up to drink mint juleps, I see."

Not answering, Asher pushed past her. "Where are my paintings?"

"Safe," she murmured, following him into the room.

"For God's sake, shut the door. You're mostly naked."

"You noticed." Miranda sauntered to the door and closed it. Turning, she walked toward Asher with a gleam in her eyes and sat on the edge of the bed, crossing her long legs. "I knew you would."

He glanced at her, noting her pallid complexion and thick eye makeup. She looked like a zombie. The elegance she'd exuded when they'd first met had been a sham. She was nothing but a gold-digging piece of trash. And she was twenty pounds underweight. "I never thought I'd say this to you . . . not in a million years . . . but you are pathetic, Miranda."

She gave a harsh laugh. "Pathetic? How ironic. I was about to say the same thing to you. By the way . . . who is Carly?"

Asher stiffened.

Miranda's eyes lit up. "Ohhhh. Mmm-hmm. I see. You've gone and found yourself a piece of meat while we were having our little spat. That's fine with me. I did the same, of course." She examined her nails.

"Carly is not meat and I could care less what you do or have done, Miranda. I just want two things. My paintings and your signature."

"Aww. Why don't you ask for something else, baby? Because those are the two things I can't give you." She uncrossed her legs and opened them a few inches.

Asher shook his head in disgust. "Again. Pathetic. Sign the divorce papers and tell me where my paintings are. Now."

Miranda re-crossed her legs and glared at him. "I want half."

"Half of what?"

"Your assets, of course," she replied, rising to stand close to him. She reached out to cup his crotch.

Asher pulled her hand away. "You just don't get it, do you? I find you repulsive. Any feelings, physical or otherwise, I had for you faded fast when I realized the mistake I made in marrying someone like you."

Miranda gasped. "Like me? You didn't seem to mind *me* when I was lying naked on a platform, modeling for one of your stupid paintings. It wasn't so long ago that I had you begging. Yes, *begging* me to spread my legs."

Asher raised an eyebrow. "Stupid paintings?"

"You heard me. Stupid." Miranda shot back, "When I sat for you, you painted me as a circus freak."

"It's called abstract—"

"Who cares? I don't give a damn about your abstract art . . . or any art, for that matter. I just want half."

"Then sign the papers. And sure, you can have half. Anything to get you off my back." Asher rubbed his forehead.

A satisfied look on her gaunt face, Miranda reached for a pen and grabbed the papers out his hands. "Good. You're doing the right thing, lover. And as soon as these are filed and I have my money, I'll tell you where the paintings are." She scrawled her signature at the bottom of several pages.

"Fine," Asher mumbled as he sat down on the bed and reached for the phone on the nightstand.

"Who are you calling?" Miranda asked.

"We need copies of these," he answered.

Miranda grinned. "Yeah, copies of my soon-to-be fortune. Well, what's left of it. I spent a lot already."

"Oui, hello? We are ready," Asher said and replaced the receiver.

"Wow, you had this all planned? I'm almost insulted how quickly you want to get rid of me," She licked the corner of her mouth. "Almost."

Asher reached for his bag and pulled out another set of papers. "Sign these too. Originals for my lawyers."

"With pleasure, Baby." Miranda sat close to him and brushed his chest with her hand as she reached for the folder. "Mmm, it's a shame we couldn't work it out, Asher. You were always a good lay."

"And you were always a crude bitch. I just wish I realized it sooner. Put on a shirt, Miranda. They will be here any minute."

"They? You mean the bellman?" Miranda laughed as she signed her name. "Oh, baby . . . he's seen me with less on that I have right now . . . and at a pretty close distance, I might add."

Asher shook his head and crossed the room to rummage through a drawer. Finding a slinky dress, he tossed it to her. "Could you just tell me one thing, Miranda?"

"What's that, baby?" she replied as she wiggled into the dress.

"Why did you steal my paintings and run for Europe?"

She shrugged. "Because, Asher, they turned out to be more valuable than you were." With a bitter laugh, she crossed the room to stand in front of him. "And I have discovered that the only thing I can trust in life is money."

Asher narrowed his eyes. "I never gave you a reason not to trust *me*. You're the one who slept with anything that moved, even after we were married." he said.

Miranda shrugged again. "You weren't enough for me."

"I never gave you a reason not to trust me," Asher repeated.

"Yes, you *did*," she shouted, "I could see it in your eyes the last few weeks we were together. You thought that I was a slut. That I was common. That I was a bitch and a whore and you were sorry you married me so quickly. Right? It's true, isn't it?" She was screaming now, her lovely eyes bulging, her flawless face red.

Asher stared at her in silence. "Yes," he finally said. "Yes . . . I was a fool to be blinded by your beauty, Miranda. An utter fool. Because you turned so ugly so fast."

Tears shone in her eyes and she clenched her trembling hands. "I knew it. So I took the paintings and ran. I had to have something. You wanted to divorce me . . . and after only two months of marriage. What made you think I was so stupid? I was never going to sign those papers. Asher, you're a bastard."

"You may say that now, but you'll certainly believe it soon,"

A sharp knock sounded at the door.

"What?" Miranda yelled.

"Open the door, Madame," said a deep voice on the other side.

Miranda stalked to the door and yanked it open.

"What the fuck?"

Four uniformed officers stood in the hallway.

"Miranda Day, you are under arrest for international trafficking."

She gasped in shock and turned a murderous glare on Asher.

"I'll kill you," she whispered.

He gave her a sad smile. "Miranda, after this moment, you will never see me again. And by the way . . . according to the divorce papers, I'm penniless. I sold everything I had left and gave the money to charity. I barely had the cash to cover my plane ticket to Paris and back. Of course, that won't be true after I recover what paintings you didn't sell, but you'll be in prison by then. Have a nice day."

He shook the hand of one of the officers, grabbed his bag, walked out the door and into the hallway.

"*Wait,*" she screamed. "I'll give your paintings back. Asher . . . Asher . . . please." Her voice caught on a sob.

He turned around and stared at her. Her lovely face was splotched red and the expensive dress hung like a sack on her thin frame.

"I have three conditions."

"Anything . . . just . . . please. I can't go to jail," she pleaded, wiping a thick track of wet mascara from her cheek.

"Tell me where my paintings are. Don't contest the divorce. Never contact me again."

"Oh. O . . . o . . . okay," she hiccoughed, shrugging off the hand of the officer holding her. She smiled at the man and then examined his body with her eyes.

"You are not pressing charges now, Monsieur?" the officer asked, shifting under Miranda's gaze.

Asher didn't answer him. "Miranda, I am not joking. Tell me where they are. Right now. Or I swear to God you're going to prison."

Eyes wide, she glanced backward through the open hotel room door. Her gaze rested on the bed. "Um, they're under there," she offered.

Asher strode past her back into the room and jerked up the duvet. The edge of a frame peeked out from under the bed. Reaching down, he pulled on it. Six more rolled up canvasses slid out as well.

"Where's the rest?"

"In the shower." Miranda cowered in the doorway, her arms limp by her sides.

"Nice," he commented and retrieved the rest of his paintings. They were still intact in frames. He ripped a sheet from the bed and began to wrap them up, but hesitated. A small smile played at the corners of his lips. Sifting through the stack, he retrieved one, stood it on the bed and then rewrapped the rest.

"A parting gift," he said and gestured toward the abstract nude propped on the pillows. "Because you love this one so much." He grabbed his bag, lifted the bundle of paintings and headed for the door, stopping only to glance at Miranda one last time. She stared at him in loathing.

"Don't cross me, Miranda. You know what will happen if you even try," he said in an even voice. "Oh, and by the way . . . you could use a bra."

She gasped and her hand flashed out to slap him. The officer standing next to her caught it in midair.

"It's over, Madame," he said.

"Thank God," Asher muttered as he headed for the elevator.

Chapter Twenty-Two

"Shit," whispered Ross as he peered into the darkness, listening to the sound of breaking glass. A second later, he heard screams, and the truck engine roaring to life. And finally, a sickening thud. Jumping up from the ground, he groped in the darkness for Nicky's arm to pull the other man to his feet, but he was already running into the clearing.

"Someone got run over. Oh my *God*," Nicky flung over his shoulder.

At the same instant, the FBI agents emerged from the trees carrying rifles, black figures in the rainy darkness. They ran for the truck, their weapons ready.

Ross stood rooted in fear, watching in horror as the sky illuminated with a crack of thunder and a flash of lightning. The truck was headed for a cliff. Four shots sounded in the night, the exploding noise ricocheting through the clearing.

Why couldn't he move?

Another burst of lightning flashed. The truck was out of control, bumping along the uneven grass, its tires shot to ribbons. A second later, it rolled over and landed with a crash next to a boulder, only inches from the cliff.

Ross heard the determined yelling of an agent giving orders. "Go. GO!"

Flashlights snapped on and the agents swarmed the truck. He saw the shape of Carly's body inside. It wasn't moving. Ross found his feet again. Sprinting, he ran, slipping on the wet grass and reached the cluster of men holding rifles on the wrecked vehicle. One of them, close to his size, grabbed his shoulders and held him back.

"Stay back, sir."

"Carly's in there. The baby. Carly. Don't shoot . . . God, don't shoot."

"We know that, sir. Just let us do our jobs."

Ross struggled against his strong grasp. "Then why the guns?"

"We have not secured the area, sir."

"What do you mean, not secured?" Ross demanded, "You're just going to scare the shit out of her."

"The suspect is not in custody. We are not secured. So let me do my job, sir," the agent replied.

"Good God . . . she must have hit him with the truck," Ross muttered, allowing the agent to push him backward.

The agent pushed again, more gently this time. "Go back to the trees until we say we are clear, Ross."

"I need to see Carly," he replied through his teeth, rooted to the ground.

"No."

"But—wait. How do you know my name?"

The agent approached him, looming near. He lowered his voice. "Look man, what is it going to take to get you to follow my orders? You're hampering the mission. Can't you understand that?" His voice was deep and soothing as he placed his hand on Ross's chest.

Ross became aware of the man's breath near his ear. It felt good and he shivered in spite of his anxiety. What the hell was wrong with him? Feeling lust at a time like this? The guy was probably straight and would be totally pissed if he knew, too. He shoved the large hand away from his shoulder. "Fine."

"All secure here," came a shout from near the truck.

The agent glanced backward and stepped closer to Ross. "Look. I'm sorry if I pissed you off, but I had to do my job." He gave a small smile. "My name is Bruce. When all of this shit blows over, I'd like to make it up to you." He squeezed Ross's shoulder and walked back to the wreck. Stunned, Ross followed him.

"Is the baby okay?" Carly's voice was muffled, but strong.

"Ma'am, just hold still so we can cut this seatbelt—

"I'm not a ma'am . . . I'm a *miss*," she corrected. "Dammit, don't make me sound so old."

Ross chuckled, his eyes bright with unshed tears. All flashlights trained on the truck as an agent lifted Carly out and laid her gently on the ground. A scowling, tiny Daniel in the car seat followed and was placed next to her.

"It's all over now, Miss," the agent said.

"Thank God," she breathed, reaching a hand toward the car seat. "He's OK?"

"Yes ma'am. We're getting paramedics to make sure. Just be still until they arrive."

All was quiet for a few seconds and Ross crouched on the ground next to her. "You all right, partner?" he whispered.

She peered at him in the dim light. "Do I have any cuts on my face?"

"No, why?"

She shrugged and cradled her right arm. "Just didn't want to end up disfigured over an asshole like Wheeler."

Ross's answering chuckle was cut off by a shout in the distance. Instantly, the agents mobilized.

"Fuck you, surfer. And your fat whore, too," Wheeler's screaming voice sent a surge of alarm through Ross's body. He knelt beside Carly and took her in his arms.

"Oh my God," Carly whispered.

The baby began to cry again.

Ross pulled the car seat next to his hip and stroked the baby's head. "Shh." He leaned down and placed a kiss on Carly's forehead. "That goes for you, too. If Wheeler hears your voice, he'll go even crazier. Is your arm hurt, sweetie?"

"Maybe. I don't know. But . . . Ross . . . I hit him with a moving vehicle. He should be unconscious," she said.

"The FBI can handle it, Carly."

A shot rang out in the distance, followed by a scream and a thud. Instinctively, Carly screamed, too.

"Agent down!" came a shout.

Ross clapped his hand over Carly's mouth and listened with sick apprehension to the escalating argument in the darkness.

Wheeler's drunken shout reverberated through the clearing. "Stay the fuck away from me. All of you are crazy. I'm a cop. You can't shoot another cop. Stand down."

"*You* shot another cop, you worthless bastard," came Nicky's answering shout, "Now let go of me before I tear your balls off."

"The only thing that's gonna be torn off is your face, surfer. You're the one with a gun pointed at your head."

"Lower your weapon, Barstow. Let the hostage go," an agent shouted.

"That's Bruce," murmured Ross. He pressed his lips together.

Carly frowned. "How do you . . ."

He waved her away. "Just stay still."

*

"I'm not lowering my weapon until you bring me my girl. Then you can have this blond bitch boy back." God *damn*, his whole body hurt. He needed to go home and go to bed. Shoving Nicky away from him but keeping the weapon trained on his head, Wheeler let out a laugh.

"Hey, bitch. You sure you ain't gay? You look like a pillow biter to me." Pain shot through his abdomen and his arm began to shake.

"What the hell does that matter?" asked Nicky.

Surfer boy didn't look concerned. *Why was he so calm?* Wheeler felt cold seep into his body.

"I don't like fags," he replied. Why did his own voice sound so far away? A choking cough clogged his throat and warmth flooded his mouth. Blood began seeping from his lips and he lowered his gun. "What the fuck?" He sank to the ground. "Jesus, she must have hit me harder that I thought she did."

Through the black spots in his vision, he watched as agents

swarmed around him. In seconds, he was thrown onto his stomach, his arms wrenched behind his back. His sight went black.

"I need an ambulance."

"You need a prison cell," someone answered.

Wheeler barely heard the voice. The only sensation he had was that of warm blood gushing out of his mouth and onto the ground in front of him. It pooled around his forehead. Then the darkness claimed him.

*

Two agents turned over Wheeler's body and trained a flashlight on his face. His bloodshot blue eyes stared at the sky. His bloody mouth was slack.

"Is he dead?" Nicky asked, rubbing his jaw where Wheeler had punched him minutes earlier.

"Yeah, man, I think so," answered Bruce as he squatted next to Wheeler's limp body. "What possessed you to come after him, anyway? That was really dangerous."

Nicky blew out a breath. "Hell, I don't know. I'm sorry but I didn't think . . . I just acted. I guess I assumed it was Carly who had been hit by the truck. I don't know. When I reached Wheeler, he was already on his feet, pulling a gun out of one of his boots." He squatted on the ground. "It happened really fast. I lunged for him and he knocked the shit out of me. Next thing I knew, I had a gun to my head." His cell phone rang and he reached for his pocket.

"Hi, Marilyn."

"Nicky, oh my God, we heard shots and then a crash and it sounded like lightning but I couldn't be sure and then Sophie said it was a car crashing and I knew that you had been run over and your leg severed and one of your eyes shot out and then you'd look like a pirate and in a way that's sexy, but please tell me that's not true," Marilyn shouted into the phone. The unmistakable sound of an ambulance whined in the background and she raised her voice above it. "But if you need an eye patch that's fine, I'll still love you."

Nicky held the phone away from his ear. "Nope. No pirates here. Love you too," he said, and then hung up on her still-chattering voice.

"Pirates?" Bruce asked.

"Never get involved with an actress." Nicky shook his head.

"Don't worry," Bruce said with a chuckle, holstering his weapon. He lowered his voice. "I don't shop in that aisle, man."

"Oh. Oh! Hey . . . I know someone who does," Nicky said.

"Ross? Already taken care of."

Nicky grinned and glanced over Bruce's shoulder. The siren was closer now and the sudden beam of headlights bounced off the mountains peaks as an ambulance made its way into the clearing. Two agents, supporting a third, raised their hands in greeting.

"Oh Jesus, I forgot about him. Is he OK?" Nicky asked.

Bruce snorted. "Yes. Wheeler barely grazed his leg. For his own protection, he stayed down, though."

"Oh. It all happened so fast," Nicky commented.

"It usually does man . . . it usually does."

"I would rather it *hadn't* happened altogether," Ross said as he approached the cluster of men.

"Hey," Bruce glanced at Ross and then away, a smile playing on his lips.

"Hey," Ross answered with a grin. "How long until we get out of here? Carly is kinda stressed. She's mumbling about eating her own weight in cheeseburgers and fifty cats eating her alive because she's stuck in a wheelchair." He rolled his eyes. "Can I take her home, please?"

"The EMTs have to check her over and if she and the baby are OK, then, yeah," Bruce replied, "We'll interview her later. We'll need to."

Holding his gaze for a moment, Ross cleared his throat and then turned to Nicky. "You all right?"

Nicky gave him a knowing grin and glanced at Bruce. "Yep. But Wheeler's not." Nicky pointed.

"Holy shit. He's dead." Ross backed away from the body. "Who shot him?"

"Nobody did," said Bruce, "He probably bled to death internally. She hit him really hard with that truck, you know."

Nicky watched as Ross walked over to Bruce and grabbed his arm. "No. No she didn't. As far as *she* knows, he was shot, okay?"

The ambulance pulled up next to them and provided enough light for Ross to search Bruce's impassive face.

"OK?" Ross repeated.

Bruce's expression hardened. "I don't lie," he said.

"You will this time. Knowing she killed someone . . . even him . . . would haunt her for the rest of her life. Why does she deserve that?" Ross's eyes pleaded with Bruce.

"She doesn't," answered Bruce after a long silence. He shifted his weight and pulled away from Ross. "Don't worry. She won't know." He turned away and walked back toward the ambulance.

"Thank you," Ross muttered at the retreating figure.

Nicky walked to Ross and pulled him into a bear hug. He looked to the sky. The rain was letting up and the stars floated behind translucent clouds. "And I know I don't say this much but thank *you*. For everything."

*

Daniel Day made soothing noises as he rocked his son. Reaching over to the porch railing, he grabbed a bottle and plunked it in the crying baby's mouth. The sobs ground to a halt.

"That was fast." Sophie pushed open the screen door and joined him on the sunny front porch of the hotel. She lowered herself into one of the rockers.

"Yeah. He was hungry. So am I," Daniel winked at his wife. God, she was gorgeous.

"Ew," she replied. "How can you think about that at a time like this?"

"At a time like what? Wheeler's been dead for almost a week. The show is spectacular and it opens tonight. Asher is back and he seems like he's going to be okay . . . " he trailed off.

"Maybe." Sophie gave him an appraising look.

"Maybe he's going to be okay . . . or maybe we can go downstairs?" Daniel asked, waggling his eyebrows.

"Maybe to both, but it will have to be later." Taking their son from his arms, she stood up and walked back to the doorway. "I need to feed him. And *you* still need to go down to the costume shop to be fitted for your opening night outfit."

"Aw, hell . . . I don't want to put all those itchy clothes on," Daniel whined.

"Hmm. You never know what a handsome man dressed like an old west gunslinger will discover in his bed later tonight. Could be that some women find that look completely irresistible," Sophie uttered from the lobby before letting the screen door bang shut.

Daniel's eyes widened. "I'm going," he muttered to himself and picked up his crutches. He hobbled down the street and opened the door to the hardware store.

"Nancy?"

"I'm back here, Daniel. But hang on a sec; I need to finish with Carly."

Daniel plopped down on a window seat. "Fine, but I need to you make me look like the most dangerous gunslinger in Wild West history, okay?"

"Already taken care of," Nancy called. "You want to see Carly?"

"Sure." Daniel pushed aside a rack of clothing and headed for the back of the store. On a makeshift platform covered with shag carpeting, Carly stood, glaring into the mirror. Her right arm was in a cast, but she looked beautiful.

"Hey," she greeted him in a dull tone. "This thing itches." She scratched around the edge of the cast.

"You are preaching to the choir, sister." He shifted a crutch so he could pat her good arm. "At least yours is just a hairline fracture."

She sighed. "Yeah and I was hoping I wouldn't have to have a cast . . . but I guess it's for the best."

"I didn't want a cast either, but the doctor told me it was for the best, too."

Bursting into laughter, Carly surveyed him. "Daniel, your thigh bone was practically poking through the skin. Of course she told you that. I'm surprised you're even out of traction."

"The Day men heal up in no time," he replied and then winced. *Oops.*

She laughed again, but it was bitter this time. "Yeah, that's what I hear. So fast that they can go from one *wife* to another lover in a matter of weeks."

"Carly . . . Asher didn't mean for—"

"How do I look?" she interrupted him. Smoothing her cream-colored silk bustle gown, she stared into the mirror again, her chin held high.

"Beautiful, of course," he said.

*

Carly stared into the mirror. And so it was true. The corset pushed everything into the right places and the graceful sweep of the skirt made her compact figure almost statuesque. Sleeveless, the bodice hugged her curves and a long, gleaming satin glove encased her left arm. Her hair was piled on top of her head and a feather ornament curled by her right ear. She smoothed it and shot a glance at Daniel. "I guess so."

"Of course. You're a lovely woman, Carly."

"You look just like a bride," added Nancy. She clapped her pudgy hands together and beamed at Carly.

"A . . . what?" Carly said. Her heart plunged. *Oh, great.* That was all she needed . . . to go to the opening of the show dressed in a wedding gown. How more pathetic could she get?

Daniel groaned. "Nancy, that was not cool."

"What?" she retorted, "She does so. What's wrong with that?" Realization dawned and her red face became rosier. "Oh crap, I'm sorry, Carly." She plucked at Carly's skirt. Here, take that off. I'll throw it in a dye bath. How do you feel about blue?"

"Blue? Perfect." Carly replied. "Just get me out of this corset, okay?"

Daniel made a hasty retreat as Nancy reached for the back of the dress, releasing the tiny buttons on the back. "I'll come back," he muttered.

"I'm sorry," Nancy said again, her eyes shimmering with tears.

"Oh, Nancy, it's fine."

Nancy shook her head. "No, it's not. That was careless of me and I should just learn to keep my big mouth shut sometimes."

Carly turned to her. "I have the same problem. You know what someone once said to me?"

"What?" Nancy sniffed.

"That I care way too much about what other people think of me."

Nancy shook her head and wiped away tears. She reached for the gown and lifted it over Carly's head. "Ha. Yeah. That describes me to a 'T'."

Scratching at her cast, Carly gave her a rueful smile. "I just can't seem to take my own advice."

"Well, you should." Nancy surveyed her. "You know . . . this color is great for you. Just wear it as it is. And hell . . . why don't you just go all the way and add a veil? I have one that would look beautiful on you."

Carly's mouth dropped open. "Are you crazy? A wedding gown on purpose?"

Nancy shook her head. "No. I am not crazy. I am a good designer . . . that's what I am. And *I* am taking your advice. So should you."

Carly stood still for a minute, staring into Nancy's eyes. "Me dressed as a bride would make Asher really uncomfortable wouldn't it?"

Nancy sputtered. "Oh. That's not what I was thinking. No . . . I just meant . . . well . . . I just thought you'd look pretty. I don't have anything against Asher."

"I do." Carly's eyes narrowed. "I'm not leaving Ruby Spring with a happy ending, Nancy. But by God, I'll leave with a flourish." She held out her hand. "Now let me see the veil, please."

Chapter Twenty-Three

Letting out a deep breath, Asher stood at the edge of the trees, staring down at Ruby Spring. He'd hid in the cabin for five days and he hated himself for it. Although the mess with Miranda was over, he had let Carly down. He wasn't able to protect her when she needed it most. And now he was too much of a coward to face her. Cursing, he kicked at some loose rocks with his booted foot. From what his brother said, Carly had refused to talk to . . . or about him.

He didn't blame her, really. Everything that had happened was his fault. If he hadn't flown to France, she wouldn't have a broken arm . . . or a broken heart. Oh, who was he kidding? The broken heart would have happened anyway. His gaze fell on the buildings below him, hoping for glimpse of the woman he loved. The streets were dusty and bare. Everyone was at the hotel, having a late lunch in preparation for opening night.

Sighing, Asher began to pick his way down the rocky trail. He had to face the love of his life sooner or later. And the day of opening night, the day before she intended to *leave* his life, was cutting it close. Walking slowly into town, he stopped at the theater for another glance at the paint on the ceiling. Just one more look to remind him of the happiness he'd known with Carly before he faced her. Music floated out of the open backstage door. He stepped inside, squinting as his eyes adjusted to the semi-darkness.

"Hello?" he called.

*

Carly, high up on a ladder next to the proscenium, gasped and dropped her paintbrush. *Dammit.* She hadn't expected to see Asher until tonight . . . and even then not face to face . . . and especially not alone. All she wanted to do was smile and nod, congratulate Ross, and then leave Ruby Spring with her dignity intact. What she most of all did *not* want to do was deal with her real feelings for Asher. She bit her lip as Asher walked onto the stage.

"Carly," he whispered. His face was a mask of pain and regret.

From her perch on the ladder, she turned her head and stared into his familiar eyes. A shot of electricity raced through her body. Trembling and gripping the ladder, she turned away to stare out into the house of the theater.

Why? Why did it have to be like this for her always? Here she was in her oldest, ugliest shorts with unshaven legs. Her hair was messy, her eyes were red and her fingers were stained with gold paint. It wasn't fair.

"Carly," he said again. His deep voice caused the tears swimming in her eyes to slide down her face. Oh yeah. She was sick of crying, too. It was getting very old.

She heard him walk closer to the ladder, and then felt the shift as he stepped on the first rung. "Come down from there, Carly."

"No," she whispered, not trusting her own voice.

"You can't stay up there. It's not safe. You have a broken arm and besides, the show is starting in two hours. You're finished painting." He stepped up another rung. She started as his warm hand encircled her calf. He began to rub it with gentle fingers.

Suddenly, she lost it. "*Stop*," she sobbed, wiggling her leg to get it free. "Don't touch me there."

His hand left her. "Oh, God. I'm sorry . . . is your leg hurt?"

"N . . . o . . . ooo," she managed through her tears.

"What's wrong then?" He replaced his hand, this time massaging around to the front of her leg. He squeezed her knee.

"What's wrong with *you*?" she countered, "Can't you feel that my legs are like a hairy mammoth's?"

"No. They're not." He replied, stepping up another rung. He

let his hand trail up her thigh and rested it on her waist. He leaned forward, resting his head on her back as his other hand came around to hold the ladder steady. "They are perfect. Just like you."

Carly melted into his touch. God help her; she couldn't help herself. "Perfect. Perfectly stupid, you mean," she ground out. "Stupid me. Falling in love with a married man. That's a new one for my collection of failed romances, I must add."

He slid his arm closer around her middle and kissed her lower back. "I'm not married anymore, Carly." Raising her T-shirt, he laid his head on her smooth skin. "God you feel good."

She was silent for a moment and then pushed back against him. "Asher, I don't like this. Climb back down, please. I hate being put at a disadvantage like this."

Good. Her voice sounded as cold as her heart felt.

He did as she requested and stood on the stage floor, his large hands stuffed into jeans pockets.

"You're an asshole," she said to the wall. "What makes you think you can touch me . . . and . . . and attempt seduction and expect that everything is all better? I can't trust you, Asher. You broke my heart and you know it. I'm too vulnerable for this, and you know that, too. You're not a good person. You're not . . . . a good *man*."

There was a dead silence for an entire minute. Finally Carly cleared her throat.

"Well?"

"Sorry," he muttered, "I just . . . Carly. I am so sorry. I love you. I just want to be near you. I love you. Carly, please." His voice broke and she turned her head to look down.

He was crying. Alarmed, she climbed down the ladder and stood before him, motionless. His eyes were as full of pain as hers were. But what could she say? He had broken her heart into a million pieces. She should still be angry as hell. But it wasn't possible. He was in pain . . . and she loved him. She loved him with all of her broken, bruised heart. Her face softened.

"Asher," she whispered, placing her left hand on his arm.

With a cry, he reached for her, gathering her in his strong arms. She closed her eyes with a sigh, clinging to him for all she was worth. Sobs wracked his strong shoulders, and still she held tight, caressing the back of his neck, his hair, the planes of his face.

"I'm sorry, I'm so sorry," he mumbled into her shoulder.

"Asher," she repeated, pulling away and leading him to the settee stage right. She sat down on the edge, drawing him with her.

"What?" he sniffled in embarrassment.

"You don't cry like that very often, do you?" she murmured, a smirk forming around the corners of her mouth.

He raised his head from where it was buried in her shoulder and surveyed her through tear-stained lashes. God, his eyes were beautiful.

"No. I'll bet you don't either," he replied, beginning to smile.

"Almost never," she whispered, caressing his cheek. She kissed where her fingers had been and then allowed her lips to trail to the corner of his mouth. She kissed that, too.

"I should cry more often," he murmured against her lips.

"How about this?" she asked, their breath mingling, "Let's try our best to make sure we don't make each other cry ever again. There's been far too much crying around here."

His answer was the best kiss she had ever experienced. Ever. When they came up for air she pushed his hair back and winked.

"By the way, just so you know, crying men are sissies," she teased.

His mouth fell open and then he narrowed his eyes.

"Sissy, huh?" his voice rumbled as he reached for her and pulled her close. In one fluid motion, he held her under her breasts and lifted her up onto his lap, her knees folded on either side of his legs. He leaned back on the settee and pulling her forward, he adjusted his hips so that she was sitting squarely on his crotch.

"Good God," she gasped into his neck. "I take it back. No sissies. Nope. None here."

"Thought not," he replied as his hands began to roam over her back . . . and lower.

She shifted in his lap and they both moaned. "Asher, um . . . this is probably not a good idea. We are kind of in a public place."

"Oh, really?" he murmured, his large hands sliding her T-shirt up and over her head.

She caught it just in time and pulled it back over her face. Her breath came in gasps. He was hard as a rock between her thighs and all she wanted to do was rip the jeans from his body. Shaking her head to clear it, she jabbed a finger in his chest. "Yes. Public. Not good. Potential embarrassment. Very high."

He gave a low chuckle and stretched, which only served to push his erection farther into Carly's crotch. "Oh, *God*," they moaned together, and then burst into laughter.

"The cabin?" he asked her, an eyebrow quirked.

"Yes . . . and right now," she agreed, scrambling off his lap.

Adjusting the front of his jeans, Asher eyed her chest with appreciation. "Your bra's crooked," he commented.

"Not my fault," she shot back, holding out her hand. He accepted it and she hauled him to his feet. "Now we just have to get out of here with nobody seeing us."

Asher walked to the open backstage door and peered out. "I don't see anyone . . . oh, shit."

"What?"

"My brother. He's standing on the hotel porch making a—"

Almost as if on cue, Asher's pocket rang. " . . . phone call," he said with a groan.

"Don't answer it," Carly demanded, running her hand down his back. He shivered.

"I have to. You ought to know by now that one unanswered call with my family results in a giant search party."

Sighing, Carly dropped her hand and grabbed the phone out of Asher's. "Hi Danny," she answered.

"Carly? What the hell are you doing answering Asher's . . . oh. Oh. Well, good. Good. Uh . . . I interrupted something important, didn't I?"

"Mmmm."

"Okay. Sorry. You two *are* going to make it to the opening tonight, right?"

"Mmm-hmm."

"Okay. Good. Well I'll let you go, then. So everything's good then?"

"Mmmmmmmmmmm," Carly said through her giggles.

Daniel cleared his throat. "Um, what?"

"Danny, I have to go now . . . your brother is . . . Oh my God, Asher, can't you wait for ten minutes before you . . . ohhh."

"Ew. Bye."

*

Daniel shook his head in disgust before flipping it shut. After shuddering, he grinned to himself. All things . . . and not just most things . . . were going to work out in the end. Happy, he pried open the screen door with a crutch and called out to his wife.

"Soph?"

"What, hon?"

"Good news!"

*

Carly panted as she reached the top of the trail. Holding her side, she glared up at Asher. "Jeez. This isn't very romantic. Couldn't you at least act like you plan to ravish me ten minutes from now?"

"Ravish? Oh, sweetheart . . . ravish doesn't begin to cover it." He reached back for her hand and pulled her to his side.

In silence, they both looked out over the valley. The setting sun glimmered on the water, turning it a translucent shade of red.

"Ruby Spring," Carly breathed, "It's beautiful. No wonder you love the cabin so much."

"I do. But I love you more," he murmured. Turning her into his arms, he kissed her and then led her to the cabin. Carly's head swam.

Asher opened the door and pushed her inside. Trembling with anticipation and lust, Carly looked around and moistened her lips. His hand on the small of her back trailed up and around as he pulled her body up close; his need for her was more than evident.

"Why are you nervous, sweetheart? You weren't earlier." His deep voice close to her ear sent shivers of delight through her body. They pooled somewhere around her pelvis.

"I . . . well . . . I'm not really nervous. It's just that this place is so *yours* . . . I feel like I'm invading or something. I don't want you to think that I'm expecting that . . . oh, I don't know," she finished with a shrug.

Asher sighed behind her. "Carly. Promise me something."

"What?"

"Stop caring so much about what other people think of you. I want you here. Yes, it's an intensely private place for me but having you here is what I want, okay? Is that what you wanted to hear?"

She nodded, turning in his arms. "Am I a psycho neurotic?"

He laughed, backing her up to the bed. "No more than any other artist."

"Asher. Are you stereotyping artists as crazy people?"

"No." He pulled her T-shirt over her head.

"I would hope not, because you *are* an artist, you know."

"I know." He reached behind her and unsnapped her bra.

"Then why would you—"

Asher's hot mouth closed over a nipple.

"Why would you . . . would you . . . ohhhhh," she sighed, gripping at his muscled arms.

Groaning at her response, Asher kissed a path up to her mouth, even as his strong hands unbuttoned her shorts. "Carly, my love. Can we have this discussion later? Or in a year? How about twenty years?"

Her eyes huge, she nodded at the implication in his his request. "Yes. And yes, and yes."

"Good."

With quick hands, Asher pulled her shorts and panties off and pressed her down to the bed, hovering over her, just as he had a few weeks ago.

"But this time is different," she whispered.

"This time I know that I love you," he responded, as if reading her thoughts.

"And I love you," she whispered. "And I want to make love to you. But I can't get your clothes off with this damned chunk of plaster wrapped around my arm." She held up her cast, pouting.

Asher chuckled deeply and sat back on his heels, unbuttoning his shirt. As he stood to remove his jeans, Carly scrambled up to stand next to him. His eyebrow raised in question.

"I want what we were doing at the theater," she said.

His other eyebrow rose to meet the first one. "Good idea." He stripped the rest of the way, and then reclined on the bed, reaching for her.

With a sigh of pleasure, Carly straddled him, holding herself up with her left palm pressed on his chest. His stormy eyes met hers as his hands gripped her hips. She watched in fascination as his biceps bunched and then she was being lifted. Reaching between them, she clasped his erection in her hands.

Asher's nostrils flared as she slowly stroked him. "Can I be inside?" he gasped, still holding her aloft.

"Oh, God, yes. Now, in fact," she moaned and guided him to the perfect place.

He entered her as he had the first time . . . with agonizing slowness, his eyes locked on hers. The fullness, the satisfaction was almost heaven enough itself as he pushed himself to the hilt inside of her.

Barely able to breathe, Carly placed her hand back on his chest and rocked forward. "Oh, Asher," she whispered, leaning in to kiss him.

The grip on her hips tightened and his mouth claimed hers, plundering. His strong fingers urged her hips into a rhythm and then they slid up her body to cup her breasts.

His kneading fingers drove Carly to the brink. Increasing the pace, she moaned and bit her lip.

"God, yes," Asher breathed, letting go of her breasts to pull her down fully on top of him. She buried her lips in his neck as he cupped her hips again, thrusting upward to meet her rocking. An orgasm began to surge through her.

"More," she said. Her heart hammered.

He increased the pace to a frantic rhythm and thrust once more, at the height of her orgasm and so deep inside that cried out.

"Asher . . . Asher," she groaned, even as his shout of completion echoed through the cabin. Shock waves ran through her body and she collapsed on top of him. The only sound in the stillness of twilight was their ragged breathing.

"Asher?" Carly repeated some moments later, but in a much calmer tone of voice, "I almost hate to ask . . . but what time is it?"

"Oh shit."

Carly giggled as he rolled her to the side and fumbled in his jeans for his cell phone. His handsome brow wrinkled with worry, he looked at the screen to check the clock. A grin split his face. He sank back onto the quilt and pulled her close.

She inhaled the scent of his skin and closed her eyes, smiling. "What time is it?"

"No worries, sweetheart."

She cracked open an eye. "Yes, worries. We had to have been up here for at least an hour and I need to get dressed for the opening, which includes putting on a corset and—"

"An hour?" Asher interrupted, "Try fifteen minutes."

Carly's jaw dropped open and then she began to laugh. "We did all that in fifteen minutes? I guess we were . . . ahem . . . eager."

He nodded, staring at her. His tongue snaked out to wet the sculpted lips she couldn't resist. "Care to see if we can double our time?"

Holding up her broken arm, Carly scrambled over him and

reached for her panties. "Let's double it later. If I stay in that bed ten more seconds, we will never even make it to the show."

Asher sighed and flopped an arm over his eyes. "Oh, all right. Does it matter that I have my van up here and we don't have to hike back?" He peered out from under his arm.

She shook her head, her eyes full of love. "Let's not chance it, handsome. Besides . . . it will be fun to flirt with you during the show. You'll like what I'm wearing."

"Oh?" He rose onto an elbow, interest sparking in his eyes. "Describe."

"Just wait," she said, winking at her man. Her wonderful, strong, man-who-cried-for-her-and-then-rocked-her-world-afterwards-man. "I love you, Asher."

He winked back and then snapped her bare butt with his shirt. "I love you too."

Chapter Twenty-Four

A hand fluttering to her chest, Carly raced down the street to the costume shop and yanked open the door.

"Nancy, I'm here. Please don't kill me," she panted.

"For God's sake, Carly, the show starts in ten minutes. What the hell took you so long?" Nancy, wearing a ratty ankle length housecoat, grumbled as she waddled forward with the cream silk gown draped over her arms.

"I had to take a shower."

Nancy looked at her with a jaundiced eye. "Mmm-hmm. That's what your man said, too." She jerked her thumb toward the back of the shop. "He's back there putting on his costume."

Carly blushed and smoothed her wet hair self-consciously. "Thanks. I guess I'll need the corset . . . " she trailed off.

Sighing, Nancy pulled her behind a rack and tugged her T-shirt up. "Take it off. I will now demonstrate the fastest corset lacing in the entire Wild West."

Moments later, Carly grabbed at a rack of clothes as Nancy jerked the last corset string tight and then tied it. She lifted her arms and the lovely silk flowed down over her body. Turning her around, Nancy buttoned the back, grabbed her hair, twisted it up and stuck the feathered comb in place. She shoved a satin glove on Carly's left hand. "Done." She raised her pudgy arms in victory.

"Thank you," Carly said with a laugh.

"No, let *me* thank you," said Asher, emerging from the back of the building.

Carly caught her breath at the sight of him. He looked dangerous. A black cowboy hat sat low over his eyes and a long black coat swirled around his calves as he walked forward. A tight, striped vest accentuated his lean torso and the gun belt slung low on his hips made her bite her lower lip.

"Um . . . Nancy? Did I say thank you?" Carly murmured. Asher met her smoldering gaze and reached for her hand.

"Yikes. The show starts in five minutes. Enough thank-yous already." Nancy removed her housecoat with a flourish to reveal a bright purple and pink gown covered in layers of lace. Grabbing an equally lacy hat from a table near the door, she plunked it on her head. "Ready?"

Asher's lips curved upwards as he slipped an arm around Carly's cinched waist. "You're ravishing, Nancy."

"I know," she flung over her shoulder as she sailed out the door and up the dusty, dark street.

Peering after her, Carly noticed the overflowing parking lot and the large crowd of people waiting outside the front entrance to the theater. Most of them had blue hair. Some of them had walkers.

"Wow. Marilyn sure has a following, doesn't she?" she commented, leaning against her man.

"Hold still," he answered. "And close your eyes."

"Asher, we have to go. After the show we will have plenty of time for—"

"Hold still and close your eyes," he repeated and she sighed, complying.

Taking her plaster covered arm in his, Asher silently pulled a marker from his pocket. It squeaked as he began to write.

"What are you doing?" she said.

"Signing your cast."

"Now?"

"Just wait. You'll like it, I promise. At least I hope you will."

The squeaking stopped and Carly peered at him through her lashes. "May I look?"

Asher dropped to a knee and clasped her left hand.

"Yes, my love. Take a look."

Smiling, Carly held out her plaster-covered right arm and her eyes widened.

On her snowy white cast, in bold black letter were the words: *Marry Me.*

Shock buzzed through her. She looked down at Asher and watched as he removed his hat and placed it on the floor, clearing his throat. He looked up. His eyes were anxious.

"Carly, will you?"

"Asher," she whispered, her eyes full of love, "Yes. And yes and yes. Forever and always."

"I don't have a ring yet. I . . . well . . . I wanted to design one for you," he murmured.

She tugged on his hand until he stood up. "Let the ring for now be the plaster one around my arm, then," she said, gazing into his eyes.

"I don't care what it is for right now, to tell you the truth. I'm just so grateful you said yes. You said yes to me." He cupped her face in his hands and drew her close. "Thank you."

Their lips met and elation swelled in Carly's heart. He loved her. Despite everything.

"Fun proposal, by the way," she commented after her heart stopped hammering from his kiss.

"I thought so, too."

A bell sounded outside.

"The curtain's about to go up . . . shall we?" He offered her his arm.

She grinned and him and then stopped, snapping her fingers. "I almost forgot."

"Forgot this?" Asher pulled a cream lace veil from an inside pocket of his coat. He removed the feather from her hair and replaced it with the delicate fabric. He adjusted the comb at the crown of her head. Pride shone in his eyes. "My bride."

"Damn straight I am." She grinned. "Broken arm, big mouth and all."

He winked. "You're perfect." Now let's go terrorize some old ladies."

Carly walked beside Asher to the theater on a cloud of air, unmindful of the dust swirling around her feet. As they rounded the corner to the front of the building, she spied Ross. He was dressed in a plain black suit and black T-shirt, pacing nervously back and forth.

"Hey partner, where's your costume?" she called out to him.

He rushed forward and gripped her arms. "For God's sake, woman, do you know how late you are? The curtain's going up any minute and I had to leave my date to come look for you and—"

"Date?" She and Asher interrupted in unison.

Ross blushed. "Bruce."

Carly squeezed her best friend's arm. "Good for you."

"Yeah. No kidding. He's hot as hell," Ross shot back, pulling away to survey Carly's costume. "Wait a minute. Why the F are you dressed like a bride?"

"She is one," replied Asher, grinning from ear to ear.

"Oh my God. Congratulations . . . can I see the ring?"

Carly held up her broken arm and burst into giggles.

Ross looked at it, rolled his eyes and then slapped Asher on the back. "That's a huge ring, man. Very impressive."

Chuckling, Asher reached out to hug him. "Thanks."

"So I guess this means you're not leaving tomorrow?" Ross asked as he pulled her into a bear hug.

"Oh hell, no," she shot back, "You?"

"Not a chance," Ross answered. "I already lined up a job in Phoenix for next month. It's a drive, and I hate driving, but for the meantime Danny told me I could stay put here. You want to come do my set and props for me when I go to Arizona?"

Carly's mouth opened and she wrinkled her brow.

He waved it away. "Never mind. We can talk about it later. You have a wedding to plan anyway. Oh, and about that . . . Bruce thinks—"

"Ross. *Ross*," A frantic whisper came from the open double doors a few feet away. "We're two point five minutes behind. I need to start the show but I won't do it without you. Come on. *Please*."

Parker jumped up and down, trembling, a stopwatch in his hand.

Carly tried to wipe the smile from her lips but failed. Leaning in to Ross, she whispered, "Drama Trauma."

"Totally," he agreed. "I'm coming, dammit. And no, you can't start the show without me." He stomped to the door and stepped over the threshold. "Now you can start."

"What a diva," Asher chuckled.

"You have no idea," said Carly, tugging on his hand.

"I'll have years to find out, though," he murmured against her ear as they entered the theater.

Carly smiled with satisfaction as she surveyed the gorgeous restoration. Walking down the aisle, hand in hand with Asher, she looked overhead at the glimmering ceiling.

"What do you think?" she asked, and then corrected herself, "Not that I care too much what people think about me." Asher threw his head back and laughed. A gaggle of old ladies turned to glare at him.

"Again, sweetheart, we have years. Someday you'll quit asking me that."

"You wish." Carly stuck out her tongue.

A hush fell over the murmuring crowd as the lights dimmed. Asher and Carly took their seats next to Ross in the front row and looked up. A spotlight appeared as the oleo curtain rose.

Marilyn stood center stage in her magnificent wine gown, her regal gaze sweeping the audience. Applause and cheers burst forth, and she held court, loving every minute of it. When the adulation finally died away, she swept downstage and paused for just the briefest of seconds. Finding Carly in the front row, she gave her a lascivious wink and then raised her chin, again the consummate diva. A pin dropping would have made noise as the audience waited with hushed anticipation for Marilyn to speak.

Asher clasped Carly's hand in his, lacing their fingers together. She turned, noting the lust in his eyes as his gaze wandered over her. Squeezing his hand, she traced the edge of her open mouth with her tongue and winked.

He leaned in close and whispered, "You're a naughty bride."

She kissed the corner of his lips softly. "Just wait."

Happier than she had ever been in her life, she turned her attention toward the stage and beamed.

About the Author

After spending twenty years in professional theater as a costume designer, Laura Simcox abandoned the nomadic lifestyle to sit at a beat up enormous second hand oak desk and write. The result? Romance novels! Her favorite thing ever since she was, oh, about twelve. She writes contemporary, light novels and enjoys creating quirky characters and funny dialogue. Still, the love story is the focus and Laura has a huge soft spot for a sappy, happy ending.

She lives in North Carolina with her husband (True love is real!) and her adorable, high-energy three year old son who is currently obsessed with pirates. And that's cool, because she loves 'em too.

She enjoys connecting with readers and more information, including links to Facebook, Twitter and others are on her website.

Reach Laura at: *www.laurasimcox.com*

In the mood for more Crimson Romance? Check out *The Sleepover Clause* by Barbara Barrett at *CrimsonRomance.com*.